PRAISE FOR THE NOVELS OF AMANDA GRANGE:

"Grange hits the Regency language and tone on the head."

—*Library Journal*

"Grange... tells Darcy's story in her own style, with charm and a gentle wit. While her characters are true to Austen's creations, a couple of surprises lurk, only adding to the reader's pleasure... Grange's humor and warmth shine."

—Susan Higginbotham, author of *The Traitor's Wife*

"Written with charm, elegance, and style. Amanda Grange... will make you fall in love with Fitzwilliam Darcy once again!"

—Single Titles

"Amanda Grange tells an engaging, thoroughly enjoyable story!"

—Romance Reader at Heart

"Amanda Grange does a great job of keeping both the language and the behavior authentic to Jane Austen and the early 19th century... she is one of the best at doing so that I have found."

—Epinions.com

"I really didn't want this book to end, as Grange's description of events following *P&P* were excellent."

—Revisiting the Moon's Library

"A treat for *Pride and Prejudice* fans, this tells the story from Mr. Darcy's point of view. Sensitive to the original but lots of fun, this is the tale behind the alpha male."

—*Woman* magazine

"Amanda Grange has taken on the challenge of reworking a much loved romance and succeeds brilliantly."

—Historical Novels Review

"Delightful. I devoured this book more greedily than *Pride and Prejudice* itself."

—Historical-Fiction.net

"A lighthearted and sparkling rendition of the classic love story."

—Historical Novel Society

"*Mr. Darcy's Diary* is an enjoyable journey into the mind of one of the most popular characters in literary history... a gift to a new generation of Darcy fans and a treat for existing fans as well."

—Austenblog

"Captures the essence of romantic and eternal love… If you want to fall in love with Mr. Darcy all over again, order yourself a copy."

—Royal Reviews

"The characters—new and old—will leave you wanting more, and the everlasting love between Darcy and Lizzy will leave more than one reader swooning."

—A Bibliophile's Bookshelf

"The way Ms. Lathan allows the relationship between Darcy and Elizabeth to evolve is wonderful and will surely induce a contented sigh from all romantics."

—Once Upon a Romance

"I felt like I slipped away into the pages of another time… I really fell in love with Lathan's continuation of Elizabeth and Fitzwilliam's story."

—One Literature Nut

"This is one of the most romantic takeoffs on *Pride and Prejudice* that I have read… Sharon Lathan's take on the couple is my all-time favorite… It's a *Pride and Prejudice* version that cannot be missed."

—This Book For Free

ALSO BY AMANDA GRANGE

Mr. Darcy's Diary
Mr. Darcy, Vampyre
Captain Wentworth's Diary
Edmund Bertram's Diary
Mr. Knightley's Diary

ALSO BY SHARON LATHAN

Mr. & Mrs. Fitzwilliam Darcy: Two Shall Become One
Loving Mr. Darcy
My Dearest Mr. Darcy
In the Arms of Mr. Darcy

A Darcy Christmas

AMANDA GRANGE
SHARON LATHAN
CAROLYN EBERHART

sourcebooks
landmark

A *Darcy Christmas* anthology copyright © 2010 by Sourcebooks, Inc.
Cover and internal design © 2010 by Sourcebooks, Inc.
The publisher acknowledges the copyright holders of the individual works as follows:
"Mr. Darcy's Christmas Carol" copyright © 2010 by Carolyn Eberhart
"Christmas Present" copyright © 2010 by Amanda Grange
"A Darcy Christmas" copyright © 2010 by Sharon Lathan
Cover design by Renee Witherwax
Cover image Portrait of a girl in a winter landscape, Weyden, Harry van der (1868–1952) / Private Collection / © Christopher Wood Gallery, London, UK / The Bridgeman Art Library International

Published by Sourcebooks Landmark, an imprint of Sourcebooks, Inc.
P.O. Box 4410, Naperville, Illinois 60567-4410
(630) 961-3900
FAX: (630) 961-2168
www.sourcebooks.com

Library of Congress Cataloging-in-Publication Data

A Darcy Christmas / Amanda Grange, Sharon Lathan, Carolyn Eberhart.
   p. cm.
 1. Christmas stories, American. 2. Christmas stories, English. 3. Darcy, Fitzwilliam (Fictitious character)--Fiction. 4. Bennet, Elizabeth (Fictitious character)--Fiction. 5. England--Social life and customs--19th century--Fiction. I. Grange, Amanda. II. Lathan, Sharon. III. Eberhart, Carolyn.
 PS648.C45D37 2010
 394.2663--dc22
                          2010027072

Printed and bound in the United States of America
VP 10 9 8 7 6 5 4 3 2 1

CONTENTS

Mr. Darcy's Christmas Carol

CAROLYN EBERHART

OLD MR. DARCY'S GHOST

OLD MR. DARCY WAS dead to begin with. There is no doubt whatsoever about that. The clergyman, the clerk, the undertaker, and the chief mourner had all signed the register of his burial. His son signed it. And Fitzwilliam Darcy's name was as good as his father's before him. Old Mr. Darcy was as dead as a doornail. Darcy was dreadfully cut up by the sad event.

There is no doubt that Old Mr. Darcy was dead. This must be distinctly understood, or nothing wonderful can come of this story.

Darcy was often proud and conceited, arrogant and disdainful to those whom he did not know. Friends, on the other hand, might stop him in the street to say, with gladsome looks, "My dear Darcy, how are you? When will you come to see me?" Children and dogs often seemed able to see beneath his exterior to the real Darcy. Yet many never saw in him that which did not appear on the surface.

Darcy's soul and heart had sustained an injury in the spring from one who had yet to see beyond his outward façade. Elizabeth Bennet had refused his proposal of marriage—refused it in a manner that seemed as hard and sharp as flint.

"I had not known you a month before I felt that you were the last man in the world whom I could ever be prevailed on to marry."

Darcy could now admit that his offer, sincere as it was, had been given in an abominable manner, and he winced at the still vibrant memory. But her harsh words had not struck out the fire of his love. He had tried to conquer his feelings but he could not. Hope had bloomed anew for a few sunlit days last summer, when he had unexpectedly run into Elizabeth at Pemberley. She had seemed more inclined to think well of him than she ever had before. A few halcyon days had been all that had been allowed before news of Lydia Bennet's fall from grace had separated them yet again.

Darcy had done what he could to restore respectability to the wayward girl. *No,* Darcy thought, *he had done what he could to restore Elizabeth's peace of mind.* He cared naught of Lydia's reputation—only that the loss of it caused pain to Elizabeth.

Darcy had seen Elizabeth perhaps a dozen times since taking care of Lydia's folly. The most awkward was when he had accepted her thanks for his actions but could not bring himself to speak further. The most painful occasion had been when he and Elizabeth met at the altar during the nuptials of Bingley and Jane. He had been best man, while Elizabeth was maid of honor. He wanted to be the one exchanging vows before God. On both occasions, he had almost renewed his addresses to Elizabeth but he had not. The memory of the hurt and anger he experienced at her first rejection had kept him silent. And yes, his damnable pride had also held his tongue. Now, with Christmas fast approaching, his hope for a future with Elizabeth had almost withered away.

Christmas Eve dawned with cold, bleak, biting weather and a fog settled over the city like a gray greatcoat. The fog came pouring in at every chink and keyhole, and was so dense without that the houses opposite were mere phantoms. When the mantel clock had only just gone three, it was already quite dark, for there had barely been light all day and candles were flaring in the windows of the neighboring houses, like shining beacons upon the palpable white mist. Few people ventured into the street outside Darcy's door, the weather keeping them inside or hurrying from warm houses to carriages where blankets and hot bricks awaited.

Darcy sat busy in his study. The door of the study was open so that he might keep his eye upon his sister, who, in a pretty little room beyond, was playing the piano. Darcy had a very good fire going, and Georgiana's fire was also blazing merrily away—so much so that Georgiana had to put off her white shawl.

Darcy was going over his Christmas accounts. Most of the household staff would receive their usual gifts before departing to visit family in or around the city. Then he allotted funds to various benevolent organizations. In the past few years, he had continued to support those charities that his father felt were worthy of his largesse and he would continue with those obligations in the foreseeable future. *Perhaps the time has come for me to take a more personal interest in such matters*, he thought. His thoughts were interrupted when he recognized the tune Georgiana was playing; it was one his father had favored.

He rose from his desk and crossed the room.

"Fitzwilliam? Is my playing bothering you?" Georgiana asked.

"No, my dear, it is as delightful as always. It is just that I remember that piece. Father was quite fond of it."

"It is this time of year that I miss Papa the most. Do you miss him too?"

"Yes, very much, and our mother too. She enjoyed the Christmas season."

"I regret that I have few memories of her now. I do remember coming into the parlor on Christmas day and watching her play the piano. She had me sit on the bench beside her and let me play with her. It must have sounded horrible."

Darcy smiled at the memory, "Never that, just a trifle unharmonious. It is a good remembrance to keep. It is a pity you do not have more."

"I do have many good memories of my childhood that include you and papa," Georgiana sought to assure him. "I remember a snowball fight between you and my Fitzwilliam cousins and the vicar was just leaving when a stray snowball hit him squarely on the back. I think father and the vicar would have laughed had it not been for Lady Catherine scolding you and saying you were all too old for such nonsense."

"And so we were. Father enjoyed hearing you play, as I do. Please continue."

So Georgiana played and Darcy listened as the fog and darkness thickened. The ancient tower of a church, whose gruff old
bell was always peeping down at Darcy's house out of a gothic
window in the wall, became invisible and struck the hours and
quarters in the clouds, with tremulous vibrations afterwards as
if its teeth were chattering in its frozen head up there. The cold
became intense. It became foggier yet, and colder! Piercing,
searching, biting cold that chilled one to the bone. Still, there
were those who chose to brave the weather.

The owner of a scant young nose, in danger of being frozen,
stooped down at Darcy's keyhole to regale him with a Christmas
carol, at the first sound of *God bless you, merry gentleman! May
nothing you dismay!* Georgiana began to accompany the caroler.
Darcy gave a footman some coins to toss at the singer.

"Thank ya, guv," was the cheery reply, as the lad went off to
the next house on the square.

At length, the hour of going to church arrived. Darcy rose from
behind his desk, and Georgiana instantly fetched her cloak and hat.

They entered the carriage and made their way to the
Christmas Eve service. "You are looking forward to tomorrow, I
suppose?" asked Darcy.

"Yes, Fitzwilliam."

"It is not as festive here in town as at Pemberley," Darcy
warned. "You will be expecting something grand for your
Christmas present, no doubt."

Georgiana smiled faintly at this teasing. What she really
wanted for Christmas was a new sister. One with laughing eyes
who made her brother smile.

"And," said Darcy, "you do not think me ill-used, that I have searched high and low for your gift."

Georgiana observed that it was only once a year.

"A poor excuse for picking a man's pocket every twenty-fifth of December!" teased Darcy lightly, buttoning his greatcoat to the chin. "But I suppose you will find much to celebrate the whole of Christmas day and all the next too, no doubt!"

Georgiana promised that she would, and Darcy smiled at her. The church was reached in a twinkling. Darcy and Georgiana, the long ends of her white scarf dangling in the wind, went into the church. The church bells rang out twenty-four times, in honor of its being Christmas Eve. The telling of the Christmas story never failed to stir Georgiana. During the service she prayed that her Christmas wish for Darcy might be granted in some way. The choir burst into song as her prayer ended. She left the church renewed in spirit, sure that her prayer would be answered.

Darcy and Georgiana feasted on a merry meal with their uncle and aunt, newly arrived in town from Bath. After dinner, Darcy beguiled the rest of the evening with friends at his club (and partook a bit more freely of the good cheer offered by these comrades than he was used to) while his sister remained with her relations. Darcy would join them on the following day for Christmas dinner.

Eventually, Darcy went home. It was an old house, but well lived-in. The yard was so dark that even Darcy, who knew its every stone, was forced to grope about with his hands. The fog and frost hung about the old, black doorway of the house.

There was nothing at all particular about the lion-headed knocker on the door, except that it was very large. It is a fact that Darcy had seen it, night and morning, during his whole residence in that place and that he had as little of what is called fancy about him. But let it also be borne in mind that Darcy had thought much of his father on this day, since the mention of his five-years dead parent that afternoon, and that he still mourned the loss of that revered personage. It should not be so surprising then that Darcy, having his key in the lock of the door, saw in the knocker, without its undergoing any intermediate process of change became not a knocker, but his father's face.

George Darcy's face was before him. It was not in impenetrable shadow, as the other objects in the yard were, but had a cheerful light about it. It was not angry or ferocious, but looked at Darcy as his father often used to look: with ghostly spectacles turned up upon its ghostly forehead. The hair was curiously stirred, as if by breath or hot air and, though the eyes were wide open, they were perfectly motionless. That, and its livid color, made it horrible; but its horror seemed to be in spite of the face and beyond its control, rather than a part of its own expression.

As Darcy looked fixedly at this phenomenon, it was a knocker again. He blinked and then traced the lion's head with fingers, feeling only cold iron beneath them. To say that he was not startled or that his blood was not conscious of a terrible sensation to which it had been a stranger from infancy would be untrue. Shaking his head, he put his hand upon the key he had relinquished, turned it sturdily, walked in, and lighted the candle that was waiting for him.

He did pause, with a moment's irresolution, before he shut the door. He did look cautiously behind it first, as if he half expected to be terrified with the sight of Old Mr. Darcy's backside sticking out into the hall. But there was nothing on the back of the door, except the screws and nuts that held the knocker on, so he closed it with a bang.

The sound resounded through the house like thunder. Every room above and every cask in the cellars below appeared to have a separate peal of echoes all its own. Darcy was not a man to be frightened by echoes. He fastened the door and walked across the hall and up the stairs, slowly too, for his candle cast eerie shadows as he went.

There was plenty of width to the old flight of stairs—a coach-and-six could drive up it with room to spare. A hearse also could have done it easily enough, which is perhaps the reason why Darcy thought he saw a locomotive hearse going on before him in the gloom.

Up Darcy went, wondering if he perhaps he was drunk. He had not thought so, for he had never truly overindulged. Yet it could explain the strange tricks his eyes were playing on him. Yet before he shut his heavy door, he walked through his rooms, which had once been occupied by his deceased parent, to see that all was right. He had just enough recollection of the face to desire to do that.

They were a cheerful suite of rooms, consisting of a sitting room and bedroom, and each was as it should be. The logs were at the ready, which Darcy quickly ignited into a large fire in the grate; the pitcher and basin were ready for use; and the decanter of brandy was upon the table, just as his valet left it before he and the rest of the servants quit the house to visit their own families and friends for the evening's celebrations. Nobody was behind the curtains; nobody was underneath the sofa; nobody was under the bed; nobody was in the closet; nobody was in his dressing gown, which was hanging up in a suspicious attitude against the wall.

Quite satisfied, he closed his door and locked himself in, which was not his custom. Thus secured against surprise, he took off his cravat and jacket, leaving his waistcoat on but unbuttoned, and shrugged into the dressing gown before sitting down in front of the fire to take his glass of brandy.

It was a very good fire indeed, nothing to it on such a bitter night. He sat close to it and brooded; the brandy remained untouched. The fireplace was an old one, built long ago, and carved all round with designs to illustrate the Scriptures. There were hundreds of figures to attract his thoughts; and yet only the face of his father, five years dead, remained in Darcy's thoughts.

"Nonsense!" said Darcy, and walked across the room. After several turns, he sat down again. As he threw his head back in the chair, his glance happened to rest upon a bell, which hung in the room and communicated to the servants in the highest story of the building. It was with great astonishment, and with a strange, inexplicable dread, that as he looked, he saw this bell begin to swing. It swung so softly in the outset that it scarcely made a sound; but soon it rang out loudly, and so did every bell in the house.

This might have lasted half a minute or a minute, but it seemed an hour. The bells ceased as they had begun: together.

They were succeeded by a clanking noise, deep down below, as if some person were dragging a heavy chain over the casks in the cellar. Darcy then remembered having heard that ghosts in haunted houses were described as dragging chains.

The cellar door flew open with a booming sound, and then he heard the noise much louder, on the floors below; then coming up the stairs; then coming straight towards his door.

"It is nonsense still!" said Darcy. "I will not believe it."

His color changed though, when, without a pause, it came on through the heavy door and passed into the room before his eyes. Upon its coming in, the flames leaped up and just as quickly fell again.

His Father's ghost! The same face, the very same. George Darcy in his favorite jacket, usual waistcoat, breeches, and boots. The chains he drew were clasped about his middle. One was very long and was made (for Darcy observed it closely) of gold studded with precious gems while the other was shorter, hardly seeming to clasp about his waist and was wrought in thick iron. His body was transparent, so that Darcy, observing him and looking through his waistcoat, could see the two buttons on his coat behind.

No, he did not believe it, even now. Though he looked the phantom through and through, and saw it standing before him; though he felt the chilling influence of its death-cold eyes and marked the very texture of the folded kerchief bound about its head and chin, which wrapper he had not observed before; he was still incredulous and fought against his senses.

"What do you want with me?" inquired Darcy

"Much!" George Darcy's voice, no doubt about it.

"Who are you?" Darcy demanded, knowing the answer but feeling compelled to ask anyway.

The ghost raised a quizzical eyebrow, "Ask me who I was."

"Who were you then?" asked Darcy.

"In life I was your father, George Darcy."

"Can you—can you sit down?" Darcy asked the question because he didn't know whether a ghost so transparent might find himself in a condition to take a chair and felt that in the event of its being impossible, it might involve the necessity of an embarrassing explanation.

"I can."

"Please do so then, sir," said Darcy, looking doubtfully at him.

The ghost sat down on the opposite side of the fireplace, as if he were quite used to it. "You do not believe in me," observed the Ghost.

"I do not," said Darcy.

"What evidence would you have of my reality beyond that of your senses?"

"I do not know," said Darcy.

"Why do you doubt your senses?"

"Because," said Darcy, "alcohol affects them. I do not usually indulge in the grape as much as I did this evening. I am sure there is more of the cask than of the casket about you, whatever you are!"

Darcy was not much in the habit of cracking jokes, nor did he feel, in his heart, by any means waggish then. The truth is that he tried to be smart, as a means of distracting his own attention and keeping down his terror, for the specter's voice disturbed the very marrow in his bones.

To sit, staring at those fixed, glazed eyes, in silence for a moment, would play, Darcy felt, the very deuce with him. It was as if he again were but twelve years old and about to be punished for some childish misdeed. There was something very awful too in the specter's being provided with an infernal atmosphere of its own.

At this, the Spirit raised a frightful cry and shook its chain with such a dismal and appalling noise that Darcy held on tight to his chair, to save himself from falling off of it. But how much greater was his horror, when the phantom took off the bandage round its head, as if it were too warm to wear indoors, and its lower jaw dropped down upon its breast!

Darcy placed his elbows on his knees, and clasped his face in his hands, as if to banish the specter. There was silence in the room, but Darcy could still feel the Spirit.

Glancing up, he looked at the Spirit, whose jaw was again shut. "Father!" he asked. "Why do you trouble me?"

"Fitzwilliam!" replied the Ghost. "Do you believe in me or not?"

"I do," said Darcy. "I must. Why are you here? Why do you come to me?"

"It is required of every man," the Ghost returned, "that the Spirit within him should walk abroad among his fellow-men, and travel far and wide; and if that spirit goes not forth in life, it is condemned to do so after death. It is doomed to wander through the world and witness what it cannot share, but might have shared on earth and turned to happiness! And, my son, you are in danger of losing your spirit within."

Again the specter raised a cry and shook its chain, and wrung its shadowy hands.

"You wear chains," said Darcy, trembling. "Tell me why?"

"I wear the chains I forged in life," replied the Ghost. "I made them link by link, and yard by yard; the gold, for all its length, is of no weight, for it is forged from the good I did during my life. However, this bit"—the Spirit touched the metal belt around his waist—"this bit of forged iron weighs heavily. For it is forged from those times when I acted without consideration for others and thought only of myself. Those times when I let pride and conceit bar the way to doing what is proper and just. I girded them on of my own free will, and of my own free will I wore it."

Darcy nodded slowly, trying to make sense his father's words.

"Do you wish to know," pursued the Ghost, "the weight and length of the chains you bear yourself? They are even, Fitzwilliam, even, identical in length to each other. However, I have come to warn you. If you persist along your present course..."

"What course?" interrupted Darcy.

"If you persist along your present course, your chain of iron will grow stronger and heavier, and the gold chain will vanish and your soul will have gone with it," the ghost continued, "you then will be condemned to wander through the world for eternity. This is not a fate I would wish for you, my son."

Darcy glanced about him on the floor, in the expectation of finding himself surrounded by fathoms of iron cable, but he could see nothing.

"Father," he said, imploringly. "Father, tell me more. Speak comfort to me, Father."

"I wish that I could, my son, but at the moment I have none to give," the Ghost replied. "It comes from other regions, Fitzwilliam, and is conveyed by other ministers, to other kinds of men. Nor can I tell you what I would. A very little more is all that is permitted to me. I cannot stay; I cannot linger anymore."

It was a habit with Darcy, whenever he became thoughtful, to fiddle with his signet ring. Pondering on what the Ghost had said, he did so now, but without lifting up his eyes to the specter.

The Ghost set up another cry and clanked its chain so hideously in the dead silence of the night.

"Many are captive, bound, and double-ironed," cried the phantom, "yet they do not know! They do not know that no space of regret can make amends for one life's opportunities missed!"

"Life's opportunities missed," faltered Darcy, who now began to apply this to himself. *Could the Spirit be talking of Elizabeth?*

Wringing its hands, the Ghost cried out, "Pemberley. The common welfare of its tenants—charity, mercy, forbearance, and benevolence—are all very easy at Pemberley. But elsewhere, Fitzwilliam? Have you shown these qualities elsewhere?"

"I try, sir," Darcy replied, shaken.

"Did you try in Hertfordshire? Did you show charity, mercy, forbearance, and benevolence there, Fitzwilliam?" Darcy was forced to shake his head, for he had not.

The spirit held up the iron chain and flung it down heavily.

"Hear me!" cried the Ghost. "My time is nearly gone."

"I will," said Darcy. "But do not be too hard upon me, Father!"

"How it is that I appear before you in a shape that you can see, I may not tell. I have sat invisible beside you many and many a day."

It was an agreeable idea. Darcy had often wished for his father's advice when making decisions.

"That is no light part of my penance," pursued the Ghost. "I have been watching you come to this precipice, and I am aware that part of it is my own doing and I must suffer for it. As a child, I taught you what was right, but I did not teach you to correct your temper. I gave you good principles but left you to follow them in pride and conceit. Unfortunately, as my only son—for many years my only child—I spoilt you; allowed, encouraged, almost taught you to be selfish and overbearing; to care for none beyond your own family circle; to think meanly of all the rest of the world; to think meanly of their sense and worth compared with your own. That is why I wear this heavy chain. I am here tonight to warn you that you have yet a chance and hope of escaping your fate. A chance and hope not just of my procuring, Fitzwilliam, but of others', who also have your welfare at heart."

"You are too harsh in your own criticism. You were always a good father," said Darcy. "Thank you, for I do not believe that I said it during your life!"

"You will be haunted," resumed the Ghost, "by Three Spirits, all of whom will appear familiar to you, for that is their way."

Darcy's countenance fell almost as low as the Ghost's had done.

"Is that the chance and hope you mentioned, Father?" he questioned in a faltering voice.

"It is."

"I—I think I would rather not," said Darcy.

"Without their visits," said the Ghost, "you cannot hope to shun the path you now tread. Expect the first tomorrow, when the bell tolls one."

"Could I not take them all at once and have it over, Father?" hinted Darcy.

"Expect the second on the next night at the same hour. The third upon the next night when the last stroke of twelve has ceased to vibrate. Look to see me no more; and for your own sake, remember what has passed between us."

When it had said these words, the specter took its wrapper from the table and bound it round its head, as before. Darcy knew this, by the smart sound its teeth made, when the bandage brought the jaws together. He ventured to raise his eyes again, and found his supernatural visitor confronting him in an erect attitude, with its chain wound over and about its arms.

The apparition walked backward from him; and at every step it took, the window raised itself a little, so that when the specter reached it, it was wide open.

It beckoned Darcy to approach, which he did. When they were within two paces of each other, Old Mr. Darcy's Ghost held up its hand, warning him to come no nearer. Darcy stopped, not so much in obedience as in surprise and fear, for on the raising of the hand, he became sensible of confused noises in the air: incoherent sounds of lamentation and regret, wailings inexpressibly sorrowful and self-accusatory. The specter, after listening for a moment, joined in the mournful dirge and floated out upon the bleak, dark night. "Hear them, Fitzwilliam! Listen to their cries, for any one of them could be you!" said Old Mr. Darcy. "Look upon them!"

Darcy followed to the window, desperate in his curiosity. He looked out.

The air was filled with phantoms, wandering hither and thither in restless haste and moaning as they went. Every one of them wore chains like Old Mr. Darcy's Ghost; some few were covered completely in chains. Darcy had personally known many during their lifetime. He had been quite familiar with one old ghost, in a white waistcoat, with a monstrous iron chain attached to its ankle, who cried piteously at being unable to assist a wretched woman with an infant, whom it saw below, upon a doorstep. The misery with them all was, clearly, that they sought to interfere, for good, in human matters, and had forever lost the power to do so.

Whether these creatures faded into mist or mist enshrouded them, he could not tell. But they and their spirit voices faded together; and the night became as it had been when he walked home.

Darcy closed the window and examined the door by which the Ghost had entered. It was locked, as he had locked it with his own hands, and the bolts were undisturbed. He tried to say "Humbug!" but stopped at the first syllable. And being, from the emotion he had undergone, or the fatigues of the day, or his glimpse of the Invisible World, or the conversation of the Ghost, or the lateness of the hour, much in need of repose, he went straight to bed, without undressing, and fell asleep upon the instant.

CHRISTMAS PAST

WHEN DARCY AWOKE, IT was so dark, that looking out of the bed, he could scarcely distinguish the transparent window from the opaque walls of his chamber. He was endeavoring to pierce the darkness with his eyes when the chimes of a neighboring church struck the four quarters, so he listened for the hour.

To his great astonishment, the heavy bell went on from six to seven, and from seven to eight, and regularly up to twelve, then stopped. Twelve! It was past two when he went to bed. The clock was wrong. An icicle must have gotten into the works. Twelve!

He glanced at the clock that rested on the mantel. Its rapid little pulse beat twelve and stopped.

"Why, it is not possible," said Darcy, "that I can have slept through a whole day and far into another night. It is not possible that anything has happened to the sun and this is twelve at noon!"

The idea being such an alarming one, he scrambled out of bed and groped his way to the window. He was obliged to rub the frost off with the sleeve of his dressing gown before he could see anything, and even after that could see very little. All he could make out was that it was still very foggy and extremely cold. It was a great relief that there was no noise of people running to and fro or making a great stir, as there unquestionably would have been if night had beaten off day and taken possession of the world.

Darcy went to bed again, thought about it over and over, and could make nothing of it. The more he thought, the more perplexed he was; and the more he endeavored not to think, the more he thought of his father's Ghost. It bothered him exceedingly. Every time he resolved within himself, after much mature inquiry, that it had all been a dream, his mind flew back to its first position, and presented the same problem to be worked through: Was it a dream or not?

Ding, dong!

"A quarter past," said Darcy counting.

Ding, dong!

"Half past!" said Darcy.

Ding, dong!

"A quarter to it." Darcy suddenly remembered that the Ghost had warned him of a visitation when the bell tolled one. He resolved to lie awake until the hour was past; and, considering that he could no more go to sleep than go to Heaven, this was perhaps the wisest resolution in his power.

The quarter was so long that he was more than once convinced he must have sunk into a doze unconsciously and missed the clock. At length it broke upon his listening ear.

Ding, dong!

"The hour itself," said Darcy triumphantly, "and nothing else!"

He spoke before the hour bell sounded, which it now did with a deep, dull, hollow, melancholy ONE. Light flashed up in the room upon the instant, and a hand drew the curtains of his bed aside. Not the curtains at his feet nor the curtains at his back, but those to which his face was addressed. Darcy, starting up into a half-recumbent attitude, found himself face to face with the unearthly visitor who drew them.

It was a not a stranger's figure. Her hair was white, as if with age, swept up with loose tendrils falling, curls framed the face that had not a wrinkle in it, and a tender bloom was on the skin. The arms were very long and feminine, her hands the same. Her feet, most delicately formed, were encased in delicate white slippers. She wore a gown of the purest white and round its high waist was bound a lustrous belt, the sheen of which was beautiful. She held a branch of fresh green holly in her hand; and, in singular contradiction of this wintry emblem, had her dress trimmed with summer flowers. But the strangest thing about her was that from the crown of her head there sprung a bright clear jet of light, by which all this was visible.

Darcy looked at it with increasing steadiness.

"Mama?" Darcy said somewhat indistinctly, for the face resembled that of Lady Anne Darcy. "Are you the Spirit whose coming was foretold to me?" asked Darcy.

"I am!" The voice was soft and gentle. Singularly low, as if instead of being so close beside him, it were at a distance.

"Who are you?" Darcy demanded.

"I am the Ghost of Christmas Past."

"Long past?" inquired Darcy

"No. Your past," replied the ghostly Lady Anne, her hand reaching out to brush a curl off Darcy's forehead.

"Mama," Darcy repeated softly. "Are you truly here?"

The ghost seemed about to nod, hesitated, then shook her head and repeated, "I am the Ghost of Christmas Past."

"What brought you here?" Darcy asked, greatly disappointed.

"Your welfare!" said the Ghost.

"I am very much obliged," Darcy thanked her.

"And your reclamation. Take heed of what you shall see!" She put out her hand as she spoke and clasped him gently by the arm. "Rise and walk with me!"

It would have been in vain for Darcy to plead that the weather and the hour were not adapted to pedestrian purposes; that bed was warm, and the thermometer a long way below freezing; that he was clad, but lightly in his shirtsleeves. The grasp, though gentle, was not to be resisted. He rose, but finding that Lady Anne made towards the window, clasped his waist-coat in supplication.

"I will fall," Darcy remonstrated.

"I would not let such a fate come to pass. Bear but a touch of my hand there," said the Spirit, laying it upon his heart, "and you shall be upheld in more than this!"

As the words were spoken, they passed through the wall and stood upon an open country road, with fields on either side. The city had entirely vanished. Not a vestige of it was to be seen. The darkness and the mist had vanished with it, for it was a clear, cold, winter day, with snow upon the ground. "Good Heavens," Darcy exclaimed. "It is Pemberley."

Lady Anne gazed upon him mildly. Her gentle touch, though it had been light and instantaneous, appeared still present to Darcy's sense of feeling. He was conscious of a thousand odors floating in the air, each one connected with a thousand thoughts and hopes and joys and cares long, long forgotten.

They walked along the drive, Darcy recognizing every gate and post and tree. Some shaggy ponies now were seen trotting towards them with a young Fitzwilliam (perhaps five or six years old) and his cousins, Edward and Frederick upon their backs, who called to their parents, riding in country gigs. Both parties were in great spirits, and shouted and laughed to each other, until the broad fields were so full of merry music that the crisp air laughed to hear it.

"These are but shadows of the things that have been," said the Ghost. "They have no consciousness of us."

The travelers passed on. Darcy and the Ghost followed them. The cart and ponies came to a stop on a large, snow-covered hill. A sled or two was removed from the back of the cart. Darcy watched as his younger self went sliding down the hill with a laugh. Darcy and his cousins continued in this amusement for some time.

"Look there," said the Spirit, as she pointed to Darcy's parents and his aunt and uncle.

"I do not see why children should be the only ones to have fun, my dear," the Countess remarked to her Earl. "And I do recall a time or two when you boasted of your prowess at building a snowman."

"I see that I shall live to regret those confessions, my love. I have not built a snowman in years," the Earl responded to his wife's teasing, but happily complied with her request.

The adults of the party began building a snowman and time slipped by quickly, for almost before the snowman was begun, he was finished.

"He looks lonely," said Lady Anne. "He needs a mate."

"And what is a more proper mate for a snowman, than a snowwoman?" asked the Countess, ready to start again.

"I fear he will have to wait for another day before he gets a partner. I fear my toes have frozen completely. I have been longing for a nice hot toddy for the past half hour," stated the Earl.

"But will we have time on another day? Catherine will be here soon, and other Christmas activities will take up a great deal time," Mr. Darcy questioned. "Perhaps we'd best do it now if it is going to be done. Who knows when we will have another opportunity?"

The matter was debated, with Mr. Darcy, Lady Anne, and the Countess arguing good-naturedly against the Earl and his cold feet. The argument was abandoned when a groom brought word that Lady Catherine had arrived at Pemberley and was awaiting their presence. The outing was over.

"They never did get the opportunity to make a mate for the snowman. He melted away come spring, all alone during that long winter," commented the Ghost, as she and Darcy stepped into the entry hall of the little Church at Lambton. Darcy had no notion how they got there.

Parishioners dressed in their best were leaving the building after the Christmas sermon. In the general melee of greetings, wishes of Merry Christmas, laughing children, and departing carriages, few noticed a tall man dressed in a gray cloak heading toward a young woman seated on a stone bench before an ancient yew tree that grew beside the church. Young Darcy was one of the few, and decided to follow.

"It is Mr. Annesley, my tutor," Darcy informed the Spirit, "and that is Miss Gordon, the vicar's daughter."

Mr. Annesley sat beside the young woman. He was smiling broadly and his eyes were shining. The only barrier between his present and future happiness lay in the ensuing answer to the most important of questions, although he felt reasonably secure of a favorable outcome.

"Miss Gordon," Mr. Annesley began as his face took on a serious demeanor, "if you could but spare me a few minutes of your time, there is a matter of great import that I wish to discuss with you."

"Of course, Mr. Annesley," Miss Gordon replied with a slight smile and happy light in her eyes.

"Miss Gordon, on this most joyous of days, will you do me the very great honor of consenting to become my wife?"

Her eyes filled with tears and her lips trembled, "I would be most happy to accept your proposal, Mr. Annesley."

A snowball hit the church wall just above young Darcy's head. Startled he looked around to see George Wickham running away with a smile on his face. No longer interested in his tutor's doings, he ran after the boy.

The older Darcy watched as the young couple approached his parents.

"Congratulations, Mr. Annesley, Miss Gordon. We were hoping that the two of you would find happiness together, and lately we have only been wondering when the announcement would be made." His father shook the tutor's hands.

"To chose this time to do so will only add to pleasures of the day," proclaimed his mother.

The Spirit touched Darcy on the arm, and he found they were now in his old schoolroom. He watching from the window as servants below loaded up a carriage.

"Why does Mr. Annesley have to go just because he is getting married?" the younger Darcy asked his father.

"It is not only his marriage, my boy, but soon you will also be going away to school."

"Cannot I go to his school?"

"No, indeed, for it would not do. He will be teaching at a school for the sons of the local tradesmen and shopkeepers. It is not the company you should be keeping. At school you will be among your peers, those whose situation in life is the same as yours."

"Is George Wickham to come to school with me or attend Mr. Annesley's school?"

"Neither, I will see that he is educated in a manner that is complementary to his position in life. Every man has his own station in life, from king to lowest beggar, and knowing where your place is amongst others is most important. You are descended from some of the oldest, most prominent families in England; be proud of that, of who you are: a Darcy of Pemberley."

Darcy looked out the window as the last of his tutor's belongings were loaded in the coach. In a few short weeks, he would also leave Pemberley. He was not looking forward to it and mentioned this to his father.

"Pemberley will always be here for you. You will be happy at your school, Fitzwilliam, just as Mr. Annesley will be happy in his new position. The school is pleased to have him and I have no doubt that he will be headmaster there before long."

The room vanished to be replaced by the nursery. Darcy and the Spirit were looking down at a peacefully sleeping baby. The Spirit tried to gently rock the cradle and was disappointed that her powers were not enough to make the shadows tangible.

The door opened. "Come meet your new sister, Fitzwilliam." Both parents ushered him into the room. He approached the baby cautiously. He looked into the cradle and was not overly impressed.

"She was so small she hardly seemed human to me. At school, I was envied for being an only child, but in turn, I envied those who had brothers and sisters," Darcy told the Spirit, looking over the shoulder of his younger self.

"And now you finally had one of your own."

"Yes, but she was not quite ready to play cricket with me, now was she?" he replied in self-deprecation.

"I imagine not." The spirit smiled.

His father said, "If you are gentle, you may hold her."

Young Fitzwilliam was not sure if he wanted to touch the baby. "I would rather not. She appears too fragile, and I could break her."

"Babies are sturdier than you think," his mother told him, "but you should do what you think is best for your sister."

"Yes, Fitzwilliam, it is your duty to look out for her and keep her from harm. You are her brother and protector." His father placed a hand upon his shoulder. "I know I can rely on you to do so."

The Ghost smiled thoughtfully and waved its hand, saying as it did so, "Let us see another Christmas!"

Darcy's former self grew larger at the words. How this was brought about, Darcy knew not. He only knew that it was quite correct; that everything had happened so; that there he was, home from school for the holiday.

He watched as Christmas day passed again, his mother, his father, Georgiana, and himself enjoying Christmas dinner, presents, reading poetry, and just being together as a family.

It was in the evening, and Darcy saw his younger self hide a yawn. His sister was already asleep upon a sofa. He watched as Lady Anne sat down beside him on the sofa, saying, "Now, William, I want to read you the verse I gave you. It is my wish for you that you become such a man when you are grown." And from *The Canterbury Tales* she began to read of the Knight:

> A Knight there was, and that a worthy man,
> Who, from the moment when he first began
> To ride forth, loved the code of chivalry:
> Honor and truth, freedom and courtesy.

As those words filled the room, Darcy knew this day. Unbeknownst to all, it had been the final Christmas he had shared with both his parents. After his mother death, his recollections of this time had him listening with keen interest to every word his mother spoke. Yet the evidence before him showed he had not attended the reading with anything more than a polite interest as his younger self tried to conceal another yawn. So he took the opportunity the Spirit provided to listen until the final words were spoken.

> ...Renowned he was; and, worthy, he was wise—
> Prudence, with him, was more than mere disguise;
> He was as meek in manner as a maid.
> Vileness he shunned, rudeness he never said
> In all his life, treating all persons right.
> He was a truly perfect, noble knight.

"Thank you, Mother, it is always a pleasure to listen to you read. I shall endeavor to live up to those expectations," said his younger self.

"'Vileness he shunned, rudeness he never said/In all his life, treating all persons right,'" quoted the Spirit. "You have not always lived up to those expectations."

"No, I have not, I have come to regret it, ma'am." Darcy frowned. He had not treated Elizabeth right, nor her sister Jane, nor his own friend Bingley. It had led to much misery for all parties.

He was walking up and down despairingly. Darcy looked at the Ghost, and with a mournful shaking of her head, the room changed to the one he had during his last year at Eton. He was pacing up and down the room in anticipation.

The door opened; the master said in a somewhat chilly voice, "Mr. Darcy, you have a caller, a female caller. As you know this is frowned upon, Mr. Darcy. However, in this case, I am prepared to make an exception for an exceptional young lady."

A little girl, much younger than Darcy, came darting in, and putting her arms about his neck and often kissing him, addressed him as her "Dear, dear brother."

"I have come to bring you home, dear brother!" said the child, clapping her tiny hands and bending down to laugh. "To bring you home, home, home!"

"Home, little Georgie?" returned the boy.

"Yes!" said the child, brimful of glee. "Father is awaiting you in the coach. I asked him if we might come and fetch you home, for the holiday will be much longer if we do not have to wait days and days for you to arrive. Papa said 'Yes, we should,' and sent me in here to bring you. And you're to go Cambridge," said the child, opening her eyes. "And are never to come back here; but first, we're to be together all the Christmas long and have the merriest time in all the world."

"You are quite a magpie, little Georgie!" exclaimed the boy.

She clapped her hands and laughed, and tried to touch his head, but being too little, laughed again and stood on tiptoe to embrace him. Then she began to drag him, in her childish eagerness, towards the door; and he, nothing loathe to go, accompanied her.

A voice in the hall cried, "Bring down Master Darcy's box, there!" and in the hall appeared the schoolmaster himself, who smiled on Master Darcy and shook hands with him. He then conveyed Darcy and his sister into his parlor. Here he produced a pot of tea and a block of curiously heavy cake, and administered installments of those dainties to the young people while at the same time sending out a meager servant to offer a glass of something to Mr. Darcy, who answered that he thanked the gentleman, but if it was the same wine as he had tasted before, he had rather not. Master Darcy's trunk being by this time tied on to the top of the chaise, the children bade the schoolmaster good-bye right willingly and, getting into it, drove gaily down the garden-sweep, the quick wheels dashing the hoarfrost and snow from off the dark leaves of the evergreens like spray.

"Always a beautiful creature," said the Ghost. "And she has a large heart!"

"So she has," returned Darcy. "You are right. I will not gainsay it, Spirit. God forbid!"

"She is now a woman," said the Ghost, "and will have, I think, many suitors."

"She has had one suitor already," Darcy returned bitterly, "but he only cared for her money. He never cared for Georgiana."

"True," said the Ghost. "Young George Wickham never cared about anyone save himself."

Darcy seemed uneasy in his mind that the Spirit should know so much about his personal business and answered briefly, "Yes."

Although Darcy and the Spirit had but that moment left Eton behind them, they now were in the thoroughfares of Cambridge, where shadowy strangers passed; where shadowy carts and coaches tumbled along the way, and all the other tumults of a city. It was made plain enough, by the dressing of the shops, that here too it was Christmas time again; but it was evening and the streets were lighted up.

The Ghost stopped at a certain pub door and asked Darcy if he knew it.

"Know it?" Darcy was incredulous. "Why, I spent many nights here while at Cambridge! It is the Fuzzy Whig!"

They went in. An old gentleman in a Welch wig was standing behind the bar. If he had been two inches shorter, he could not have seen over the top of the bar.

Darcy cried in great excitement. "It is Old Peterson alive again! Many hours we spent in the pub, talking philosophy and literature..."

"And other fancies of young men?" asked the Spirit.

Darcy blushed and nodded, and looked over this memory.

Old Peterson laid down his polishing cloth and looked up at the clock, which pointed to the hour of seven. He rubbed his hands, adjusted his capacious apron, laughed to himself, and called out in a comfortable and jovial voice as the door to the taproom opened:

"Yo ho, there! Mr. Darcy! Lord Wilkins!"

Darcy's former self, now grown to a young man, came in briskly, accompanied by his fellow classmate.

"Richard Wilkins, to be sure!" said Darcy to the Ghost. "Yes. There he is. He was so lively, it is hard to believe that he is already gone, killed in the Battle of Talavera."

"Yo ho, boys! No more work for me tonight. Christmas Eve, Lord Wilkins. Christmas, Mr. Darcy!" cried old Peterson with a sharp clap of his hands.

Peterson held a party for all those fine young scholars at Cambridge, who, for whatever reason, could not make it home for Christmas. Darcy had not been particularly eager to join his father and sister in spending the holiday with his aunt, Lady Catherine. So he accepted Lord Wilkins invitation to stay in Cambridge during the holiday.

More students entered behind Darcy and his friend. Peterson skipped around the bar with wonderful agility. "Go on up, my lads, and enjoy the party!"

Up they ventured into the public room where everyone was gathering. The floor was swept, the lamps were trimmed, fuel was heaped upon the fire; and the pub was as snug, warm, dry, and as bright as could be desired from a ballroom on a cold winter's night.

In came the musicians with their music books and made an orchestra of one corner, tuning their instruments like fifty stomachaches. In came Mrs. Peterson, one vast smile, followed by the three Miss Petersons, beaming and lovable, and the six young followers whose hearts they held. In came the housemaid with her baker, the cook with her milkman, and the boy from over the way, who tried to hide himself from the girl next door who had caught his shy heart. More friends of the Petersons and more students arrived. In they all came, one after another—some shyly, some boldly, some gracefully, some awkwardly, some pushing, some pulling—but they all came to the party.

There were dances, and there were forfeits and still more dances. There were tables laden with cake, negus, a great piece of cold roast, a great piece of cold ham, and mince pies. Plenty of beer flowed throughout the night. But the greatest event of the evening came after the roast, when the fiddler struck up "Sir

Roger de Coverley." Then, old Peterson stood up to dance with Mrs. Peterson. Four and twenty pair of partners joined in—people who were not to be trifled with, people who would dance and had no notion of walking, including Darcy.

But if they had been twice as many, old Peterson would have been a match for them and so would Mrs. Peterson.

The Spirit noticed this and said to Darcy, "She was worthy to be his partner in every sense of the term. If that is not high praise, tell me what is higher and I will use it."

"Indeed," Darcy observed from the sidelines, "all of the couples were well matched. Oh, the women laughed and flirted and danced with the students, but it was clear that they were just having an evening's fun. They were truly happy with their own partners."

When the clock struck eleven, the domestic ball broke up. Mr. and Mrs. Peterson took their stations, one on either side of the door, and shaking hands with every person individually as he or she went out, wished him or her a Merry Christmas. Everybody had retired but Darcy and his friend, so they did the same to them; and thus the cheerful voices died away, and the lads were left to find their way back to their rooms.

During the whole of this time, Darcy had acted quite unlike himself. His heart and soul were in the scene and with his former self. He corroborated everything, remembered everything, and enjoyed everything. It was not until now, when the bright faces of his former self and Dick were turned from them, that he remembered the Ghost and became conscious that it was looking full upon him.

"Were you not bored?" asked the Ghost, as they followed the young men.

"Bored?" echoed Darcy.

"I should think you would be," answered the Spirit, "at an assembly such as that, with people of little character and no breeding. Cooks and milkmen, housemaids and bakers?"

"It was not the company," said Darcy, heated by the remark, and speaking unconsciously like his Cambridge self. "Peterson could not bear to see anyone unhappy. The happiness he gave was to all who needed it, especially to those who were alone during the holidays; it mattered not if you were a Duke or a dust boy. All mingled at the Fuzzy Whig. Pretensions were not allowed."

He felt the Spirit's glance and stopped.

"What is the matter?" asked the Ghost.

"Nothing particular," said Darcy.

"Something, I think," the Ghost insisted.

"No," said Darcy. "No. I should like to have behaved better at an assembly I attended in Meryton. That's all."

His former self turned down the lane as he gave utterance to the wish; and Darcy and the Ghost again stood side-by-side, alone in the open air.

"My time grows short," observed the Spirit. "Quick!"

The address was again familiar to Darcy, a small house in an exclusive section of London. Darcy saw himself. He was older now. It was the Christmas dinner of a year ago. He was not alone, but sat across from a red-headed woman in a green dress. He was embarrassed that his mother should see him here.

"It matters little," she said softly. "Very little. Another has displaced me; and if she can cheer and comfort you in the time to come, as I have tried to do, I have no just cause to grieve."

"Who has displaced you?" he rejoined.

"I know not, but you have not been the same since you came back from Hertfordshire."

"You are mistaken," he said. "There is no-one!"

"Are you trying to convince me or yourself?" she asked gently.

"There is no-one," he repeated. "I am not changed towards you."

She shook her head.

"Am I?"

"Our *friendship* is an old one. It was made when we were both in need of comfort and companionship. You were still grieving for your father and I was *not* grieving for my husband. Still, I had much to recover from."

"He was not a gentleman," he said quietly.

"True," she returned. "Marriage, that which promised happiness when I was young, was fraught with misery. I learned that a parent does not always know what is best for their child. A fine name, good income, and a grand home will never make up for a lack of character in its owner." She hesitated a moment before continuing. "I am not the child I was upon my marriage nor am I the pathetic creature that I was after it was over. You helped me more than I can ever acknowledge nor can I sufficiently express my gratitude."

"Gratitude was never necessary," replied Darcy.

"I know that it is not, but it is what I feel. It is with much thanks that I release you."

"Have I sought release?"

"In words? No. Never."

"In what then?"

"In a changed nature; in an altered spirit; the atmosphere of another who is ever on your mind; another hope as its great end. If the past had never been between us," said the woman, looking mildly, but with steadiness, upon him, "tell me, would you seek me out now? Ah, no!"

He seemed to yield to the justice of this supposition in spite of himself. But he said with a struggle, "You think not."

"I can hardly think otherwise," she answered. "Heaven knows! How can I believe that you would choose me when I can see that there is one who you weigh every female against? Choose her; do not know the repentance and regret I did. Whatever happens, I am hopeful that we will remain friends."

She lifted her wine glass and toasted, "May you be happy with the one you love!"

Darcy remembered that he felt some inner turmoil, for he had not yet been ready to acknowledge the truth of her statements. But almost as if it acted of its own accord, Darcy's hand lifted the wine glass in an answering salute.

He turned upon the Ghost and saw that it looked upon him with a questioning face.

"Interesting, is it not, that some can see so clearly, while others blind themselves to truth?" asked the Spirit. Darcy looked at himself calming sipping wine. A year ago he would have smugly thought that the woman he wanted to marry would return his sentiments. He had been in dire need of the comeuppance Elizabeth had delivered.

As if the Spirit read his thoughts, he was in the drawing room at the Hunsford parsonage.

"Spirit!" said Darcy. "Please, show me no more! Conduct me home. Do you delight in torturing me?"

"Only one shadow more!" exclaimed the Ghost.

"No more!" cried Darcy. "No more. I do not wish to see it. Show me no more!"

But his words were in vain, for he could hear himself exclaim, "In vain have I struggled. It will not do. My feelings will not be repressed. You must allow me to tell you how ardently I admire and love you."

Darcy listened as he made avowals of all that he still and had long felt for Elizabeth. He could hear how he spoke on the subject of his sense of her inferiority—of its being a degradation—of the family obstacles which judgment had always opposed to inclination—all were dwelt on.

Darcy heard himself conclude by representing to her the strength of his attachment, which, in spite of all his endeavors, he had found impossible to conquer, and expressing his hope that it would now be rewarded by her acceptance of his hand. As he said this, Darcy cringed beside the Spirit, for he could easily see that he had no doubt of a favorable answer. He spoke of apprehension and anxiety, but his countenance expressed security. Such a circumstance could only exasperate Elizabeth, he now knew. Yet it was like being cut by a knife to hear rejection again.

"Spirit," said Darcy in a broken voice, "remove me from this place. There was no need to bring me here, madam, for not a word, not a syllable have I forgotten. Do you wish to hear for yourself?"

Darcy began to recite along with Elizabeth each and every word of her rejection. Not one word was spoken out of place.

"You could not have made me the offer of your hand in any possible way that would have tempted me to accept it. From the very beginning, from the first moment I may almost say, of my acquaintance with you, your manners, impressing me with the fullest belief of your arrogance, your conceit, and your selfish disdain of the feelings of others, were such as to form that ground-work of disapprobation, on which succeeding events have built so immoveable a dislike; and I had not known you a month before I felt that you were the last man in the world whom I could ever be prevailed on to marry."

As the last word fell, Darcy turned on the Spirit with such a mixture of anger, bitterness, and despair, that she took a step away from him. "I told you these were shadows of the things that have been," said the Ghost. "That they are what they are, do not blame me!"

"You have said quite enough, madam." It was as if Darcy was speaking to both Elizabeth and the Spirit. "I perfectly comprehend your feelings, and have now only to be ashamed of what my own have been. Forgive me for having taken up so much of your time, and accept my best wishes for your health and happiness."

"Leave me! Take me back. Haunt me no longer!"

The Ghost took a step away from him and then another, her light getting fainter, and repeated, "That the shadows are what they are, do not blame me!" each word further diminishing her light and appearance. Darcy observed a final burst of light that was burning so high and bright that he was forced to close his eyes.

When he opened them again, he was conscious of being alone, exhausted, and overcome by an irresistible drowsiness; and, further, of being in his own bedroom. He gave the pillow a welcoming squeeze as he crawled into bed; and he had barely time to lie full on the bed before he sank into a heavy sleep.

The Ghost appeared beside the bed. Gently, it brushed a lock of Darcy's hair away from his forehead. He mumbled in his sleep and the Spirit disappeared.

Chapter 3

CHRISTMAS PRESENT

WAKING SUDDENLY AND SITTING up in bed to get his thoughts together, Darcy had no occasion to be told that the bell was again upon the stroke of one. He felt that he was restored to consciousness in the nick of time for the especial purpose of holding a conference with the second messenger dispatched to him. But, finding that he dreaded the thought of not knowing which of his curtains this new specter would draw back, he put every one of them aside with his own hands and, lying down again, established a sharp lookout all round the bed. He did not wish to be taken by surprise and made nervous. Darcy wished to challenge the Spirit on the moment of its appearance.

He was ready for a good, broad field of strange appearances, and nothing between a baby and a rhinoceros would have astonished him very much.

Now, being prepared for almost anything, he was not by any means prepared for nothing; the bell struck one and no shape appeared. Five minutes, ten minutes, a quarter of an hour went by, yet nothing came. All this time, a blaze of light streamed upon the clock as it proclaimed the hour; and which, being the only light, was more alarming than a dozen ghosts, as he was powerless to make out what it meant. At last, however, he began to think that the source and secret of this ghostly light might be in the adjoining room, from whence, on further tracing it, it seemed to shine. This idea taking full possession of his mind, he got up softly and went to the door.

The moment Darcy's hand touched the lock a familiar voice called him by his name and bade him enter. He obeyed.

It was his sitting room. There was no doubt about that. But it had undergone a surprising transformation. The walls and ceiling were so hung with living green that it looked a perfect grove. The crisp leaves of holly, mistletoe, and ivy reflected back the light. A mighty blaze went roaring up the chimney. Heaped up on the floor, to form a kind of throne, were poultry, great joints of meat, mince pies, plum puddings, red-hot chestnuts, fruits, immense twelfth-cakes, and seething bowls of punch, which perfumed the chamber with their delicious steam.

In easy state upon a couch, there sat Georgiana, glorious to see: bearing a glowing torch, in a shape not unlike a horn of plenty, and holding it up, high up, to shed its light on Darcy as he came round the door.

"Come in!" exclaimed the Ghost. "Come in, and know me better!"

Darcy entered rapidly, "Georgiana, what is the meaning of this? Why are you not at Matlock House?" he demanded.

"I am the Ghost of Christmas Present," said the Spirit. "Look upon me!"

Darcy did so. She was clothed in one simple green dress, bordered with white fur. Her feet, observable beneath the gown, were bare, and on her head she wore no other covering than a holly wreath, set here and there with burning candles. Her blonde curls were long and free, her face was genial, her eyes were sparkling, her hands were open, her voice was cheery, her demeanor was unconstrained, and her air was joyful. Except for her more outgoing manner, the Spirit looked just like Darcy's sister.

"You have never seen the like of me before!" exclaimed the Spirit.

"Every day of my life, I have seen your likeness," Darcy made answer to it.

"You have never seen the like of me before!" repeated the Spirit.

"If you say I have not," agreed Darcy, "then I have not."

The Ghost of Christmas Present rose.

"Spirit," said Darcy, "conduct me where you will. I went forth last night on compulsion, and I learnt a lesson, which is working now. Tonight, if you have aught to teach me, let me learn it."

"Touch my gown!"

Darcy did as he was told and held it fast.

The greenery, food, and punch all vanished instantly. So did the room, the fire, the ruddy glow, and the hour of night, and they stood in the city streets on Christmas morning. Darcy and the Spirit began to walk down the road, where the people made a rough but brisk and not unpleasant kind of music, in scraping the snow from the pavement in front of their dwellings.

The people who were shoveling away were jovial and full of glee, calling out to one another from the sidewalk and now and then exchanging a facetious snowball—better-natured missile far than many a wordy jest—laughing heartily if it went right and not less heartily if it went wrong.

Darcy and the Spirit passed a fruit stall. As some girls went by, they glanced at the hung-up mistletoe and giggled. Darcy looked at it also; he had not understood the appeal of the plant.

"Mistletoe was sacred to the Nordic goddess of love. She decreed that whoever should stand under the mistletoe, no harm would befall them, only a kiss, a token of love. Is it any wonder that those young woman wish to indulge in the tradition?"

"I suppose not," Darcy replied as they walked on. The blended scents of tea and coffee, cinnamon and other spices filled the morning air. Darcy took a deep breath, letting the scents fill his mind. He had not taken the time to indulge in such a small but glorious pleasure in a long time.

Soon the steeples called all good people to come to church and chapel, and away they went, walking through the streets in their best clothes and with their brightest faces.

In time the bells ceased, and there emerged from the scores of bye-streets innumerable people, carrying their dinners to the bakers' shops. The sight of these poor revelers appeared to interest the Spirit very much, for she stood with Darcy beside him in a baker's doorway and, taking off the covers as their bearers passed, sprinkled incense on their dinners from her torch. There was a genial foreshadowing of all the dinners and the progress of their cooking in the thawed blotch of wet above each baker's oven and where the pavement smoked, as if its stones were cooking too.

It was a very uncommon kind of torch, for once or twice when there were angry words between some dinner-carriers who had jostled each other, she shed a few drops of water on them from it and their good humor was restored directly.

"It's a shame to quarrel upon Christmas Day."

"So it is! So it is! Have a Merry Christmas!"

Away the former combatants went, feeling that all was right in their world.

"Is there a peculiar flavor in what you sprinkle from your torch?" asked Darcy as they resumed their walk.

"There is. It is my own special spice."

"Would it apply to any kind of dinner on this day?" asked Darcy.

"To any kindly given. To a poor one most."

"Why to a poor one most?" asked Darcy.

"Because it needs it most. My spice makes each dish taste its absolute best. It will cause the food to linger on the tongue and in the belly much longer."

"Spirit," said Darcy, after a moment's thought, "I have done what I could to relieve the suffering of those in my sphere who are more unfortunate than I. No one at Pemberley ever goes hungry," said Darcy.

"Indeed not!" cried the Spirit. "You oversee those on your estate well, and though it is not wrong to concentrate your good-will in one place, the world is larger than your estate."

The good Spirit led Darcy straight to the Gardiners; for there she went and took Darcy with her, holding to her gown, and on the threshold of the door the Spirit smiled and stopped to bless Edward Gardiner's dwelling with the sprinkling of her torch.

Mrs. Gardiner, dressed in a fashionable gown that was festooned in ribbons, laid the tablecloth, assisted by Belinda Crachit, the second housemaid, also dressed in her holiday best. The oldest boy, Master Robert Gardiner, plunged his fingers stealthily into the sugarplums, surreptitiously stuffing the sweets into his mouth whenever his mother's back was turned.

And now the smallest Gardiner, a girl named Alice, came tearing in, screaming, "I smell the goose, I smell the goose!"

"I can smell it also, my dear, there is no need to shout," Mrs. Gardiner remonstrated as Alice danced merrily around the table. Taking a deep breath, the luxurious scents of sage and onion filled her senses. "Robert, if you do not stop eating those sugarplums, you will have no room for the goose, which means there will be plenty more for the rest of us. Stoke the fire so a more cheerful blaze greets your father."

Robert swallowed the last of his treats, "Yes, ma'am."

"Whatever can be keeping your father?" Mrs. Gardiner wondered aloud as she left the dining room. "And your brother, William? And Kate is also late by half-an-hour!" Kate had gone for a walk in the park with her best friend. It was the best way to show off the pretty red coat and furry white muff she received as gifts.

"Here's Kate, Mother!" As the door opened to let in the older daughter Alice cried, "There is such a goose, Kate!"

"No doubt your special spice is on that goose," Darcy remarked.

The Spirit smiled, "The little one is in no need of it. She already has all the season she needs."

"Why, my dear, how cold you are!" said Mrs. Gardiner, rubbing her daughter's hands. "I thought you would be warm enough in that new coat."

"I was more than comfortable. We had a wonderful time at the park," replied the girl, "and it was such a pleasant walk this morning, Mother! The newly fallen snow twinkled like stars."

"Yes, that is all very well," replied Mrs. Gardiner as she led the children into the parlor. "Sit down before the fire, my dear, and warm yourself!"

"No, no! Father is coming," cried Alice, who was everywhere at once. "Hide, Kate, hide!"

So Kate hid herself and in came Edward, the father, looking quite seasonable in a red silk vest; his youngest son, William, was beside him.

"Why, where is Kate?" cried Edward Gardiner, looking round.

"Still at the park," said Mrs. Gardiner.

"At the park?" asked Edward. "She will be late for Christmas Dinner!"

Kate came out of hiding prematurely from behind the door and ran into his arms. "I would never miss dinner. I swear I could smell the goose as soon as I turned the corner."

Alice grabbed her brother and bore William off to the kitchen, "You have to hear the pudding singing in the copper. You have to!"

"And how did William behave?" asked Mrs. Gardiner as the children left the room.

"As good as gold," said Edward, "and better. Coming home, he gave the guinea he received for Christmas to a crippled boy, much the same age as himself. He told me afterwards that he helped the boy because he was a cripple and on Christmas Day it is good to remember those less fortunate than himself." His voice was filled with pride when he related this deed.

Before another word was spoken, William came back, escorted by his sister, and seated himself before the fire.

A servant brought in fixings for Mr. Gardiner's special Christmas punch and he compounded a hot mixture in a jug with gin and lemons, and stirred it round and round. Master Robert, along with Alice, went to check on the goose. Soon they returned with news that dinner was ready to be served.

There was a mad scramble of children to the dining room. The Gardiners quickly sat down for dinner and grace was said. The servants entered with the bird in high procession. It was succeeded by a breathless pause, as Mr. Gardiner, looking slowly all along the carving knife, prepared to plunge it in the breast. When he did, and when the long expected gush of stuffing issued forth, a murmur of delight arose all round the board. William cried, "Hurrah!" and Alice clapped.

Everyone ate until they had enough, and the youngest Gardiners in particular were steeped in goose and sage and onion to their eyebrows!

But now, Belinda was exchanging the dinner plates in anticipation of dessert. She left the room. In half a minute she returned, flushed but smiling proudly, with the pudding, like a speckled cannon ball, so hard and firm, blazing in ignited brandy.

"Oh, what a wonderful pudding!" Edward Gardiner said. Everybody had something to say about it; all praise was sent to Cook.

At last the dinner was all done, the cloth was cleared, and the fire made up in the parlor. The punch being tasted and considered perfect, apples and oranges were put upon the table, and chestnuts were roasting in the open fire. Then, all the Gardiner family drew round the hearth.

Golden goblets held the hot stuff from the jug; Edward served it out with beaming looks, while the chestnuts on the fire sputtered and cracked noisily.

Then Edward proposed: "A Merry Christmas to us all, my dears. God bless us!"

Which all the family echoed.

"God bless us every one!" said William, the last of all.

He sat very close to his father's side upon his stool. Edward held his hand in his, for he loved his children and was not averse to showing it.

"Spirit," said Darcy, with an interest he had never felt before, "Why are we here?"

"Quiet," replied the Ghost, "for you are here to learn."

"Mr. Darcy!" said Edward Gardiner. "I'll give you Mr. Darcy!"

Darcy turned speedily on hearing his own name.

"Mr. Darcy?" questioned Mrs. Gardiner. "Why, he is not part of the family nor is he likely to be."

"My dear," said Edward, "he has done our family a very good turn this year. Should we not acknowledge it on Christmas Day?"

"It is just that I was hoping that he would be a part of our family by now," said she, "and you did too. And poor Elizabeth is pining, though she thinks she can hide it."

Darcy was startled by this information. He glanced at the Spirit who nodded slowly.

"My dear," was Edward's mild answer, "we cannot change what has passed. We can only wish him well on this Christmas Day and hope the best for both his and Elizabeth's futures."

"You are right, my dear. I will drink his health for Elizabeth's sake," said Mrs. Gardiner, "and for his. May there be a long life before him. A Merry Christmas and a Happy New Year! He will be very merry and very happy, I have no doubt, if he would only wed Elizabeth!"

"Emily!" remonstrated Mr. Gardiner, but in a playful manner. He lifted his glass in toast, "To Mr. Darcy and dear Elizabeth, may they realize that they are made for one another in the New Year!"

Edward Gardiner then read them the Christmas story from the family Bible. Other family stories were related and talked of. Kate told them that morning she had seen a lady and a lord, and how the lord "was much about as tall as Robert," at which Robert pulled himself up as tall as he was able and, walking on his toes, bowed grandly before each member of his family, who laughed in delight. All this time, the chestnuts and the punch went round and round; and by-and-by they had a song or two.

There was nothing of high mark in this. They were a happy family—grateful, pleased with one another, and contented with the time; and when they faded, and looked happier yet in the bright sprinklings of the Spirit's torch at parting, Darcy had his eye upon them until the last.

By this time it was getting dark and snowing pretty heavily; and as Darcy and the Spirit went along the streets, the brightness of the roaring fires in kitchens, parlors, and all sorts of rooms was wonderful.

The children of the house were running out into the snow to meet their married sisters, brothers, cousins, uncles, aunts, and be the first to greet them. Here, again, were shadows on the window-blind of guests assembling; and there a group of handsome girls tripped lightly off to some near neighbor's house, where the single men saw them enter in a glow!

And now, they stopped in front of one particularly grand house. "My uncle's house?" asked Darcy.

A light shone from the window of the mansion, and swiftly they advanced towards it. Passing through the wall, they found a cheerful company assembled around a glowing fire. An older man and woman, with their children and their grandchildren, were all decked out gaily in their holiday attire. The Earl was singing them a Christmas song; and from time to time, they all joined in the chorus.

Georgiana, who had been playing the piano accompaniment, stilled as the song died. Col. Fitzwilliam came over to the piano and suggested that Georgiana play the new music she had received as a Christmas present. Georgiana began to play.

"I hope you are pleased with your gift?" the Colonel inquired.

"Yes, very much, thank you. And are you pleased with your gift? Fitzwilliam said that you could use it to ward off your many female admirers."

Fitzwilliam eyed the beautifully carved ebony walking stick. "I would never be so ungentlemanly. Who am I to deny their admiration, especially as it feeds my own vanity?" Colonel

Fitzwilliam heaved a great sigh. "Though it is a terrible burden to be the object of so much admiration."

"Pish-tosh!" cried the Countess.

"Fish toss!" echoed his young niece and nephew. The adults broke into uncontrolled laughter.

Darcy smiled in amusement himself.

"What is the name of this piece?" the Colonel asked.

"*Ode to Joy* by Herr Beethoven," Georgiana replied with a sad little sigh.

"You do not appear to be very joyful, my dear," observed the Colonel softly.

"It is just that I do not believe that I shall get the present that I want the most for Christmas."

"And what present would that be?" inquired the Colonel.

Georgiana leaned over the piano to whisper into Colonel Fitzwilliam's ear, "A new sister. A particular new sister."

The Colonel whispered back, "Now that is peculiar, for I wished for a new cousin for Christmas. A particular new cousin."

And though they spoke in whisper, Darcy could hear their wishes as if they were whispering into his ears.

The Spirit did not tarry, but bade Darcy hold her robe, and passing on above the city sped on to the sea. To Darcy's horror, looking back, he saw the last of the land, a frightful range of rocks, behind them; and his ears were deafened by the thundering of water, as it rolled and roared and raged among the dreadful caverns it had worn, and fiercely tried to undermine the earth.

The Ghost sped on, above the black and heaving sea until they lighted on a ship. They stood beside the helmsman at the wheel, the lookout in the bow, the officers who had the watch—dark, ghostly figures in their several stations—but every man among them hummed a Christmas tune, "Three Ships" being the most popular. One spoke below his breath to his companion of some bygone Christmas Day, with homeward hopes belonging to it.

"And it is for certain that the Captain is having a very merry Christmas this year."

"Aye," cried the men, "here's to the Cap'n and his Missus, may many more Christmas days come their way."

Darcy was then in the Captain's cabin. A man and a woman occupied the room. Joining their hands over the rough table at which they sat, they wished each other Merry Christmas.

"If I harbor any regrets of the past, it is not being able to see your face on Christmas these last six years. Nor to witness your delight in singing Christmas songs this day, Anne," said the Captain.

"Frederick, please do not find regret in the past. It cannot be changed. Six years may seem long now, but in the sum of our existence are but a few. I fell in love with your youth in my youth. I fell in love with the man you are now, as the woman I am now."

"You harbor no regrets then?"

"I shall always have a small scar on my heart for what might have been. But it in no way damages the delight for what I have now."

While listening to the couple and thinking what a solemn thing it was to live without the woman you love for six years, it was a great surprise to Darcy to hear a hearty laugh. It was a much greater surprise to Darcy to recognize it as Bingley's and to find himself in a bright, dry, gleaming room, with the Spirit standing smiling by his side, and looking at Bingley with approving affability!

"Ha, ha!" laughed Bingley. "Ha, ha, ha!"

"I know of no man who delights more in a laugh than Bingley," Darcy told the Spirit.

"There is nothing in the world so irresistibly contagious as laughter and good-humor," the Spirit replied. Bingley laughed, and then the assembled family and friends joined in; Elizabeth even managed a smile.

"Ha, ha! Ha, ha, ha, ha!"

Elizabeth set down her cup of tea and looked out the window of Netherfield, unconsciously reenacting Darcy's typical stance. Her face was serious in contrast to those around her.

Jane, Charles, and Mr. Bennet watched her actions with concern. The rest of the party ignored her except for Miss Bingley.

"How interesting," said Miss Bingley, "that the witty Miss Bennet is not as pleasant as she might be? I should be relieved that she has finally learned to keep her tongue still."

"Caroline, Miss Bennet might hear you," cautioned Louisa.

Turning to her sister, Caroline shrugged and said, "He is so very rich, Louisa, and handsome, and he cannot have affections for Miss Bennet or else he would be here. I shall take his absence as a sign that he is over his infatuation."

Jane approached the window and laid her hand on Elizabeth arm. Shortly before Jane married, Elizabeth had confided a little of her feelings for Darcy to her sister.

"I am well, Jane, perfectly well," Elizabeth reassured her sister.

"I shall put as much faith in those words as when I voiced the same last summer," said Jane.

"At least you had some small hope of having your words proven false, while I have none."

"Oh, but I have hope for you!" said Jane. "And for him. I am sorry for him; I could not be angry with him if I tried. He also suffers, I am sure, Elizabeth."

"Jane, I wish I could I believe that."

"It is Christmas, Elizabeth. A time for wishes to come to true." She hugged her sister.

In the blink of an eye, the room filled with more guests. Everyone was talking about the dinner they had just consumed and praised it for being fine.

"Well! I'm very glad to hear it," teased Bingley, "because I do not have great faith in these young housekeepers. What do you say, Topper?"

His friend answered, "A bachelor was a wretched outcast, who has no right to express an opinion on the subject. When I find myself in your happy circumstances, I will offer an opinion." Topper cast his eyes over Elizabeth, clearly taken with this new sister-in-law of his friend. Darcy stepped in front of Elizabeth as if to hide her from the man's gaze, quite forgetting that the occupants of the room could not see him.

After tea, they had some music. Caroline played on the harp; and Elizabeth played a simple little air, which had been familiar to Darcy from childhood. When this strain of music sounded, his mind drifted to the meeting at Pemberley and memories came upon his mind; he softened with each thought and reflected that he could have listened to her for eternity. His memories were shattered when Mary Bennet took over pianoforte duties.

But the company did not devote the whole evening to music. Games came next, especially their childhood favorites, for it is good to return to childhood sometimes and there never is a better time than Christmas. First they played forfeits, then came the game of blind-man's bluff that caused Darcy's jealousy to rise.

The Spirit and Darcy gazed upon the revelers. "The way Topper goes after Elizabeth is an outrage on the credulity of human nature. I no more believe Topper is really blind than I believe he has eyes in his boots," said Darcy harshly. "Knocking down the fire-irons, tumbling over the chairs, bumping against the piano, smothering himself among the curtains, wherever she goes, there he goes. He always knows where Elizabeth is. He does not try to catch anybody else. My opinion is there is a conspiracy between him and Miss Bingley." The Ghost of Christmas Present nodded in agreement, only remarking that a pretty young lady of marriageable age often attracted admirers.

Elizabeth laughed, "It is not fair, you never try for anyone else."

At last, Topper caught her, and under the mistletoe too. Darcy was outraged as Topper stole a kiss that should have gone to him. Elizabeth seemed quite surprised by the kiss, for her mind had not been on *this* friend of Bingley's.

Jane had not joined the blind-man's buff party, but was made comfortable with a large chair and a footstool, in a snug corner, where the Ghost and Darcy stood close behind her. She did join in the game of How, When, and Where, and she was very good and—to the secret joy of Bingley—beat her sisters hollow. There might have been twenty people there, young and old, but they all played, and after awhile so did Darcy; often forgetting, in the interest he had in what was going on, that his voice made no sound in their ears, he sometimes came out with his guess quite loud (especially when it was Topper's turn to answer), and very often guessed quite right too.

The Ghost was greatly pleased to find him in this mood, and looked upon him with such favor that he begged like a boy to be allowed to stay until the guests departed. "Here is a new game," said Darcy. "One half hour, Spirit, only one!"

It was a Game called Yes and No, where Bingley had to think of something and the rest must find out what, he only answering yes or no to their questions as the case was. The brisk fire of questioning to which he was exposed elicited from him that he was thinking of an animal, a live animal, rather a disagreeable animal, a savage animal, an animal that growled and grunted sometimes, and talked sometimes, and lived in London, and walked about the streets, and wasn't made a show of, and wasn't led by anybody, and didn't live in a menagerie, and was never killed in a market. At last Mrs. Bennet cried out:

"I have found it out! I know what it is! I know what it is!"

"What is it?" cried Bingley.

"Mr. Darcy!"

"Mama, it certainly is not!" cried Elizabeth. However, there was much admiration for Mrs. Bennet's answer and only a few objections. Mr. Bingley was one who did object.

"It is not so, my dear Mrs. Bennet. He encouraged me to go after a most precious gift," said Bingley, looking at Jane, "and it would be ungrateful of me not to drink his health. Here is a glass of mulled wine ready for our hands," he said as footmen carried trays of wine around the room. "I say Merry Christmas and a Happy New Year to you, Darcy, wherever you are!"

"Mr. Darcy!" the guests cried.

"A Merry Christmas and a Happy New Year, Mr. Darcy," said Elizabeth softly.

Darcy had imperceptibly become so gay and light of heart that he would have pledged the unconscious Elizabeth in return if the Ghost had given him time. But the whole scene passed off in the breath of the last word spoken by Elizabeth and he and the Spirit were again upon their travels.

The Spirit took Darcy to foreign lands where young soldiers read letters from their faithful ladies back home. They stood beside sick beds, where husbands attended their wives and vice versa; they saw couples in poverty; they saw struggling men and their patient wives who held greater hopes, and couples whose hopes had been fulfilled and now lived in riches.

It was a long night, if it were only one night and Darcy had his doubts of this, because the Christmas holidays appeared to be condensed into the space of time they passed together. It was strange too, that while not seeming to melt, the candles on the Ghost's head grew shorter and shorter. Darcy had observed this change, but never spoke of it until they left a children's Twelfth Night party, when, looking at the Spirit as they stood together in an open place, he noticed that the lights were almost out.

"Your candles are almost burnt out; do you not need new ones?"

"These are the only candles that I need. When they are gone, I am gone."

"Are spirits' lives so short?" asked Darcy.

"My life upon this globe is very brief," replied the Ghost. "It ends tonight."

"Tonight!" cried Darcy.

"Tonight at midnight. Hark! The Time is drawing near."

The chimes were ringing the three quarters past eleven at that moment.

"Forgive me if I am not justified in what I ask," said Darcy, looking intently at the Spirit's robe, "but I see something strange and not belonging to yourself protruding from behind your skirts. Is it a foot or a claw?"

"It might be a claw, for what little flesh there is upon it," was the Spirit's sorrowful reply. "Look here."

From the folds of her dress, she brought forth two children, a boy and girl, wretched, abject, frightful, hideous, and miserable. They knelt down at her feet and clung upon the outside of her garment.

"Darcy, look down here!" instructed the Ghost.

Their appearance was that of horrible and dreadful monsters. Yellow, meager, ragged, scowling, and wolfish devils that glared out of menacing eyes. Their stained and shriveled hands looked ready to pinch and pull, and tear him into shreds.

Darcy started back, appalled. "Spirit, are they yours?" Darcy asked.

"They are yours," said the Spirit, looking down upon them. "And they cling to me, fleeing from their father. This boy is Fear.

This girl is Pride. Beware of both of them and all of their degree, for much good is prevented when they work together. But most of all beware this boy. For he will take over your life, and you will live in his shadow, instead of he in yours," warned the Spirit, stretching out her hand towards Rosings, as they were among the hedgerows now.

"See what happens when fear and pride take over a life."

Darcy and the Spirit were now in the dining room of Rosings. Lady Catherine sat at one end of the long table, her daughter about half way down, next to Mrs. Jenkins. Anne sniffed and coughed her way through dinner. Lady Catherine ignored her and kept a running monologue.

"Lady Catherine, the staff was wondering if they could have the rest of the evening off," the butler interrupted.

"They already have half a day tomorrow. That is sufficient; any more is taking advantage of my generosity and I will not allow that."

"Yes, ma'am," the butler bowed out. Lady Catherine continued her monologue, criticizing and advising on everything from Mr. Collins's sermon, to the lack of cleanliness in both stables and mangers (how on the earth the Savior was allowed to be born there, she had no reason, she only knew that she would have planned the event much better), to the presumptions of servants, through dinner and into the drawing room afterwards.

Darcy felt like covering his ears to end the monotonous sound of Lady Catherine's voice.

The mantel clock struck twelve.

Darcy looked about him for the Ghost and saw it not. As the last stroke ceased to vibrate, he remembered the prediction of his father and, lifting up his eyes, beheld a solemn site. The drawing room vanished around Lady Catherine, and as she stood, her chair vanished, fog seemed to cover the ground, and in the blink of an eye she changed.

Chapter 4

CHRISTMAS FUTURE

NOW LADY CATHERINE WAS draped in a black gown, with a hooped skirt and bodice cut low, exposing too much bony bosom. Her head was ringed by sausage curls, looking grotesquely girlish against a face that seemed to consist of little more than flesh covering bone. There was no life in her face. There was no life in her eyes. She seemed to glide towards him in a most unnerving manner.

He felt her come beside him, and her mysterious presence filled him with a solemn dread.

"Am I in the presence of the Ghost of Christmas Yet To Come?" asked Darcy.

The Spirit answered not but pointed onward with its hand.

"You are about to show me shadows of the things that have not happened, but will happen in the time before us," Darcy pursued. "Is that so, Spirit?"

The Spirit inclined her head. That was the only answer he received. It was doubly chilling, this lack of voice in the body of one usually so verbal.

Although well used to ghostly company by this time, Darcy feared the silent shape so much that his legs trembled beneath him, and he found that he could hardly stand when he prepared to follow it. The Spirit paused a moment, observing his condition, and gave him time to recover.

But Darcy was all the worse for this. It filled him with a vague uncertain horror to know that there were ghostly eyes intently fixed upon him.

"Ghost of the Future!" he exclaimed. "I fear you more than any specter I have seen. But as I know your purpose is to do me good, and as I hope to live to be another man from what I was, I am prepared to bear your company and do it with a thankful heart. Will you not speak to me?"

She gave him no reply. The hand was pointed straight before them.

"Lead on!" said Darcy. "Lead on! The night is waning fast and time is precious to me, I know. Lead on, Spirit!"

The Phantom moved away as it had come towards him. Darcy followed in the shadow of her dress, which bore him up, he thought, and carried him along.

They scarcely seemed to enter the room, for the room rather seemed to spring up about them and encompass them of its own accord. But there they were, in the heart of Bingley's London mansion.

The Spirit stopped beside one little chair. Observing that

the hand was pointed to the room's occupants, Darcy advanced to listen to their talk.

"No," said Mr. Hurst, now a great fat man with a monstrous chin, "I do not know much about it either way. I only know she's dead."

"When did she die?" inquired Louisa.

"Last night, I believe."

"Why, what was the matter with her?" asked Caroline.

"God knows," said Mr. Hurst, "a fever of some sort."

"I hope that it is not contagious?" asked Louisa.

"I haven't heard," said Mr. Hurst.

"It's likely to be a very cheap funeral," said Caroline, "for upon my life I do not know why anyone would want to go to it. I suppose we must make some show of support for her family? I have a black dress I have never worn—the workmanship was too shoddy, but it will do for her."

"I do not mind going, as long as lunch is provided," observed Mr. Hurst.

"Well, it is the most uninteresting way for you to pass the day," said Caroline. "But I will go and comfort the sisters. That way, I can see for myself that she is truly gone!"

Their conversation then turned to another subject altogether. Darcy looked towards the Spirit for an explanation.

The Phantom glided on into a street. Its finger pointed to two persons meeting. Darcy listened again, thinking that the explanation might lie here.

He knew these men, also.

"How are you?" said Sir William.

"How are you?" returned Mr. Phillips.

"Well!" said Sir William. "I am sorry to hear of your loss. Heaven has received another angel?"

"So I believe," returned Mr. Phillips. Not wishing to speak of it, he changed the subject. "Cold, isn't it?"

"Seasonable for Christmas time."

"Something else to think of. Good morning!"

Not another word. That was their meeting, their conversation, and their parting.

Darcy was at first surprised by the conversations; but feeling assured that they must have some hidden purpose, he set himself to consider what it was likely to be.

Darcy tried to think of anyone immediately connected with himself who might also be the subject of both conversations. Caroline and Mrs. Hurst kept much different company than Sir William and Mr. Phillips. The only common connection was Jane, and by extension, the Bennet family. The loss of Jane would devastate Bingley, the loss of a relation would wound Elizabeth grievously, and the loss of Elizabeth was not a thought Darcy was willing to contemplate.

He recoiled in terror, for the scene had changed, and now he almost touched a bed on which, beneath a sheet, there lay someone covered up, which, though it was dumb, announced itself in awful language.

The room was very dark, too dark to be observed with any accuracy, though Darcy glanced round it in obedience to a secret impulse, anxious to know what kind of room it was. A pale light, rising in the outer air, fell straight upon the bed and on it was the body of a woman.

Darcy glanced towards the Phantom. Her steady hand was pointed to the head. The cover was so carelessly adjusted that the slightest raising of it, the mere motion of a finger upon Darcy's part, would disclose the face. He thought of it, felt how easy it would be to do, and longed to do it, but had no more power to withdraw the veil than to dismiss the specter at his side.

"Spirit!" he said. "This is a fearful place. Let us go!"

Still the Ghost pointed with an unmoved finger to the head.

"I understand you, I know what you wish," Darcy returned, "and I would do it if I could. But I cannot, Spirit. I have not the power."

Quiet and dark, beside him stood false Lady Catherine, with her outstretched hand. Her eyes were looking at him keenly. They made him shudder and feel very cold.

The Phantom spread her dark dress before her for a moment, like a wing; and withdrawing it, they were before his house in Mayfair. His carriage pulled up and a somewhat older self exited. Darcy noticed that his face was careworn and depressed, though he was still quite young. *How odd it is to see oneself in but a few years time. It is like in a mirror, but a flawed one,* he thought as he and Lady Catherine made their way inside. He watched himself vanish upstairs.

The door to a parlor opened, and Caroline Bingley stood there. Not Bingley, Darcy noted, for she fiddled with a wedding ring. Darcy knew with an awful certainty that he was the husband. His stomach roiled in shock. "How can this be?" he demanded of the Spirit.

He turned to view this wife of the future. She walked up and down the room and wondered how everything she had ever coveted had been in her grasp, and somehow she had lost it all or perhaps dreams had never met her preconceived expectations. How Darcy knew all this was unclear, but the knowledge came to him like the vision before him.

Caroline started at every sound; looked out from the window; glanced at the clock; and tried, in vain, to settle. That she was expecting him and was waiting with anxious dread was obvious. At length the long-expected footsteps were heard on the stairs. She faced the door and met her husband.

"Madam," he ground out, but could say no more. It was clear that he was furious. He began to pace the room in a vain effort to relieve some of the anger. Finally, stopping before Caroline, he began to question her in a harsh voice, "Why, Caroline? Why did you not summon me earlier? Why must I learn from your brother that my son was ill? And what do I find when I arrive at your home? That not only was he very ill, but dying."

"That is not true."

"It is true. Our marriage has long been over, but I am still his father. You stole what time I could have spent with Charles by keeping his illness from me. I do not believe I can forgive you for that."

"Darcy, it was not like that. I did not know the seriousness of his illness at first…"

"But when you did, you still kept quiet. I do not believe you intended to inform me at all. I expect you planned to send a note stating *'Charles cannot come to Pemberley this spring. He is dead. Madame Bertine's bill has not yet been paid, could you see to it?'*"

"That was vicious," Caroline felt her own anger rising over the heart-stopping grief. "I will not justify my actions now. I am Charles's mother; I did what I thought best for him. Now I wish to see my son."

Darcy block her way, "No, you cannot see him. Not now. I will not have you contaminate the room where he lies."

Caroline felt shattered. All the dreams and fantasies she had still cherished of what it meant to be Mrs. Darcy broke to pieces like fragile glass. It angered her; in fact, everything angered her: her shattered schemes, the illness that ate away at her son, the man before her. Caroline looked him in the eye and spoke quietly, "You wish to know why? I was jealous. You called for her in your sleep, not once but many times. You should have married her when you had the chance. My disposition does not take well to being second best, so that my regard for you diminished as my jealousy grew. But I triumphed over her, because I had your child. A feat she could not accomplish. I am his mother, Darcy, and I did everything within my power to see that he would be well again. I had no wish to bring you and your ghost back into my life at such a trying time. Now, I am going to attend *my* son." With these words she left him alone. The slam of the door echoed in Darcy's ears.

Darcy seated himself before the fire and lingered there for some time before he went upstairs into his child's bedchamber above. The Spirit and Darcy followed. The room was lighted cheerfully and hung with the trappings of Christmas. Thankfully, Caroline was no longer there. A chair was set close beside the child. His other self sat down in it and gently reached for the child's hand while Darcy and the Spirit watched from the opposite side of the bed. When he had composed himself, Darcy looked down on the little face. It was a face that he had never seen before, yet it seemed intimately familiar and dear. He felt a lump rise in his throat and his eyes were suddenly scratchy and wet.

The child looked up at Darcy, "Papa, I wanted to go home for Christmas."

"Next year, my boy, when you are well again."

"Can I have a puppy and a pony?" he asked.

"Without a doubt. And what will you call them?"

"Chestnut and Pudding," came the reply after some thought.

"Very good names, I am sure, but which is for the pony and which is for the puppy?" Darcy asked.

"How will I know until I see them?" young Charles reasoned. The Spirit laid a bony hand on the child's brow, and he began to cough. Darcy watched as his older self and Caroline took turns looking after the boy. Days seemed to pass before his eyes. Every so often the Spirit touched the child and his conditioned worsened. Finally, Darcy could take no more and cried out, "Cease tormenting the child."

The Spirit looked at Darcy and grinned. She laid an emaciated hand on the child's chest and the breathing ceased.

"No!" both Darcys cried in unison.

The future Darcy broke down. He couldn't help it. Over the last several days he had watched his son die before his very eyes and felt totally helpless.

Darcy turned angrily on the Spirit and spoke through gritted teeth. "How could you? I did not want the child to die. Am I to blame for his passing now?"

The Spirit remained silent, as if his questions were of no account. Instead, she moved them into the study to witness another form of death.

His other self sat behind a desk. A pale Caroline, dressed in severe black, sat across from him and asked him faintly, "What is it that you wish of me?"

"I will make the funeral arrangements," Darcy answered in a choked voice. "After it is over, I wish you to leave. I do not care where you go. You will be attended to, wherever it is you settle. If I never see you again it will be too soon, Caroline!"

"Then I will leave your life for good. Strange how it is only now that I realize how much time I have wasted on what might been." And she walked out of the room.

"Spirit, I wish to leave here now." She nodded in agreement. He was grateful when he and the Spirit left the scene and went into the small kitchen of some unknown house.

Sitting by a fireplace was a grey-haired man, nearly seventy years of age, smoking his pipe.

Darcy and the Phantom came into the presence of this man; a woman came into the room, carrying a bundle, but she had scarcely entered when another woman came in too and a man in black closely followed her.

"What is the world coming to, Joe?" Mrs. Dilber asked the old man. "The missus is dying and her brother won't come, even though she asks and asks!"

"That's true, indeed!" said Mrs. Launders. "No man is more stubborn than he. Disowned the missus when she married the master, God keep his soul. He wasn't good enough for their fine bloodstock."

"Nor was he rich enough neither," said the man in black.

"No, indeed, Henry! Not good enough for the likes of him," said Mrs. Dilber.

"He will be the worse for the loss of a sister," Henry informed them.

"Indeed!" said Mrs. Dilber in complete agreement.

"He wanted to keep 'em apart, the master and the missus. He is a wicked old screw," pursued the woman. "Why isn't he more natural? If he was, he'd be here to look after his sister when she is struck with Death. Instead she is all alone, except for us."

"It's the truest word that ever was spoke," said Mrs. Dilber. "It will be a judgment on him."

"I hope he does get his just deserts," said old Joe, stopping in his task and looking up at them.

"Me too," returned the woman. "I ain't so fond of his company that I'd loiter about looking for him, but if he does come my way, well then, I shall certainly give him what for."

Mrs. Launders picked up the bundle and shook it out. "Ah, you may look through this dress till your eyes ache, but you won't find a hole in it nor a threadbare place. It's the best she had, and a fine one too."

"So it is," said old Joe.

"She is to be buried in it, to be sure," replied the woman with a sob.

Recovering, Mrs. Launders spoke again. "This is not the end of it, you'll see! He will frighten everyone away from him and then he will end up all alone. Serves him right, I say. I just wish I knew what is to become of young Freddy."

"Spirit!" said Darcy, shuddering from head to foot. "Merciful Heaven, what is this about?" For Darcy was again in the drawing room of his London mansion. But now the room was made horrible by obvious neglect. The wallpaper was peeling, the furniture was undusted, the windows grimy, the curtains torn and tattered.

Darcy gasped as he saw the owner of the house sitting by a meager fire. It was himself; he knew it was himself, though he aged at least thirty years!

A young man came into the room. "A Merry Christmas, Uncle! God save you!" cried a cheerful voice. It was the voice of Darcy's nephew, who came upon him so quickly that this was the first intimation he had of his approach.

"Bah!" said Darcy. "Humbug!"

This nephew-to-be of Darcy had a face that was ruddy and handsome. He had so heated himself with rapid walking in the fog and frost that his eyes sparkled from the exercise. He reminded Darcy of his cousin Fitzwilliam.

"Christmas a humbug, Uncle!" said Darcy's nephew. "You do not mean that, I am sure."

"I do mean it," said Darcy. "Merry Christmas! What right have you to be merry? What reason do you have to be merry? You're poor enough."

"Come now, I am not a pauper by any means. My mother saw that I was provided for; if not rich, I am certainly comfortable," returned the nephew gaily. "I might ask what right have you to be so dismal and morose? You're rich enough."

Darcy, having no better answer ready on the spur of the moment, said, "Bah!" again and followed it up with "Humbug."

"Do not be cross, Uncle," said the nephew.

"What else can I be," returned the uncle, "when I live in such a world of fools who believe in a Merry Christmas? And I suppose you believe in Father Christmas too."

"Oh, without a doubt, Uncle, I believe."

"I say, out upon Merry Christmas. What is Christmas time to you but a time for frittering away money on needless things; a time for finding yourself a year older, but not an hour wiser? If I could work my will," said Darcy indignantly, "every idiot who goes about with 'Merry Christmas' on his lips should be boiled with his own pudding and buried with a stake of holly through his heart."

"Uncle!" returned the nephew. "What a singularly unpleasant thought."

"Nephew!" returned the uncle sternly. "Keep Christmas in your own way, and let me keep it in mine."

"Keep it!" repeated Darcy's nephew. "But you do not keep it."

"Let me leave it alone then," said Darcy. "Much good may it do you. Much good it has ever done you!"

"There are many things from which I might have derived good, by which I have not profited, I dare say," returned the nephew, "Christmas among the rest. But I am sure I have always thought that, apart from the veneration due to its sacred name and origin, Christmas Time is a good time: a kind, forgiving, charitable, pleasant time. The only time I know of, in the long calendar of the year, when men and women seem by one consent to open their shut-up hearts freely and to think of people below them as if they really were fellow passengers to the grave, and not another race of creatures bound on other journeys. And therefore, Uncle, though it has never put a scrap of gold or silver in my pocket, I believe that it has done me good and will do me good; and I say, God bless it!"

A servant in the hall involuntarily applauded. Becoming immediately sensible of the impropriety, he entered the room with a wine decanter and one glass.

"Let me hear another sound from you," said Darcy addressing the servant, "and you'll keep your Christmas by losing your situation." Turning to his nephew, he said, "You're quite a powerful speaker, sir. I wonder you do not go into Parliament."

"Politicians certainly put believing to the test. Please do not be angry, Uncle. Come! Dine with us tomorrow."

"Why did you get married?" said Darcy.

"Because I fell in love."

"Because you fell in love!" growled the elder Darcy. "There is only one thing in the world more ridiculous than a Merry Christmas and it is love. And you are fool if you believe otherwise. Why should I subject myself and ruin my digestion to view the mockery that is a love match."

Darcy was astonished to hear these words come from his mouth. In fact, every word he heard spoken from the time he entered the room with the Spirit shocked him greatly. He could not believe the sentiments he was expressing as they were so far from those he felt now, as to be totally alien.

"But, Uncle, you never came to see me before that happened. Why give it as a reason for not coming now? I can assure the meals are much better than when I was a bachelor, so there really is no need to worry about your tender stomach," his nephew offered cheekily.

"Good afternoon," said Darcy, creakily getting up from his chair.

"I want nothing from you; I ask nothing of you; why cannot we be friends?"

"Good afternoon," repeated Darcy, as he walked over to the door.

"I am sorry, with all my heart, to find you so resolute. We have never had any quarrel to which I have been a party. But I have made the offer in homage to Christmas, and I'll keep my Christmas humor to the last. So a Merry Christmas, Uncle!"

"Good afternoon!" said Darcy, opening the door.

"And a Happy New Year!"

"Good afternoon, Frederick!" said Darcy as he left the room.

The young man waited behind in the cold room. "I tried, Mother," he said looking up at the ceiling. "I will try again next year and the next until that foolish old man accepts my invitation, just as I promised so long ago. Why you were so concerned for him, when he showed no care for you, I will never know." Placing his hat on head, he left so his uncle could leave Christmas alone.

Frederick! Darcy thought. He turned to the Spirit. "This is my future? This is my fate? I turn into a man so heartless that I would leave my sister alone to die?" The Spirit looked at him but gave no answer.

"So far the future you have shown is bleak and awful. Let me see some happiness connected to the future," demanded Darcy.

The Ghost conducted him through several streets familiar to

his feet. They entered the Bingleys' house and found Jane and her children seated round the fire.

The room was very large and handsome, and full of comfort. Near to the winter fire sat a beautiful young girl, so like Jane that Darcy believed it was the same, until he saw her, now a comely matron, sitting opposite her daughter. The noise in this room was perfectly tumultuous, for there were children all about and they were failing to conduct themselves in a civilized manner. But no one seemed to care; on the contrary, the mother and daughter laughed heartily.

A knocking at the door was heard and a rush towards it immediately ensued. Jane made her way toward the center of the boisterous group just in time to greet Bingley, who came home attended by a footman laden with Christmas toys and presents. The shouts of wonder and delight with which the development of every package was received!

Now Darcy looked on more attentively than ever, when the master of the house, having his daughter leaning fondly on him, sat down with her and Jane at his own fireside.

"Jane," said Bingley, turning to his wife with a smile, "I thought I saw an old friend this afternoon."

"Who was it?"

"Guess!"

"How can I? You know I fare poorly at such games. I do not know." Then she added in the same breath, laughing as he laughed. "Mr. Darcy."

"Darcy it was. I passed his window; and, as it was not shut up and he had a candle inside, I could scarcely help seeing him. There he sat alone. Quite alone in the world, I do believe. I hesitated to called upon him, as my efforts would have been rebuffed as they have been so many times in the past."

"Poor Mr. Darcy," said Jane.

Bingley was pensive for a moment, the loss of friendship still keenly felt even after many years. "He saw me, he looked out the window and saw me, and there was an expression on his face and in his eyes for a few seconds, and I saw the friend that I had lost. I made a step towards the door, but he turned away."

"The death of their child affected both him and Caroline greatly," Jane comforted.

"Caroline has found contentment in Bath. She derives much satisfaction from being a big fish in a small pond. Darcy has never been consolable."

Bingley's nature was such that soon he was cheerful again and spoke pleasantly to all the family. He looked at the work upon the table and praised the industry and speed of Jane and his daughters.

Bingley told them of the meeting General Fitzwilliam in the street that day.

"'Merry Christmas, Mr. Bingley,' he said, 'and the same for your good wife.' By-the-by, how he ever knew that, I do not know."

"Knew what, my dear?"

"Why, that you are a good wife," replied Bingley.

"Everybody knows that," said Peter.

"Very well observed, my boy," cried Bingley. "I hope they do. The General was off to invite Darcy for Christmas, though with little expectation of his invitation being accepted."

"He is such a good soul!" said Jane.

"You can be sure of that, my dear," returned Bingley. Changing the subject, Bingley remarked casually that Mr. and Mrs. Gardiner would be joining them for Christmas.

"Only hear that, Peter," said Jane.

"Peter," cried one of the girls, "Peter will try to keep Alice's attention on himself."

"Get along with you!" retorted Peter, grinning.

"It's just as likely as not," said Bingley, "one of these days; though there's plenty of time for that, my boy. Come, it is time for bed. You would not want to sleep through Christmas tomorrow, would you?"

"Never, Father!" cried they all.

"And I know," said Bingley, "I know, my dears, that you will be patient and kind and shall not quarrel easily among yourselves tomorrow."

"Of course, Father!" they all cried again.

"I am very happy," said Bingley. "I am very happy!"

The children kissed their parents and retired for the evening.

"Specter," said Darcy, "something informs me that our parting moment is drawing close at hand. I know it, but I know not how. Tell me who was the woman that we saw lying dead?"

The Ghost of Christmas Yet To Come conveyed him out of London and into the countryside.

Darcy wondered where they were going as he accompanied the Spirit until they reached a rusted iron gate. He paused to look round before entering. A churchyard. Here, then, the woman whose name he just had to learn lay underneath the ground.

The ghostly Lady Catherine stood among the graves. She was

exactly as she had been all evening, but he feared that he saw new meaning in her solemn shape as she pointed down to one particular grave. He advanced towards it trembling.

"Before I draw nearer to the stone to which you point," said Darcy, "answer me one question. Are these the shadows of the things that *will be*, or are they shadows of things that *may be* only?"

She only pointed downward to the grave by which it stood.

"The paths men take will foreshadow certain ends, and if the path is never deviated from, they must lead to that outcome," said Darcy. "But if they departed from one path and chose another, then the ends must change. Say it is thus with what you show me!"

The Spirit was immovable as ever.

Darcy crept towards the tombstone, trembling as he went and, following the finger, read what was carved into the grave-stone. The inscription read:

ELIZABETH BENNET
25th August 1791–22nd December 1815
Beloved daughter
She will make the angels laugh

"She was the woman who lay upon the bed?" he cried, falling upon his knees. It was the vision he dreaded almost from the start of this visitation

The finger pointed from the grave to him and back again, and then laughed. Darcy was shocked by the sound, for it chilled him to his bones.

"'Tis your own fault, Darcy. Your pride would not let you ask

Elizabeth again. Fear of rejection would not let you ask her again. She never gave up on you, but then she caught a fever from her younger sister's sniveling brat and had not the strength to go on. I believe she asked for you a time or two, but you could not be found until it was too late." Lady Catherine smiled in malicious delight.

"No, Spirit! Oh no, no!"

"But it is the truth, Darcy. You are always so keen on the truth, are you not?" The Spirit continued in what could only be described as a cheerful voice. "What did your pride and fear get you in the end? Loneliness, for you have lost all your friends and turned your back upon your remaining family."

The finger still pointed accusingly at Darcy. "And the name you were so proud of is the subject of many course and scurrilous jests. You have become a laughingstock."

"Spirit!" he cried, tightly clutching at her dress. "Hear me! I am not the man I was. I will not become the man I might have been but for this intercourse. Why show me this if I am past all hope?"

For the first time the hand appeared to shake.

"Good Spirit," he pursued, "your good nature intercedes for me. Assure me that I yet may change these shadows you have shown me by living an altered life!"

The hand trembled.

"I will honor my love in my heart and keep it in all the years yet to come. I will remember the Past, live in the Present, and look to the Future. The Spirits of all Three shall strive within me. I will not shut out the lessons that they teach. Oh, tell me I may remove away the writing on this stone!"

In his agony, he caught the spectral hand. She sought to free herself, but he was strong in his entreaty and detained it. The Spirit, stronger yet, repulsed him and laughed.

"Bravo," the Spirit called out, while clapping with the polite and insincere applause usually bestowed upon amateurs. "Such melodramatic drivel," she sneered. "Such maudlin sentimentality. I find it highly entertaining."

In defeat, Darcy leaned back against the gravestone, his arms resting upon his bended knees. He did not feel that he was defiling the grave; in fact, he felt comforted sitting there. He looked up at that grinning face. "Just go," he said wearily, "and leave me in peace. The future you showed is not worth living. I will just sit here until winter overtakes me."

"Are you giving up so easily? No more dramatic entreaties? No sobs, no weeping? Is your love so ready to accept failure? Not thirty seconds ago you were crying out how much you had changed. You have learned *nothing*," came the Spirit's unkind reply.

Darcy looked at her with open dislike. "I asked but a simple question and received nothing but mockery in return."

"Your question is a mockery," the Spirit answered scornfully, "of all that was shown you this night." And she began to cackle. "A life you richly deserve."

Anger coursed through Darcy. He gazed hotly at the figure before, now seated on an opposing headstone. He lunged at her, crying out, "I will not live such a life, do you hear me!" as her laughing grew louder. He reached to grab her shoulders, but she was no longer before him and he was falling into blackness.

Chapter 5

THE END OF IT

DARCY AWOKE IN THE bed that was his own in the room that was his own. The morning light was just beginning to filter into the room. Three spirits had come and gone, and his travels and travails with them were over. Past, Present, and Future had all shown him the course he should and must take.

"The Spirits of all three have striven to show me what I already knew within me. The past cannot be changed and while some memories cause pain, others provide comfort; the present requires action, and the future is the best and happiest time of all because the time before me is my own, to make the most of and it will be different—quite different than the one played out before me," Darcy promised himself. "Father, Heaven, and the Christmas Time Spirits, thank you for being around me last night!

"I know just what to do!" cried Darcy, laughing. He felt lighter than he had in months; happiness that had been so elusive in his life lately had returned, making him feel as merry as a schoolboy, as giddy as a drunken man.

Running to the window, he opened it and gazed at the wonder before him. A layer of pristine snow covered the ground and sparkled in the golden sunlight. The heavenly blue sky made a stunning backdrop to icicles that shone like diamonds. The air was cold but invigorating. It had been a long time since he had taken the time to notice the beauty of a winter morning.

But Darcy did not linger, for there was too much to be done and he was eager to get started. He strode into the sitting room and was now standing there replaying the memories of the evening. "Here is the decanter of brandy and still full!" cried Darcy, starting off again and going round to the fireplace. "There is the door by which the ghost of my father entered! There is the window where I saw the wandering Spirits! There is the corner where the Ghost of Christmas Present sat!" He bent down and retrieved a lone holly leaf. "It is all true; it all happened."

He was checked in his transports by the sound of church bells ringing out the lustiest peals he had ever heard—*clash, clang, hammer, ding, dong, bell.* Oh, what a glorious noise!

The door opened and in walked his valet. "Good morning, sir, and a Merry Christmas to you."

It is Christmas Day! thought Darcy to himself. *I have not missed it. The Spirits have done it all in one night. They can do anything they like; they are Spirits after all.*

"Thank you, Marks, and also to you."

"Shall I tell Cook to prepare breakfast?"

"No. There is a change of plans. I require my riding gear. Send a message to the stables to ready my horse. I wish to leave within the hour."

"You wish to go for a morning's ride?" asked Marks.

"No, I will be traveling to Hertfordshire. Going by horseback will be quicker. You will follow in the carriage on the morrow. Just pack a satchel for overnight."

Darcy delivered his orders and set about making himself presentable. Shaving was not an easy task, for his hand continued to shake very much and shaving required attention. He dressed himself all in his best.

A boy came in with his cleaned boots.

"Hallo there!"

"Hallo, sir!" returned the boy.

"Do you know Matlock House, in the next street but one, at the corner?" Darcy inquired.

"I should hope I do," replied the lad.

"I will give you a shilling to deliver a letter there. No, I will give you half-a-crown!"

"A half-a-crown, sir, it is far too much!" protested his valet.

"Nonsense, it is Christmas after all."

The hand in which he wrote the letter was not a steady one, but write it he did. After giving the lad his letter and coin, he went downstairs to open the street door and watched the lad run down the street. As he stood there, the door knocker caught his attention.

"I shall love it as long as I live!" cried Darcy, patting it with his hand. "I scarcely ever looked at it before. What expression it has in its face! It is a wonderful knocker!"

A groom arrived with his horse from the stable. Straddling his horse, he started the journey into Hertfordshire.

Meanwhile, Georgiana had made her way down into the breakfast parlor. She was alone when the butler handed her a note on a silver platter. The Earl entered the breakfast as Georgiana finished her letter, "Good morning, sir! A Merry Christmas to you!"

"And to you, my dear!" replied the Earl. "Who sends you greetings on Christmas morning if I may ask?"

"It is a letter from Fitzwilliam, sir. He says that he will be unable to join us for Christmas dinner."

"I am sorry to hear that. Are you greatly disappointed?"

"Oh no, sir. For he says he is going to fulfill my greatest wish for Christmas."

"And that wish is?" enquired the Earl.

"A new sister, sir. A new sister," Georgiana returned happily, before taking a sip of hot chocolate, leaving the Earl quite speechless.

Darcy was by this time on the outskirts of London, heading for Netherfield. If the visions of Christmas Present were true, he would find Elizabeth there.

He did not mind the cold; in truth he barely felt it. His mind was so busy with the images of the previous night that he barely noticed the world around him. The sound of the horse's hooves hitting the cold ground penetrated his thoughts occasionally. He would smile, for each step brought him closer to Elizabeth.

Finally, in the afternoon, he arrived at Netherfield. A groom rushed out to take the horse. Darcy patted the horse on the neck, thanking him for making the journey as quickly as he had. "Give him a good rub down, some extra oats, and an apple if you can find one."

"Yes, sir," replied the groom. Darcy tossed him a coin.

"And a Merry Christmas."

"Thank you, sir."

He looked up to the window and spied Elizabeth gazing out the window. He had never dreamed that any ride could give him so much happiness. He turned to go up the steps of Bingley's house but stopped. Instead, he turned to the window and, realizing that Elizabeth had spotted him, he pointed to her, then to himself, and out to the winter-cloaked garden, silently asking her to meet him there.

He saw Elizabeth nod from the window. Eagerly, he strode into the garden.

Elizabeth was filled with gladness when she saw Darcy arrive. When he silently asked to be met in the garden, she could only nod, for the rest of her seemed frozen in place. Only when she saw him stride away did she regain movement. She began to move to the door.

"Where do you think you are going?" Mrs. Bennet asked.

"I am going for a walk in the gardens. The room is overheated and a walk would do me some good."

"It would do you some good to stay and talk with Mr. Topper. He has almost three thousand a year! And he has shown an interest in you!" cried Mrs. Bennet.

Curious, Bingley looked out the window, and recognizing the horse his groom was leading away, said, "I do believe some fresh air would do you a world of good, Elizabeth." He quickly made his way to the door and opened it for her.

"I hope so, Charles, I hope so," replied Elizabeth, as she left the room. Outside the room she raced down the stairs and ran down the hall to the doorway, only skidding to a halt when she saw a footman with her cloak, gloves, and bonnet. Hastily putting on these outer garments, she hurried into the garden where Darcy was waiting and pacing.

"Miss Bennet." They were the only words he could get out of his mouth. Elizabeth was also stricken with silence. Darcy offered his arm, Elizabeth took it, and they began to walk in silence.

When they came upon a sheltered bench, they stopped and sat down. Elizabeth looked down at her clasped hands, until Darcy covered her hands with his. Then she looked up into his eyes, his bright, shining eyes that held a touch of shyness, determination, and another emotion that she was afraid to name.

"Miss Bennet, last April you said that I could not have made you the offer of my hand in any possible way that would have tempted you to accept it. Even if your answer remains the same as it was then, please allow me to speak a second time upon this subject."

"As you wish."

"Miss Bennet, few people get to see into the future and what joys or calamities may be waiting there. Last night I was fortunate to get a glimpse of my future. I do not know if it was a dream or a vision, I only know that the future that lay before me was bleak and stark and lonely because you were not in it."

Elizabeth knew from the look in his eyes that he was telling the truth.

"So I am asking you to share the future with me, to change that wretched existence I saw into a one of great joy and happiness. I love you. I shall always love you. I am willing to wait with a hope that someday you will return my regard. Please say that I may have some hope."

"You may, for it would not be a very long wait," said Elizabeth. "Not long at all."

"Dearest, loveliest Elizabeth, would you do me the very great honor of accepting my offer of marriage?"

Elizabeth, feeling all the common awkwardness and anxiety of the situation, now forced herself to speak. "I wish you to understand that my sentiments have undergone so material a change since that time, that your present assurances fill me with gratitude and pleasure and the only answer I can give is… yes."

The happiness that this reply produced was such as he had never felt before, and he expressed himself on the occasion as sensibly and as warmly as a man violently in love can be supposed to do. "Thank you," he raised her gloved hands to lips and kissed each one. "Thank you, I will endeavor to make sure you never have cause to regret your decision."

Had Elizabeth been able to encounter his eyes, she might have seen how well the expression of heartfelt delight diffused over his face became him; but, though she could not look, she could listen, and he told her of feelings which, in proving of what importance she was to him, made his affection every moment more valuable.

"You are cold," he noticed and was immediately concerned. "Let us return to the house so that you can be warmed."

Elizabeth shook her head. "No, it is too soon to return to others, to be amongst them. Let us walk for a bit; that will take off any chill."

So they walked, without knowing in what direction. There was too much to be thought and felt and said for attention to any other objects.

"I should not have waited so long to come to you. Last fall, I had a visit from my aunt, who called upon me in London, and related her journey to Longbourn, its motive, and the substance of her conversation with you, peculiarly denoting your perverseness—her words—as she sought to obtain that promise from me, which you had refused to give. But, unluckily for her ladyship, its effect had been exactly contrariwise. It taught me to hope," said he, "as I had scarcely ever allowed myself to hope before. I should have come then."

"Why did you not come? Surely you knew enough of my disposition to be certain, that had I been absolutely, irrevocably decided against you, I would have acknowledged it to Lady Catherine, frankly and openly." Elizabeth colored and laughed as she continued, "After abusing you so abominably to your face, I could have no scruple in abusing you to all your relations."

"Fear, doubt, pride. My aunt can be quite overbearing, and I feared you simply would not provide her the satisfaction of giving her the assurance she demanded. Your previous refusal has weighed heavily on my mind. I was doubtful that even if your feelings for me had changed for the better, they may not have been strong enough to accept a proposal, and I felt my pride could not withstand another rejection, no matter how gently or kindly given."

"And I had not treated your feelings so kindly in the past."

"My behavior to you at the time merited the severest reproof. It was unpardonable. I cannot think of it without abhorrence and was doubtful that you could ever forgive me."

"We will not quarrel for the greater share of blame annexed to that evening," said Elizabeth. "The conduct of neither, if strictly examined, will be irreproachable. But since then we have both, I hope, improved in civility."

"I cannot be so easily reconciled to myself. The recollection of what I then said—of my conduct, my manners, and my expressions during the whole of it—is now, and has been for many months, inexpressibly painful to me. Your reproof, so well applied, I shall never forget: 'Had you behaved in a more gentlemanlike manner.' Those were your words. You know not, you can scarcely conceive, how they have tortured me, though it was some time, I confess, before I was reasonable enough to allow their justice."

"I was certainly very far from expecting them to make so strong an impression. I had not the smallest idea of their ever being felt in such a way."

"I can easily believe it. You thought me then devoid of every proper feeling; I am sure you did. The turn of your countenance I shall never forget, as you said that I could not have addressed you in any possible way that would induce you to accept me."

"Oh! Do not repeat what I then said. These recollections will not do at all. I assure you that I have long been most heartily ashamed of it."

"My letter, did it," asked Darcy, "did it soon make you think better of me? Did you, on reading it, give any credit to its contents?"

She explained what its effect on her had been: "My feelings as I read your letter can scarcely be defined. With amazement did I understand that you believed any apology to be in your power; and I was steadfastly persuaded that you could have no explanation to give that would be acceptable. It was with a strong prejudice against everything you might say that I first read your letter," Elizabeth was embarrassed to confess.

"Your belief of Jane's insensibility I knew to be false. Your account of the real and the worst objections to the match made me too angry to perceive any justice in your words." Elizabeth gave Darcy a wry little smile. "And it was some time, I confess, before I was reasonable enough to allow their justice. As to Mr. Wickham, every line proved more clearly that in matters between you and him, you were entirely blameless throughout the whole, which I would have believed to be impossible before reading your letter."

Darcy wanted to offer her some comfort, but Elizabeth spoke before he could do so. "I was absolutely ashamed of myself. I had been blind, partial, prejudiced, and absurd. It was a hard realization to face, for I had prided myself on my discernment!" Elizabeth shook her head at her folly.

"I knew," said he, "that what I wrote must give you pain; but it was necessary. I hope you have destroyed the letter. There was one part, especially the opening of it, which I should dread your having the power of reading again. I can remember some expressions which might justly make you hate me."

"The letter shall certainly be burnt if you believe it essential to the preservation of my regard; however, though we both have proof that my opinions are not entirely unalterable, they also are not, I hope, quite so easily changed as that implies."

"When I wrote that letter," replied Darcy, "I believed myself perfectly calm and cool; but I am since convinced that it was written in a dreadful bitterness of spirit."

"The letter, perhaps, began in bitterness; but it did not end so." Elizabeth stopped to look at him. "The *adieu* is charity itself. But think no more of the letter. The feelings of the person who wrote it and the person who received it are now so widely different from what they were then that every unpleasant circumstance attending it ought to be forgotten. You must learn some of my philosophy. Think only of the past as its remembrance gives you pleasure."

A quick flash of those memories he experienced the night before came to mind. "Many retrospections are so totally void of reproach that only contentment arises from them. The moment you agreed to marry me I will always treasure. However, painful recollections will intrude, which cannot, which ought not, to be repelled. They can teach one a lesson, hard indeed at first to learn, but really most advantageous."

"You are becoming quite philosophical, Mr. Darcy."

"So formal, Miss Bennet? I would wish that you would call me by my given name."

"Fitzwilliam, then," Elizabeth said before continuing on their walk. "I am almost afraid of asking what you thought of me when we met at Pemberley. You blamed me for coming?"

"No, indeed, I felt nothing but surprise."

"Your surprise could not be greater than mine in being noticed by you. My conscience told me that I deserved no extraordinary politeness, and I confess that I did not expect to receive more than my due."

"My object then," replied Darcy, "was to show you, by every civility in my power, that I was not so mean as to resent the past; and I hoped to obtain your forgiveness, to lessen your ill opinion, by letting you see that your reproofs had been attended to. How soon any other wishes introduced themselves I can hardly tell, but I believe in about half an hour after I had seen you."

He then told her of Georgiana's delight in her acquaintance: "I know she will be quite happy to learn that you are to be her new sister. She was quite disappointed not to further the acquaintance last summer."

"If Lydia had not eloped," she began, "this happy day may have come about much sooner. I wish to tell you how grateful I am, again, at your intervention in the matter."

"I thought only of you," Darcy told her. "Before I quit the inn, I had resolved on quitting Derbyshire in a quest for your sister. Your distress I could not bear, and as I believed it to be within my power to relieve it, I set about doing so."

This is what love truly is, Elizabeth thought, her heart thumping joyfully. She gave him a wistful smile. "I was sure that I would never see you again. The moment that you walked out the door of that inn, I knew I loved you, and I felt it would all come to naught. Now such a painful subject need not be dwelt upon further.

"So, what persuaded you to renew your addresses now? Was it the vision you spoke of earlier? It must have been a very convincing one. Do tell me about it."

"Someday perhaps. It is a rather long and somewhat fanciful tale, too much to relate just now. The afternoon sky has darkened and I can see a servant has been sent out to search for us. I will say that the vision served to reinforce the wishes and desires I already possessed and gave me the courage to pursue them."

They headed back to Bingley's house. Elizabeth entered before Darcy did. Alone in the garden he spoke aloud, "Thank you, Father and all the Spirits. I appreciate what you did for me and I will remember it always. I will do my best to see that Elizabeth is happy, for in her happiness is mine. I shall be worthy of the gift you have given me."

As Darcy entered, he saw that Elizabeth was standing under a ball of mistletoe, brightly trimmed with evergreens, ribbons, and ornaments. And his eyes lit up.

"Elizabeth, do you realize where you are standing?"

Elizabeth looked up for a moment. "Certainly, I have very good eyesight."

So Darcy gathered Elizabeth in his arms and used the kissing bough for it proper purpose. So engrossed were they in the activity, neither heard the approaching footsteps.

"Elizabeth Bennet!" cried her shocked mother.

"Mr. Darcy!" exclaimed the equally shocked Miss Bingley.

"At last," Bingley said as he winked at his wife, who smiled happily in return.

CHRISTMAS 1843

"Look at Grandmama and Grandfather under the kissing bough," cried young Master Timothy Darcy from the top of the stairs.

"It is a long-standing Christmas tradition," his father, Bennet Darcy, informed him.

"Is everyone here? Will there be dinner soon?" Timothy asked.

Several Bingleys made their way into the hall. "Are we the last to arrive?" asked Jane.

"We are only awaiting the arrival of Uncle Gardiner. Now, Timothy—and is that Belinda and Bettina?—why don't the three of you run along to the back parlor and visit with your other cousins," Elizabeth told them.

"Yes, Grandmama, but will he be here soon?" he called out.

"Very soon, my dear, very soon."

"Do you ever find yourself losing track of who's who among our minor relations? Lord, there are more of them every year it seems," declared Charles Bingley.

"Well, you would have a large family," Darcy reminded him.

"It is not all my fault you know; between our children and grandchildren, the Gardiner progeny and your sister's offspring, family gatherings can get overpopulated rather quickly."

They made their way into the parlor where the adult members of the party had gathered. Darcy thought it a good thing that not all the connected relations were able to come. The ballroom would have had to have been opened to accommodate them all for dinner.

Jane and Elizabeth lingered in the hallway, wishing each other a Merry Christmas and exchanging tidbits of family news when the front door opened and Mr. Gardiner entered.

"The most extraordinary thing happened today," Mr. Gardiner exclaimed as a footman helped him remove his coat. "A most extraordinary thing."

"And a Merry Christmas to you also, Uncle," Elizabeth cheerfully greeted them.

"I apologize, my dear," returned her uncle with a twinkle in his eyes. "The very best of Christmases to you both. You are looking well, very well indeed. And best wishes on your anniversaries. Neither of you look older than when you were brides."

"You are a flatterer, sir, but my appearance is appropriate for a matron of my years."

"You cannot be that old, Elizabeth, for that would make me ancient."

"I regret to inform you that you are indeed ancient"— Elizabeth smiled at him—"and I am glad to have it so. Shall we join the others in the parlor?"

After greetings were exchanged and everyone was made comfortable, Jane asked, "What is the extraordinary thing that happened to you, Uncle?"

"Do you have a story to tell, Uncle?" asked Bingley. "I for one would be delighted to hear it."

"Part of my tale is already known to Darcy, for he was there at its beginning and can attest, in part, to the truth of my words. Yesterday, our Gentlemen's Benevolent Society went about asking for donations from various businesses. Darcy and I came upon the most miserly gentleman I have yet to meet. His office was so cold that it was impossible to know inside from out by temperature alone." The servant offered some wine to Mr. Gardiner. "Thank you. It is just what I needed."

"Do continue your tale, Uncle, for you have whetted our curiosity," Jane begged and the others in the room also begged for the tale.

"Well, my dear, Darcy and I went forth to gather funds in the area of town where Mr. Scrooge has his business. 'Have I the pleasure of addressing Mr. Scrooge or Mr. Marley?' asked Darcy.

"'Mr. Marley has been dead these seven years,' Scrooge replied. 'He died this very night.'

"Now, a chill went down my spine when I heard this, but whether it was from the lack of warmth in the office or in Scrooge's tone, I cannot tell, but Darcy carried on, 'We have no doubt his liberality is well represented by his surviving partner,' he said.

"Scrooge frowned and shook his head. The cold seemed to freeze his features, nipped his pointed nose, and shriveled his cheek. Frost had settled on his head and on his eyebrows and his wiry chin."

"Stop teasing, Father," Alice exclaimed.

"I do not exaggerate," claimed Uncle Gardiner.

"At least not very much," Darcy responded dryly. "I explained the purpose of the visit, of gathering funds to provide some slight provisions for the poor and destitute."

Mr. Gardiner continued, "I swear his eyes turned red, and his lips compressed into a thin blue line. In a grating voice he demanded 'Are there no prisons? Are the workhouses still in operation? Are the Treadmill and the Poor Law still in full vigor?'

"When we agreed that indeed these institutions were still in operation, he said, 'I was afraid that something had occurred to stop them in their useful course.'

"I then explained that these places could hardly supply much in the way of a Christmas celebration and asked how much he wished to contribute.

"'Nothing!' Scrooge replied.

"'You wish to be anonymous?' asked Darcy.

"'I wish to be left alone,' said Scrooge. 'Since you ask me what I wish, gentlemen, that is my answer. I don't make merry myself at Christmas and I can't afford to make idle people merry. I help to support the establishments I have mentioned—they cost enough; and those who are badly off must go there.'"

"Oh, he sounds a horrid fellow, Father," exclaimed Alice.

The door to the parlor opened, and a young girl of perhaps six or so came into the room.

"Grandpapa!" she exclaimed and made her way to Mr. Gardiner for a welcoming hug. "Did you know we are to have turkey and stuffing and Christmas pudding? Very soon, I hope."

"Rebecca, you should be in the back parlor with the rest of the children; the turkey will be in the dining room when it is ready," her mother scolded.

"I can remember a time when you liked a roast goose well enough yourself, Alice," recalled Mr. Gardiner, setting his grand-daughter on his knee.

"I did not forever go on about it," Alice said.

"Oh, did you not? Rebecca, your mother used to—" Robert started.

But Alice quickly interrupted. "Father has not finished his story. What happened then?"

"Where was I? Ah, yes, the poor were to go to the publicly supported institutions. I then replied that many would rather die than go to such places. 'If they would rather die,' said Scrooge, 'they had better do it, and decrease the surplus population.'"

"The man is positively dreadful," exclaimed Elizabeth.

"Seeing clearly that it would be useless to pursue the point, we withdrew. We agreed that we had never met a more tight-fisted old sinner! Luckily for the Society, most of the businesses we approached were generous enough to give at least a little to our cause."

"I agree that he was most unpleasant, but as there is nothing extraordinary in that part of the tale, misers are not uncommon," Darcy remarked.

"I am getting to that part, never fear." He took another sip of wine and leaned forward to continue his tale when the door to the parlor opened yet again.

"Dinner is served," announced the butler.

"Can it not wait until the tale is done?" asked Alice.

"No, no, my dear, the turkey is ready and must not be kept waiting; I shall finish the tale after our grand feast. Come along, Rebecca." Taking his granddaughter's hand, he led the exodus out of the parlor and into the dining room.

Sometime later, when bellies were full of a bountiful Christmas repast, the family retired to the large drawing room, where a Christmas tree stood tall and proud.

"What think you of this new fashion, Darcy?" Mr. Gardiner asked, surveying the tree.

"I like it very much," exclaimed Rebecca. "It is very pretty."

"Yes, indeed, but I did not ask *you*, my dear."

"It is an old custom in some parts of the world, I am told. Whether it will remain in fashion here, only time will tell, but I like it well enough."

"As do I. Now dear Uncle, you have kept us in suspense long enough, do finish your story," Elizabeth demanded.

"Very well, my dear. Some members of the Benevolent Society gathered this morning, so we could deliver the goods we had purchased."

"Well, what happened to you?" demanded young Timothy Darcy.

"I had decided to walk to our meeting, it being such a

beautiful morning. I had not gone far when I beheld Mr. Scrooge coming toward me. Having no wish to remember the unpleasantness of the day before, I did my best to ignore the old gentleman, only to be waylaid by a hail from Scrooge himself.

"'My dear sir,' he exclaimed, taking both my hands. 'How do you do? I hope you succeeded exceptionally well yesterday. It was very kind of you. A Merry Christmas to you, sir!'

"'Mr. Scrooge?' I asked, for I was dumbfounded and wondering if my memory was so faulty that I had attributed Scrooge's faults onto an innocent look-alike.

"He answered in the affirmative. 'I fear my presence may not be pleasant to you. Allow me to ask your pardon. And will you have the goodness to accept a substantial donation to your cause, say £5,000?'"

"Lord bless me!" croaked Bingley, his breath being taken away.

"Was he serious, do you think?" commented Robert.

"Very serious, for while I was still doubting what I heard, he continued, 'Not a farthing less. A great many back-payments are included in it, I assure you. Will you do me that favor?'

"'My dear sir,' I began to shake his hand most violently. 'I don't know what to say to such munificence—'

"'Don't say anything, please,' retorted Scrooge. 'Come and see me. Will you come and see me?'

"'I will!' I cried.

"'Thank you,' said Scrooge. 'I am much obliged to you. I thank you fifty times. Bless you!'

"Well, I stood in the street for a good five minutes, trying to grasp what had just befallen before hurrying on to our meeting. I entered the room with such a stunned expression on my face that the others could not but wonder what had happened to me. So I told them the same story that I told you. The members rejoiced at what £5,000 could provide to those we serve. I mean to visit Scrooge at the earliest opportunity, for one cannot know how long such a transformation will last."

"I will believe it when the money is received and not a moment before," Darcy stated, such was his ill impression of the man.

"What could have occurred to cause such a transformation?" Elizabeth commented.

"I wondered that myself and so I asked him."

"You spoke with him about it?" asked Jane.

"Scrooge again hailed me as I was on my way here, he looked so pleasant and also younger. Yesterday I would have figured he was as old or older than myself."

"As ancient as that then?" Bingley asked with a twinkle in his eye.

"Quite ancient, but it was his spirit and demeanor that made him appear so aged—in reality he is only a little older than yourself and Darcy. One of the Society members vaguely remembered that he was a young man when he established his business some thirty years ago. But let us return to the present Mr. Scrooge. 'Good day, sir! A Merry Christmas to you! It seems to be our day for chance meetings. You are still coming to see me tomorrow?'

"'I nodded in agreement.'

"'And where are you off to?' he asked.

"I explained that I was going to have Christmas dinner with my family and he said he was about to do same. I thought he seemed excited yet anxious about the visit. He was about to turn away when I again thanked him very much for his generosity this morning.

"He commented that he had not known that generosity could make a man feel so happy.

"Emboldened by his response, I asked what had occurred to change him so, that only yesterday a penny was too much to give to the poor and today his liberality is overflowing.

"'I have been blessed by the Christmas Spirits, Mr. Gardiner, the Christmas Spirits have the way to making a man change his destiny,' he said, before turning and walking away."

He did not see Darcy stiffen upon these words, but Elizabeth did and her hand reached out to clasp his.

"At first, I thought he meant some sort of liquor, but I could tell he was not drunk. So, I wondered who are these spirits and how can I get hold of one of them?"

"They only come when one is in need of them," Darcy answered without thinking. And he was grateful for them every day. He looked around the room, at the faces of his family and friends, and knew he would be thankful until the day he died. Elizabeth reached over to him and clasped his hand.

"What did you say?"

"I say that it is time to light the candles upon the tree," Elizabeth interrupted. "Now children, you must be very careful. Light only one candle and then back away. All the candles will be lit, never fear."

When the task was completed and the room aglow, Elizabeth began to play Christmas carols and the family joined in singing until their throats grew dry. Luckily, the servants were just then bringing in a large punch bowl. As soon as everyone had a cup, Bingley exclaimed, "I think we need a toast. Mr. Gardiner, will you do the honors?"

"I propose we drink to Mr. Scrooge, for changing his heart in such a dramatic and generous manner, so God bless Mr. Scrooge."

Everyone drank to the toast.

"Can I make a toast?" asked Timothy, tugging on Bingley's coat.

"Certainly. Come with me." Bingley led the boy over to the piano bench and helped him stand upon it. "Your attention everyone, Master Timothy would like to make a toast."

"God Bless Grandmama and Grandfather, and Father and Mother and Uncle and Bingley and..." He broke off, looking around at the all faces in the room. "Ah, God bless us, every one!"

Christmas Present

AMANDA GRANGE

IT IS A TRUTH universally acknowledged, that a married man in possession of a good fortune, must be in want of an heir, and Mr. Darcy of Pemberley was just such a man. Moreover, he was soon to have that want satisfied, for his wife, Elizabeth, was expecting their first child. As he watched her reading her mail at the breakfast table, his heart swelled with pride.

She opened a second letter and smiled.

"Jane has had the baby!" she said. "A boy!"

"So Bingley is a father," said Darcy with evident pleasure.

"And Jane is a mother. Oh, my dear Jane, how proud and pleased she must be. Bingley is besotted," said Elizabeth, returning to her letter. "Jane says she can scarcely persuade him to leave the nursery to eat and sleep. She adds, *and it is not to be wondered at, for little Charles is the most beautiful baby you have ever seen.*" Elizabeth looked up at Darcy. "Jane would like us to stay with her for Christmas. She says she can wait no longer to show us the new baby, as well as the new house. I am sure I cannot wait to see them. I will give orders for the packing at once."

"No, we cannot go and see them just yet," said Darcy. He looked at his wife's full figure as she rose unsteadily to her feet. "You forget your condition."

"I never forget my condition," she said with a rueful smile, resting her hand on her rounded stomach.

"We will wait a few weeks nevertheless," he said. "It will be better that way."

"What nonsense! I am perfectly able to climb into the carriage, and that is all I need to do," she said, laughing at him.

"But you might have the baby on the way!" he said.

"And I might not," she replied.

"We might be in a lonely spot, with no midwife to hand, and nothing but the coach to shelter you," he protested. "No hot water, no maids, no Mrs. Reynolds. No, Lizzy, it will not do. I am sorry, my love, but I forbid it."

Instead of meekly obeying his command, Lizzy's eyes sparkled and she said, "Ah! I knew how it would be. When we were newly married, you would deny me nothing, but now that a year and more has passed, you are showing your true colours and you expect me to obey you in everything!"

"I doubt if you have ever obeyed anyone in your life," he returned, sitting back and looking at her with a smile playing about his lips.

"No, indeed I have not, for I have a mind of my own and I like to use it," she said. "Otherwise, it might grow rusty with neglect."

He laughed. But he was not to be so easily talked out of his fears.

"Only consider—"

"I have considered!" she said. And then, more seriously, "Believe me, I have. I have scarcely ventured beyond the flower gardens these past few weeks and for the last sennight I have barely set foot out of the door, but I cannot do so forever. It is very wearing and very tedious. Mama's first child was three weeks late, and if I am the same, there will be plenty of time for us to go and see Jane's baby and still return to Pemberley before our baby is born. And besides, I want a family Christmas."

"Then let us invite your family here."

"No, it would not do," said Lizzy, sitting down again. "Jane and the baby cannot travel. Besides, it is already arranged that the family will visit Jane's new residence, Lowlands Park. Jane's housekeeper has been preparing for the event for weeks. The rooms have been aired, the larder stocked, and the beds made up." She took pity on him and said, "Jane's new house is not so very far away. If we leave Pemberley after lunch we will be there in time for dinner, scarcely time for anything to happen. I promise you, if I feel any twinges before we set out then we will delay the journey."

"And what if you feel a twinge when we are halfway to Jane's?"

"Then we will carry on our way and I will be well looked after as soon as we arrive." As he still looked dubious, she continued. "You know what the midwife said: ladies in my condition must be humoured, and my mind is made up," she told him.

Even before their marriage, Darcy had learnt that Elizabeth had a strong will, so that at last, he conceded to her wishes.

"Then I had better let them know in the stables, and you had better tell Mrs. Reynolds that we intend to leave tomorrow.

There will be a great many arrangements to be made if you are to have a comfortable journey."

"Thank you, my dear. I knew you would see sense!"

He made a noise which sounded suspiciously like harrumph, and Elizabeth returned to her letters.

"Is there any other news?" he asked.

Elizabeth opened a letter from her mother and began to read it to herself. Every now and again she broke out to relate some absurdity.

Darcy, now that he was at a safe distance from Mrs. Bennet, found that he could enjoy her foibles.

"She thanks me for my letter," said Elizabeth. Then she said, "Oh dear! Oh no!" She shook her head. "Poor Charlotte!"

Darcy looked at her enquiringly and she read aloud from her letter.

"Charlotte Lucas—although I should say Charlotte Collins, though why she had a right to Mr. Collins I will never know, as he was promised to you, Lizzy—called on us last Tuesday, for you must know that she and Mr. Collins are staying at Lucas Lodge. I saw at once what she was about. As soon as she walked in the room she ran her eyes over your father to see if he showed signs of illness or age. I am sure she will turn us out before he is cold in his grave. Thank goodness you have married Mr. Darcy, Lizzy, so that when your father dies we can all come and live with you, otherwise I do not know what we should do. My sister in Meryton does not have room for all of us, nor my brother in London, but at Pemberley there is room to spare—"

"Then we must hope your father lives to a ripe old age!" interposed Darcy.

Elizabeth laughed. "I am sure he will." She began to read again. *"We are setting out for Jane's tomorrow and we mean to travel by easy stages, arriving on the 19th."* She broke off and said, "So they will be there in two days' time. If we leave tomorrow then we will have Jane and the baby to ourselves for a day before Mama arrives."

She finished reading the letter to herself, then told him what it had contained, shorn of her mother's ramblings.

"Maria Lucas is going to Jane's as well. She and Kitty have become firm friends and so Jane has invited her to keep Kitty company. I am glad of it. Mary is not much of a companion, as she spends her time either practising the pianoforte or reading sermons and making extracts from them. With Jane and I living our own lives and Lydia in the north, it must be lonely for Kitty."

"Your mother will no doubt find a husband for her before too long," said Darcy.

"I rather believe that is what she is hoping for this Christmas. There will be no other guests staying in the house, only family, but Mama hopes there will be entertainments in the evenings and visitors during the day, and that one of them might suit Kitty."

"But only if he has ten thousand a year!"

"Yes," said Lizzy. "You have quite spoilt Mama for other men!"

"Or at least, for other fortunes!" said Darcy.

"And now I must go and see Mrs. Reynolds, then in an hour, you must take me round the park in the phaeton."

Elizabeth left the room and Darcy finished his breakfast, then went out to the stables where he gave orders for the journey on the following day. As well as the usual instructions, he made it plain that he required one of the under grooms, a lad who was an expert horseman and a very fast rider, to be amongst the party and that he expected the lad to ride Lightning. This produced a startled reaction from the head groom, for Lightning was one of the most expensive horses in the stables. But Darcy was adamant. Although he did not say so, he wanted to be sure that help could be brought quickly if Elizabeth unexpectedly went into labour.

At the mere thought of it, he almost decided to cancel the journey after all, but he knew it would give Elizabeth such pleasure that he could not deny her the treat.

On leaving the stables he returned to the house and went upstairs to speak to his valet. As he did so he passed the foot of the stairs leading to the second floor, wherein lay the nursery, and on a sudden impulse he mounted them.

They gave way to a corridor which was looking bright and cheerful, having been newly renovated. The windows had been cleaned and the view they gave over the Pemberley park was beautiful. Sweeping lawns spread in every direction, and beyond them lay the Derbyshire moor.

He trod on the squeaking floorboard and smiled. Elizabeth had at first wanted to replace it, but she had relented when he had told her that it reminded him of his childhood. When he had slept in the nursery, its sound had heralded the approach of visitors.

His had been a happy childhood, roaming the grounds and climbing trees, loved by both parents, his beautiful mother and his austere father. From his mother had come open demonstrations of affection; from his father had come a solid feeling of security.

"The Darcys have lived at Pemberley for over two hundred years," his father had said to him. "It is a name to be proud of."

And he had been proud. Too proud on occasion, he thought uncomfortably, as he remembered his early relationship with Elizabeth. But she had taught him that too much pride led to incivility and, worse, blindness. Blindness to the qualities of others, regardless of their rank. And so he had mended his ways, and in doing so he had won his dearest, loveliest Elizabeth.

He paused on the threshold of the nursery. It had been decorated in a sunny yellow and the window seat had been upholstered in a matching fabric decorated with rocking horses. The inspiration had been his old wooden rocking horse, which had been freshly painted and varnished. He had spent many happy hours playing on it, as he had spent many happy hours kneeling on the window seat and looking out at the gardens, his excitement brimming over as he had seen his first pony standing below.

He turned to look at the cot in which he himself had slept, and he had a sudden memory of his mother bending over him illuminated by a halo of light coming from the candles on the landing behind her. He could almost hear the swish of her brocade dress as she bent over him, and feel the soft fall of powder on his cheek as she kissed him goodnight.

And then the memory faded and he thought that here, soon, his own child would be sleeping, climbing on the window seat, riding on the rocking horse.

He had always known he must marry and provide an heir for Pemberley, but with Elizabeth it was so much more than that. It was not just marrying and then having done with it; it was going through life together, exploring its new experiences side by side. And it was this, having a child together, becoming a family.

He smiled and, with one last look around the room, he went down to the first floor. He gave instructions to his valet for the morrow, then he went downstairs and rang for Mrs. Reynolds.

"Mrs. Darcy has no doubt told you of our plans for tomorrow," he said.

"Yes, sir, she has."

"I want to make sure that everything is done for her comfort. Blankets in the coach, a hot brick for her feet, a hamper of food with some tempting delicacies, and plenty of cushions."

Mrs. Reynolds assured him that everything would be done. Content that he had made all the necessary plans, he made ready to escort his wife around the park in the phaeton.

As they set out, Elizabeth looking radiant in a new blue cloak, Darcy privately thought that the ride might show her she was not capable of making such a long journey by coach on the morrow. But instead of finding it uncomfortable she found it exhilarating. She was by nature active, and if she could not walk round the park, then to drive was the next best thing.

"You did not find it too tiring?" he asked her as he handed her out of the phaeton after an hour.

"Not at all. And I will not find the coach journey too tiring either," she said mischievously.

"Then I admit myself beaten. We will set off at two o'clock," he said.

There was a light covering of snow the following day. The white-ness glittered in the sunshine as it lay across the open expanse of the moor.

When Elizabeth stepped outside after lunch, the sharp, clean air stung her cheeks and made them glow. Darcy handed her into the coach. She settled herself, with some difficulty, on the comfortable seats, and he wrapped her round with blankets. She put her feet on the hot brick, the door was closed, and, with a crunching sound as the wheels began to roll across the frosted gravel, they were off.

Elizabeth felt her spirits rise as they bowled down the drive and turned into the road. She had not set foot beyond the gates for a week, and she was looking forward to the journey.

It was now almost three months since Jane and Bingley had left Netherfield. It had been a comfortable house and it had created many happy memories for them, but it was too near to Mrs. Bennet to be truly home. Mrs. Bennet had had a habit of visiting every day, sometimes two or three times a day, and if it was not Mrs. Bennet, then it was one of the other relations. Jane, always softhearted, had not liked to tell them that, although she loved them, she did not want to see them quite so often; and even Bingley, the most mild-mannered of men, had been heard to remark on several occasions that he wished the Bennets were not quite so near.

Since the Bennets could not be expected to move, and since Netherfield was only rented, the problem was solved once Jane and Bingley found a house of their own to buy. They had wisely ignored the suitable houses in Hertfordshire and looked further north, near Lizzy and Darcy. After many months of searching, they had found the perfect house and they had taken up residence there at the end of summer.

The house had at first not been fit for visitors, and afterwards, Elizabeth's condition had made travelling difficult, so that Elizabeth and Darcy had not yet visited, and Elizabeth was eager to see it.

The coach drove through Derby, a bustling city, and Darcy asked Elizabeth if she would like to stop for some refreshment, but she was eager to arrive. So they travelled on into Nottinghamshire, where the countryside became softer and more smiling. Gone were the moors and instead there were fields, separated from the road by hedgerows, which were covered with glittering spiders' webs.

The snow gradually disappeared as they moved further south and, as they approached Jane's new neighbourhood, they saw open fields with a river meandering through.

"We are almost there," said Elizabeth, her excitement mounting at the thought of seeing Jane again.

The coachman took a wrong turn and had to ask for directions, but they were soon on the right road and turned in between tall gates. They travelled through a deer park until the house came into view. It was an imposing house in the English Renaissance style, its pale stone looking serene in the midday light.

The coach came to a halt outside the front door, which opened immediately, and Bingley came down the steps, hands outstretched to greet them.

"My dear Darcy! And Elizabeth! Upon my honour, I have never seen you looking better. But it is cold out here. Come, let us go inside."

He asked them about the journey as they went indoors, and they remarked upon the splendour of the house, but there was only one thing Elizabeth really wanted to do and that was to see her sister and her new nephew.

Bingley conducted them to the nursery, where a large fire crackled cheerily in the grate. And there was Jane, looking matronly and happy, by the side of the crib.

"Lizzy! Oh, how glad I am to see you!" she said, jumping up and kissing Lizzy affectionately. "I hoped you would come, but with the weather being against us and your time being so near I did not depend upon it."

"I could not resist. The opportunity to see you was too tempting, and the chance to see little Charles was irresistible," said Elizabeth.

She embraced Jane and then bent over the crib, where the newest addition to the Bingley family lay sleeping. His little fists were curled up sweetly, and his expression was contented.

"He has your nose and Bingley's chin," said Elizabeth. "I cannot yet tell about his eyes. Oh, Jane, he is beautiful."

"I think he is the most beautiful baby I have ever seen," said Jane.

"As our baby has not been born yet, I will not argue with you!" said Elizabeth. "He shall be the most beautiful baby in England until then. Have you decided what to name him?"

"Charles Edward Fitzwilliam Bingley," said Jane.

"A very large name for a very small baby!" said Darcy, who was looking down at the infant with some interest.

"He will grow into it, never fear," said Bingley, who looked at his son with adoration.

"I did not expect to find you up," said Elizabeth to her sister. "I thought you would still be lying in."

"And so I would be, if we were still at Netherfield, for Mama would have been scandalised otherwise, but here I am mistress in my own home. I felt well enough to rise this morning, although I must admit the birth was very tiring."

As the conversation seemed to be in danger of moving into realms that Bingley and Darcy would rather know nothing about, the two gentlemen excused themselves, whilst Elizabeth settled down for a long and interesting conversation with Jane about the birth of little Charles.

"Well, what do you think?" asked Bingley as the two men went downstairs.

"I think it is a very fine house," said Darcy. "You have done well. You remembered to ask about the chimneys, I hope?"

"Oh, the chimneys!" said Bingley. "I did not mean the house, I meant—"

"I know," said Darcy with a laugh.

"Of course! I had forgotten that Elizabeth has taught you how to tease people! Well, what do you think? Is he not the most handsome baby you have ever seen? Is he not the strongest, the healthiest, the happiest baby it has ever been your pleasure to meet?" he asked as he led Darcy into the drawing-room.

"I have met very few infants and so yes, I can say he is."

"Darcy!"

"Very well then! I agree with whatever you say. He is a very fine boy. I can say this in all sincerity: he is lucky to have such a father."

"Do you really think so?" asked Bingley. He beamed whilst looking anxious at the same time. "I was elated when he was born. When I first heard him cry I felt an enormous sense of pride—"

There came a snort from the sofa, where Mr. Hurst, Charles Bingley's brother-in-law, was lying, apparently asleep.

"Ah, yes," said Bingley, momentarily diverted. "My family are here. Caroline arrived a month ago to run the household whilst Jane was indisposed, and Louisa arrived with her husband last week. My brother-in-law, as you see, is resting."

Darcy raised one eyebrow. Mr. Hurst spent most of his life on the sofa and Bingley knew, as well as Darcy, that indolence, not the need for rest, was the reason.

The snort resolved itself into words as Mr. Hurst opened one eye.

"Felt an enormous sense of pride?" he asked. "Thought nothing of the sort. As soon as you heard that cry, you said, 'I've killed them!' and strode around the room like a man demented, moaning, 'They're dead. It's all my fault!'"

"Nonsense!" said Bingley, but his laugh was a little sheepish.

Darcy smiled, but beneath his smile was a sense of understanding. He had been elated when Elizabeth had told him that she was expecting a child, but he had been anxious too and, try as he might, he could not rid himself of the anxiety. If anything should happen to her...

He was luckily saved from further reflections by the appearance of Caroline, who, together with Louisa, now entered the room.

"Mr. Darcy," said Caroline warmly.

She had at first been incensed when she had discovered that he meant to marry Elizabeth Bennet, but she had quickly come to realise that unless she put on a glad, or at least a polite, face, she would lose Darcy's friendship, and she would never be invited to Pemberley.

"You have brought the bad weather with you I fear," said Caroline.

It was true. The snow, which had been falling lightly in sporadic showers, was now falling thick and fast outside the window. It was melting as it hit the ground, but here and there, patches were settling and the lawns were already white.

"I do hope it will not discommode your mother-in-law," said Louisa.

"No, indeed," said Caroline in a droll voice. "It would be a tragedy if she was delayed and did not manage to arrive tomorrow as expected. But where is Elizabeth? You cannot have left her behind?"

"She is upstairs with Jane," said Darcy.

"It quite reminds me of old times, when Jane was taken ill at Netherfield," said Bingley. "She had a cold, I remember, which she had caught from riding in the rain. Elizabeth sat with her upstairs and then the two of them came down after dinner."

"Dear Jane will not be well enough to come downstairs today," said Caroline. "She needs her rest."

"She was talking of it only this morning," Bingley contradicted her.

"My dear Charles, you must not allow it," said Caroline. "It will be too much for her. I am at your disposal for as long as you need, you know that. I have managed the household not too ill this last month, as I am sure you will agree. Dear Jane need do nothing more than remain in the nursery until she is quite recovered." She turned to Darcy. "I kept house for Charles before his marriage and as soon as Jane was no longer able to manage affairs, owing to her condition, I arrived at once to care for the household."

"That was very good of you!" remarked Darcy with a speaking glance at Bingley.

"Yes, was it not?" said Bingley. "Caroline did not even wait for an invitation."

"I thought it my duty to come. The inconvenience was nothing to me, and family, you know, never wait for an invitation," said Caroline.

She walked across the room, displaying her figure, and then seated herself at the pianoforte and began to play.

"This is your favourite song, is it not, Mr. Darcy?" she asked.

He was forced to admit that it was, but he was saved from further attentions by Bingley saying, "I still have not shown you the billiard room, Darcy. Would you care for a game?"

Darcy agreed with alacrity and the two men left the room.

"Why did you not tell Caroline that she was not needed?" asked Darcy. "You have a house full of servants to look after you, and I am sure Jane does not want her here."

"Oh, you know, Darcy, Caroline is not so bad. She is very efficient and she frightens the servants into honesty."

"Honesty?" asked Darcy in surprise.

At that moment, a movement caught his eye and he saw Elizabeth coming down the stairs. She had evidently overheard their conversation for she said to Bingley, "So my father was right! He said that you and Jane were both so complying that nothing would ever be resolved upon and that every servant would cheat you."

"Yes, well, perhaps we are too easygoing," admitted Bingley. Then he asked eagerly, "How is Jane? Do you think she is looking well?"

"I think she is looking very well," Elizabeth assured him. "And very happy."

"And the baby?"

"He is contented. He is sleeping. Jane is resting now, but she hopes to join us in the drawing-room after dinner."

"There you are! What did I say?" asked Bingley in delight. "I knew she would join us. Darcy and I were just going into the billiard room, but we will gladly return to the drawing-room with you if you wish."

"Caroline is in the drawing-room," remarked Darcy.

"Ah!" said Elizabeth. "Then I will come and watch the two of you play."

They went into the billiard room. Darcy and Elizabeth commented on its fine proportions and remarked on the beauty and elegance of the house.

"It took us a long time to find it, but it has repaid our efforts," said Bingley. "Jane and I are both settled here and we mean to make this our ancestral seat. Perhaps one day it will be as renowned as Pemberley."

Darcy and Bingley began to play and Elizabeth looked around the room, thinking that Jane had chosen very well. The house was comfortable and elegant, and she knew that Jane was very happy with it. It gave her great pleasure to think of Jane being so well settled, and within an easy distance of Pemberley.

The three of them exchanged news as the two men played. When the game was over, Elizabeth and Darcy retired to their suite of rooms to dress for dinner. Jane and Charles kept country hours and dinner was served, in the winter, almost as soon as it was dark.

"Now, are you glad I talked you into coming?" Elizabeth asked her husband as she sat down at her dressing table and began to unpin her hair.

He helped her in her task, taking the pins out of her dark hair and letting it fall about her shoulders. He stroked it, letting his hands linger on the soft tresses.

"Yes, I am, as long as you are not feeling any ill effects from the journey."

"No, none at all other than a little fatigue. I think I will lie down for half an hour before changing for dinner."

She suited the action to the words and Darcy rubbed her feet in a way she found relaxing and pleasurable. She was glad to have some time alone with him. She had greatly enjoyed talking to Jane, and she had adored seeing the baby, but she had grown used to having Darcy to herself and she treasured their time alone. They stayed together, talking, until the clock struck the hour, and then they changed for dinner.

Elizabeth took Darcy's arm and they descended the stairs. Jane and Bingley were in the hall, and together they went into the drawing-room.

Elizabeth's eye ran round the room as she entered, noting the grand fireplace, the comfortable sofas, and the rich gold drapes, which had been drawn across the tall windows to keep out the December darkness. By the fire, which was burning with a cheery glow, was a screen which Jane had painted herself and a small table on which were several ornaments from the Bennet household, remembrances of home.

"Elizabeth, how well you look," said Caroline, rising and greeting her. She turned to Jane. "My dear sister, are you sure you should be downstairs?"

"I am quite well, I do assure you," said Jane.

Caroline opened her mouth, but Elizabeth looked at her, and Caroline quickly shut it again, for she had no wish to cross wits with Elizabeth. If she did, she was uncomfortably aware that she would come off the loser.

Bingley conducted Jane over to the fire and then arranged the screen to keep her out of any drafts.

"And how is my nephew?" asked Caroline.

"He is very well and sleeping," said Jane.

"I do declare he is twice the size he was when he was born. He will be a fine boy before long," said Louisa.

"He is a fine boy already," said Bingley. "I never saw finer. His little fingers and toes, you never saw the like!"

"Do not encourage him or Charles will talk of nothing else," said Caroline.

Indeed, the new son and heir formed most of Bingley's conversation over dinner, and although Jane and Elizabeth managed to talk of other things from time to time, the new arrival formed most of Jane's conversation too.

"And how is Pemberley, Mr. Darcy?" asked Caroline.

"The estate is thriving, thank you."

"And your sister? Dear Georgiana, how I long to see her again."

"She too is well. She is spending Christmas with friends."

"Is she not young for such a visit?" asked Caroline.

"She is almost eighteen," Darcy reminded her. "She will be coming out in the spring."

"You will be going to town for the Season then," said Caroline. She turned to her brother. "I told you, Charles, that you must buy a house in town, and see, I was right. If you will only bestir yourself, you can spend the spring in town and help Georgiana by escorting her to balls and such like."

"I will be busy here," said Charles.

"Then let me find a house for you."

"We really couldn't put you to so much trouble," said Jane.

"It is no trouble. I would like nothing better," said Caroline. "There, it is settled."

Jane and Bingley looked at each other helplessly and Elizabeth thought that Caroline would very likely carry the day. She refrained from interfering but managed to say to Jane, as the ladies withdrew, "If you wish me to dissuade her, you have only to say the word."

"Say nothing yet," said Jane. "It will give her something to think about."

"Something other than running the household and telling you what to do, do you mean?" asked Lizzy mischievously, as the two ladies crossed the hall behind Caroline and Louisa.

"She has been very kind, really she has," said Jane. "Although I cannot think so well of her as I once did, for there is no denying that she tried to separate me from Charles, I believe she has seen the error of her ways and I think she is trying to make amends. She has been very helpful over the last few weeks; indeed, I would have found it difficult to manage without her. She has taken over everything."

"I do not doubt it!"

Jane smiled but said, "Really, Lizzy, I think you misjudge her. I truly believe she is trying to be friends."

"Jane, you are too good."

"No, not too good, for I do not repose the same confidence in her as once I did. But she has been a help, there is no denying it, and I hope she will continue to be so. When Mama arrives, I am intending to leave her with Caroline."

Elizabeth laughed at the thought of Caroline entertaining Mrs. Bennet. The two ladies had little liking for each other. Caroline thought Mrs. Bennet was excessively vulgar, and Mrs. Bennet had little time for anyone who was not an eligible young man.

"Perhaps they do not get on well together," Jane conceded, "but it will be someone for Mama to talk to if I am indisposed."

"And are you planning to be indisposed when Mama arrives?" teased Elizabeth.

"Really, Lizzy! I am looking forward to seeing her. But even so, I feel I will need some respite from her ways. She is to stay for a fortnight, and that is a long time."

"With luck, she will be so enamoured of little Charles that she will be able to talk of nothing else, and you, my dear Jane, will, I am sure, be happy to talk about him all day long."

"Indeed I will. But Mama will not be able to forget her daughters so easily, even whilst talking about her grandson. She has already told me that she expects me to give a ball, so that Kitty and Mary can find a husband," said Jane.

"And are you giving a ball?" asked Lizzy.

"Yes. Caroline has been good enough to arrange it!"

Having reached the drawing-room, where Caroline and Louisa were already seated, the other two ladies joined in the conversation, and a discussion of the forthcoming ball ensued. Refreshments were discussed, the guest list reviewed, clothes spoken of, so that the time until the gentlemen joined them was agreeably spent.

After that, there was some general discussion about Bingley's relatives and the new estate, but Jane soon began to tire and excused herself. Bingley followed her out of the room and their footsteps could be heard climbing the stairs to the nursery.

Elizabeth and Darcy continued to talk to Caroline and the Hursts for half an hour, but then they too excused themselves and retired for the night.

Elizabeth was not altogether looking forward to seeing her mother, particularly at such a time when her mother would no doubt interfere in everything she wished to eat, drink, or do, but she was longing to see her father again. He had always been very dear to her. He had defended her when her mother had tried to force her to marry Mr. Collins, and he had obliged her by discovering the good qualities in her husband, even though, at first, he had doubted they existed. He had come to realise that underneath Darcy's reserved and proud exterior there was a man who was worthy of his daughter, and Mr. Bennet knew no higher praise than that, for he had always had a soft spot for his Lizzy.

So when, the following morning, she caught sight of the Bennet carriage appearing through heavy snow, she was delighted.

Bingley went out to greet them, quickly bringing everyone into the drawing-room, where a large fire and some refreshments awaited them.

"Lizzy, my dear," said Mr. Bennet. His face was a picture of delighted surprise as he saw his favourite daughter. "This is an unexpected pleasure. We did not think to find you here. How are you?" He ran his eyes over her full figure. "Well, I hope?"

"Yes, Papa, very well," said Lizzy, kissing him on the cheek. "When Jane invited us, I could not resist seeing her new house and my new nephew."

"You should not have travelled in your condition. If I had known what you intended, I would have put a stop to it," said Mrs. Bennet.

"Then it is as well that you did not. I am sure Lizzy was just as excited about seeing the newest addition to the family as we are," said Mr. Bennet. There was a trace of unaccustomed pride in his voice. "Jane is well?"

"Very well. She will be down directly."

Mr. Bingley urged them all to sit down and they settled themselves by the fire.

"It is perhaps a good thing you are here, after all, Lizzy," said Mrs. Bennet. "I hope you will learn from your sister. I knew how it would be. I said, did I not, Mr. Bennet—did I not, Mary, Kitty, Maria?—that Jane would have a boy." She looked around the drawing-room. "This is a very elegant drawing-room, far better than the one at Lucas Lodge, and better than Netherfield too, is it not, Mr. Bennet?"

"The relative merits of various drawing-rooms are, I am afraid, beyond me," said Mr. Bennet.

Kitty looked around the room and pronounced it very fine. But it lost all its interest when, a moment later, Jane entered the room with little Charles in her arms. The talk was then all of the baby, with Mrs. Bennet predicting a great future for him and Mr. Bennet being quietly pleased. Kitty cooed over her first nephew and addressed herself as Aunt Kitty several times, whilst Mary said, "It is usual on such occasions to predict that the infant is destined for greatness, but I have often observed that very few of those who have greatness foretold for them manage to achieve such greatness when the full measure of their maturity unfolds."

Elizabeth laughed. Mrs. Bennet said, "Hush, Mary, whoever asked you?" and Mr. Bennet said gravely, "Very wise, Mary. I am glad to see that your hours of study have not been wasted, but have been productive of such wisdom."

Mary gave a gracious smile.

Little Charles was passed round all the females and, as they made a great fuss of him, Mr. Bennet said to his eldest daughter,

"You have found yourself a fine house here, Jane. The situation is good and it seems comfortable. It is a true family home."

Having passed the baby round everyone in turn, little Charles was returned to his mother.

"There is nothing finer than a fire in winter," said Mrs. Bennet. She added complacently, "I am sure Lady Catherine will like it. She will be used to the very best fires at Rosings Park, for the chimney piece cost eight hundred pounds, and no one would wish to find a niggling fire beneath a chimney piece of such value. But even Lady Catherine, I am persuaded, will have no fault to find with this."

Elizabeth looked at her mother in surprise, wondering why Lady Catherine had entered the conversation.

Before she had time to speak, Jane said, "Lady Catherine, Mama? Why should it matter whether or not Lady Catherine likes my fire?"

"Why, because I have invited her to stay here, of course. We have travelled up from Hertfordshire in the same party. Lady Catherine called in at Lucas Lodge on her way north to visit relatives, something to do with telling Charlotte that she was breeding the wrong sort of poultry, and as the weather was so poor, she was condescending enough to say that we could all travel on together. Two carriages are so much better than one when it snows, you know, for if one is stuck in a snowdrift, then the extra horses can be used to pull it out."

"Lady Catherine is here?" asked Jane, looking out of the window in expectation of seeing her ladyship's carriage.

"She is at an inn, not an hour's drive away. It was as we stopped there to change the horses and take some refreshment that a party of gentlemen came in, telling us that the road further north was completely blocked. They themselves had tried to get through and had had to turn back. Lady Catherine decided that she would have to take rooms at the inn until the weather improved, but I assured her that she would have to do no such thing, for she would be welcome here. I knew you would not mind," she said to Jane. "You have plenty of room, and Lady Catherine is family, you know."

"Mama!" said Lizzy. "You had no right to issue an invitation on Jane's behalf, especially when Jane is not yet recovered."

"Now, Lizzy, do not take on so, it is not your house, you know, and Jane is delighted. Are you not, Jane?" Mrs. Bennet went on without waiting for Jane to reply. "Besides, Lizzy, Lady Catherine is your aunt. I could not leave her to a lengthy stay in the inn, for who knows when the roads will be clear. I dare say Mr. Darcy, at any rate, is pleased."

If it was so, then Mr. Darcy hid his pleasure well.

"I had better arrange for a room to be aired," said Jane.

"Two rooms," said Mrs. Bennet. "Mr. Collins is with her ladyship. He has a brother nearby, and as he happened to mention it when Lady Catherine was visiting Lucas Lodge, she offered him a place in her carriage so that he could visit his brother without any trouble or expense."

"I am sorry, my dear," said Mr. Bennet to Jane. "I was too late to prevent the invitation being issued, and the best I could do was to encourage Lady Catherine to pause for something to eat so that we could arrive here first and give you some warning."

"Never fear, Papa, Lady Catherine is welcome," said Jane amicably.

"I did not know that Mr. Collins had a brother," said Elizabeth, learning this new knowledge with interest.

"Oh, yes, a very fine young man by all accounts, I am sure he is everything that is charming and delightful. And what a good thing for Kitty!" said Mrs. Bennet, looking complacently at Kitty. "I have often wondered what would become of her, but now my mind is at ease."

The smile left Kitty's face.

"How can the fact that Mr. Collins has a brother be good for Kitty?" asked Elizabeth in surprise.

"Because Kitty will be able to marry him, of course."

"No, Mama, I will not marry Mr. Collins's brother!" said Kitty vehemently.

From the tone of her voice, it was obvious she had heard the suggestion before.

"Of course you will. He is a very eligible gentleman," said her mother. "You will be delighted with him, no doubt."

"I will not be delighted with him. I am not delighted with Mr. Collins," said Kitty stubbornly.

"No one is asking you to be delighted with Mr. Collins; you are not expected to marry Mr. Collins. His brother is no doubt as different from him as you are from Lizzy. I am sure he is everything that is handsome and agreeable."

"And I am sure he is nothing of the kind," said Kitty. "I am determined not to marry him!"

"But, only think, my love. When Mr. Collins dies, as I am sure he will before very long—for he eats and drinks a prodigious amount and he will no doubt have an apoplexy before the year is out—his brother will inherit all his worldly possessions, so he will also inherit the entail. Then, when Mr. Bennet dies and you and your husband inherit Longbourn, you, Mary, and I may live there, all three of us together, till the end of our days."

This prospect did not appear to cheer Kitty, who, instead of smiling with delight, looked as though she was ready to cry.

"There, there," said Mr. Bennet, patting her hand. "I mean to live for a good long time yet, and neither Mr. Collins nor his brother shall have Longbourn until I am gone."

Mrs. Bennet opened her mouth but Bingley, with a great deal of tact, silenced her by the simple expedient of offering her a piece of seed cake. She accepted with relish, saying that she was famished, and fell mercifully silent for a full two minutes.

"Then I must have preparations made for our unexpected guests," said Jane. "Is Charlotte with Lady Catherine too?"

"No," said Mr. Bennet.

"Charlotte very much wanted to accompany her husband, but she felt that it would be better if Mr. Collins went alone, as she did not like to crowd her ladyship in the coach," said Mrs. Bennet.

Elizabeth's eyes sparkled and she murmured under her breath, "Sensible Charlotte."

"Indeed," said Mr. Bennet, sharing a smile with Lizzy.

"I will tell the housekeeper to ready two rooms," said Jane.

"Three rooms. Do not forget Mr. Collins's brother," said Mrs. Bennet, finishing her cake. "I told Mr. Collins that he must invite his brother to stay as well. He was delighted with the idea and promised to invite him as soon as he saw him. The poor young man is in lodgings close by the inn, and there is nothing more dreary than a Christmas spent in rented rooms."

"Well," said Bingley, clapping his hands together good-naturedly, "that is all to the good. I like a large party at Christmas."

Mr. Bennet gave a dry laugh.

"What did I tell you, Jane? You and your husband are both so amiable that you are being taken advantage of already."

"In this case, I do not mind my mother's—"

"Interference?" put in Lizzy.

"Suggestions," said Jane mildly. "I do not like to think of Lady Catherine being trapped by bad weather in an inn, nor do I like to think of Mr. Collins's brother spending Christmas alone. We shall be a merry party, I am sure." She turned to her mother. "Will you not come with me, Mama? I will show you and my sisters to your rooms. I am sure you will want to rest after your journey."

"Not at all!" said Mrs. Bennet.

"Yes, my love, you will," said Mr. Bennet firmly. He rose to his feet. "Jane, lead on, my dear."

Jane led her family out of the room, and Bingley followed.

Elizabeth and Darcy exchanged looks as Mrs. Bennet left the room. Having spent some time away from her mother, Elizabeth had forgotten how tiring she could be.

"So, my aunt, it seems, is to join us. Then we are to have a family Christmas after all," said Darcy.

"Yes," said Lizzy. "Full of quarrels and tantrums no doubt! It is a far cry from the Christmas we were expecting at Pemberley. No, do not say it!"

"Say what?" enquired Darcy wickedly.

"That I have only myself to blame! That we could have stayed at Pemberley quietly."

"But then we would not have seen little Charles, and you would not have been able to speak to your sister."

"No, you are right. I do not regret it. We do not have to spend every minute of every day with them, after all. I love my family dearly but there are times when it is good to be away from them!" She glanced out of the window, attracted by a gleam of sunshine. "Look, the snow has stopped. Let us go outside. I am longing for a breath of air."

They wrapped up warmly and were soon outdoors.

"Jane and Charles have a very pretty park here," said Elizabeth.

She let her eyes wander over the spacious lawns with the sweeping driveway and the shrubbery beyond. Specimen trees were dotted here and there, casting patches of blue shadow across the whiteness. The clouds had rolled away and, up above them, the sky was a startling blue.

"If this continues, the snow will soon melt," said Darcy.

"You sound pleased with the idea," said Elizabeth teasingly as they strolled down the paths. "Do you mean to tell me you are not delighted with the idea of your aunt's visit?"

"Other things have delighted me more!" he said, adding, "Such as seeing you so happy."

He stopped and turned to face her. She was radiant. The sharp winter air had given her cheeks a healthy colour and brought a sparkle to her eyes, so that she was glowing with health.

"I love to be out of doors," she said. "There is nothing like the feel of the wind on my cheek—unless it is the feel of your hand," she said saucily.

He drew her to him and stroked her cheek, then, looking down into her eyes, he kissed her.

"We are very near the house," she said. "Someone might see."

"The drawing-room looks the other way. Besides, we are married," he said.

"So we are," she said, and he kissed her again.

"Do you think your aunt will really stay here for Christmas?" Elizabeth asked Darcy some time later.

The cold had driven them indoors and they had chosen to sit in the library.

"If she has a choice, no, but the weather appears to be worsening and it may be impossible for her to leave."

"I only hope the weather does not mean that Jane has to cancel the ball. I know that she is looking forward to it."

"It is still a few days hence, and travelling a few miles to a private ball is not the same as travelling across the country," said Darcy. "It will only take a bright evening to encourage people to leave their firesides, the more so because they will have been deprived of company, and I will sit beside you the entire evening."

"Thank you, but I have no intention of sitting down all evening; I intend to dance. You look surprised."

"Nothing you could ever say or do would surprise me! But are you sure it is wise?"

"Wise or not, I intend to do it. I am looking forward to it. I have not danced for months," she said.

"Then I will make sure Mr. Collins keeps a dance free for you!" Elizabeth laughed.

"I thank you, but I believe that, if Mr. Collins asks for my hand, I will confess to fatigue and sit the dance out. It was barely tolerable dancing with him at Netherfield. I do not believe I could endure the mortification a second time. Charlotte was very wise to stay at Lucas Lodge. I am sure she is far happier with her baby! A girl for Charlotte, a boy for Jane. I wonder which it will be for us?" she mused, resting her hand on her stomach. "Do you mind?" she asked him.

"No."

"Not even a little bit? You do, after all, need an heir."

"A girl will do as well as a boy; in our family it has never mattered. Besides, if we do not have a boy this time, we will have one next time."

"If there is a next time."

"Do you not want more children?" he asked, looking at her with interest.

"I will let you know, once I have had this one!" said Lizzy.

She had spoken mischievously, but her words had reminded him of his fears and his brow clouded.

"I wish there were another way or that I could take this from you," he said seriously.

"What, have the baby for me? You would be the first man in history to do so!"

He smiled, but there was something troubled in his smile.

"If anything should happen to you…"

"Nothing will happen to me," she said, stroking his hand.

"No, of course not. I just do not like to think of you in pain."

"Then do not think of it. Think of the ball instead—though, if I cannot escape the attentions of Mr. Collins, you will no doubt have to think of me in pain, and, even worse, see it, for he is sure to step on my toes!"

"That, at least, I can prevent," said Darcy. "If he claims your hand I will rescue you, I promise you."

"Will you ride up on a white charger?"

"I brought one with me from Pemberley especially," he remarked. Lizzy laughed.

"I am very glad we came," she said, leaning back against him and smiling contentedly. "It has done me good to see Jane again. In particular, it has done me good to be able to talk to her as it has set my mind at rest on a few things which were worrying me."

They continued to talk, but as they did so, Darcy continued to be troubled. Elizabeth had had her sister to talk to, but he had talked of his fears to no one. He knew that she would soon be facing an ordeal that neither his wealth nor his position in the world could help her with. Worse, it brought back dark memories of the night of his sister's birth, when, as a ten-year-old boy, he had wandered, desolate, through the halls of Pemberley, whilst anxious voices had echoed down the corridors.

So troubled was he by these memories that he was glad when Elizabeth exclaimed, "I believe your aunt is here!" and looking out of the window, he saw Lady Catherine's coach.

The coach rolled to a halt. Footmen jumped down from the roof and opened the door, and Lady Catherine stepped out. Behind her followed Mr. Collins.

Lady Catherine's commanding voice could be heard through the window, even though it was closed: "… terrible roads… small park… intolerable drive…"

Interspersed were Mr. Collins's exclamations, "So noble… so good… so condescending…"

And so the odd couple proceeded from the coach to the front door.

"Poor Jane!" said Elizabeth. "We had better go and help her make her unexpected guests welcome."

"I would rather stay here with you," said Darcy.

"Do not tempt me! But I cannot leave my sister to face your aunt alone. If I do not miss my guess, Lady Catherine will be criticising everything and everyone roundly."

And so it proved. As Lizzy and Darcy left the library and crossed the hall, Lady Catherine's voice could be heard saying, "And so you are settled in Nottinghamshire, Mrs. Bingley. A very inconvenient country. It has the worst weather in England, I believe."

As Lizzy and Darcy entered the drawing-room, the scene was revealed. Jane stood by the fireplace, with her husband beside her, endeavouring to welcome Lady Catherine. Lady Catherine, however, would not let them speak. Mr. Collins was bobbing up and down behind her ladyship, endeavouring to agree with everything she said, whilst at the same time ingratiating himself with Jane and Bingley and smiling pompously at Mr. and Mrs. Bennet.

Mr. Bennet picked up a newspaper and began to read it assiduously, but such a scene was as welcome to Mrs. Bennet as it was unwelcome to her husband, and she replied firmly to Lady Catherine, "On the contrary. Nottinghamshire has some of the finest weather in the country."

"If it had some of the finest weather in the country, then it would not be snowing," said Lady Catherine.

"Quite so," said Mr. Collins. "Oh, indubitably so."

"I believe that any country may have snow in December," said Bingley peaceably.

"We would not dream of it in Kent," said Lady Catherine.

"In every way a superior country," said Mr. Collins. "And Rosings Park is one of its finest houses."

"Only *one* of its finest houses?" enquired Mr. Bennet with a wink at Lizzy.

Lady Catherine turned towards Mr. Collins with raised eyebrows.

"That is to say, *the* finest house in Kent," said Mr. Collins, "a positive jewel in the crown of the countryside, a most noble and elegant dwelling of magnificent and munificent proportions that vies with its illustrious owner in its sagacious and splendid proportions of magnificent munificent sagacious…"

He trailed away in some confusion, having lost himself in the labyrinthine excesses of his compliment.

"You express yourself very well," said Mr. Bennet gravely.

"Papa!" said Elizabeth, trying to control her laughter. "You forget yourself!"

"Do I, my dear?" he asked mildly.

"That is to say, you forget to welcome Jane's guests," she said.

"Ah, yes. Never mind. I am sure Jane is capable of welcoming them herself. If you will excuse me, I believe that Mr. Bingley has a library and I am eager to explore its riches."

"Lady Catherine, will you not sit down?" asked Jane, as her father left the room.

Lady Catherine looked at the sofa as though wondering whether it was fit to carry her illustrious personage, then said, "I think I will retire to my room."

"You must be fatigued after your journey," said Mrs. Bennet.

This was a challenge Lady Catherine could not resist.

"I am never fatigued," she said. "I do not believe in fatigue. Pray ring for some tea."

And so saying she removed her cloak, which she handed to Mr. Collins. She sat down on the sofa, peeling off her gloves as she looked around.

"You have a few fine pieces of furniture," she said to Jane. "The table is pretty." She looked at the other pieces as if to say, *But the rest is not.*

Jane thanked her politely.

"And so, you have just had a baby. A boy, I understand."

"Yes, your ladyship," said Jane, sitting down in a chair by the fire.

"I saw no point in having a boy myself," said Lady Catherine. "Since my sister had already had one, I decided I would have a girl instead."

They were by now all seated.

"It is all very well deciding to have a girl when there is no entail," said Mrs. Bennet with a heavy sigh. "Once an entail is involved there is no knowing what will happen."

"The de Bourghs have never believed in entails," replied Lady Catherine grandly.

"And I am sure I have told Mr. Bennet the same thing until I am blue in the face, but will he listen to me? No. We must have an entail, though why we must have one I cannot imagine," said Mrs. Bennet. "If not for Kitty, I do not know what we should do."

This remark surprised everyone who was not privy to Mrs. Bennet's plan of marrying her younger daughter to Mr. Collins's brother and her hopeful belief that Mr. Collins himself would soon be dead.

Lady Catherine ignored her and said to Elizabeth, "You must have a girl."

Mrs. Bennet shook her head firmly.

"No, Lady Catherine, with that I cannot agree," she said. "Girls are a great deal of trouble."

"Not if they have a governess," said Lady Catherine. "A great deal of trouble is just what a governess will prevent. I have been the means of supplying a great many governesses to a great many deserving families and they have all thanked me for the attention most effusively. Four nieces of Mrs. Jenkinson are most delightfully situated through my means, and I have sometimes recommended young ladies who were merely accidentally mentioned to me. The families are always delighted with them. You, girl," she said to Kitty. "Do you have a governess?"

"No, your Ladyship," said Kitty.

"And you?" she said to Maria Lucas.

"No," admitted Maria.

"And you?" she asked Mary.

"I have found that personal study is much more effica-cious than the exhortations of another female," said Mary. "By virtue of reading and making extensive extracts, I have, without any assistance, become the most accomplished young lady in the neighbourhood."

"Indeed? And how large is your neighbourhood? No, do not reply. It is the size of a pocket handkerchief, I suppose. It is clear to me that you have all been sadly neglected," said Lady Catherine. "Mrs. Bennet, you must take your remaining daughters in hand. It will not to do have them running off with stewards' sons like your other girl. A nice, sensible curate would do for them, I am sure."

"I hope I know my girls' entitlements better than to think them fit for nothing more than a curate," said Mrs. Bennet. "Now that Jane and Lizzy are so well settled, I see no reason why they should not marry lords. I am sure they are good enough."

Lady Catherine ignored her and turned to Elizabeth.

"If you have a girl, she will be able to marry the Duke of Wexington's son. He is at present two years old and will remain two years her senior throughout his life. It is a good age differ-ence, and of course he comes from the very best family."

"Since the baby is not born yet, it seems a little early to be finding her a husband, particularly as she may be a boy," remarked Elizabeth.

"It is never too early," said Lady Catherine.

"In this I have to agree, Lizzy," said Mrs. Bennet. "It really is never too early to think of suitable matches, for you have no idea how difficult it is to find people later on."

"And then there is the Devingshire boy," said Lady Catherine. "He might do, although Lord Devingshire looks like a sheep, and it would perhaps be wise to wait a few years and see which of his parents the boy favours."

"I thank you for your interest, but I am sure our son or daughter will be able to choose their own spouse with very little help from us. Darcy and I managed to find each other. Our child will only need to follow our example to make the best match possible."

Mrs. Bennet, completely misunderstanding Elizabeth, gave a happy sigh and said, "You are right, Lizzy, you caught a man with ten thousand a year and an estate in Derbyshire. I am sure your daughter will do just as well."

As the days passed, the house began to take on a festive air. Greenery was brought in from the gardens to decorate the house with holly, ivy, and mistletoe adorning the pictures or threading their way through the banisters. Rich smells wafted up from the kitchens, and the scent of winter spices and rich fruit cakes filled the air. Kitty and Maria could be heard giggling as they hastily hid half-wrapped presents whenever anyone unexpectedly entered their rooms, whilst Mary began making Christmas extracts.

The day of the ball approached. It had been arranged for Christmas Eve, a time of celebration, and there was an air of excitement when the day arrived.

"How is everything coming along?" asked Mrs. Bennet.

"It is all well in hand," said Caroline before Jane could speak. "Mr. Collins and his brother will make two extra gentlemen, but that is never to be deplored. They dance, I hope?"

"Mr. Collins certainly takes to the floor with alacrity," said Darcy. "I remember him dancing with Elizabeth at the Netherfield ball. It was a most edifying spectacle!"

Elizabeth laughed outright.

"Poor Mr. Collins! He tries very hard, but I pity the lady who stands up with him. He turns in all the wrong places and is constantly treading on his partner's toes or the hem of her gown."

"I am sure the young ladies hereabouts will not mind. They are used to dancing at the local assembly, and assembly balls, you know, do not produce the best dancing..." She turned to Mr. Darcy "... as I am sure you remember only too well."

"Perhaps not, but they produce a great deal of pleasure for those who know how to enjoy them," said Darcy.

"Aye, they do very well, but they are not to be compared with a private ball. Are there any eligible young men about?" Mrs. Bennet asked Caroline.

"Never fear, your daughters will have a choice," said Caroline in a droll voice.

"And you too, I hope. You are not getting any younger, and if you do not look sharp you will soon be an old maid."

"Mama!" said Jane.

But Caroline was not at all put out.

"I thank you for your kind concern," she said with a superior smile.

"Well, my dear, someone must be concerned, and as you have

no mother then I will take it upon myself. I found three good husbands for my own girls last year and I have found another one for Kitty only last week, so I am sure I will be able to find someone for you before the end of the year."

"Ah, yes, you did an admirable job of finding a husband for your youngest daughter. Darcy's steward's son, was it not? And acquired in such an unusual fashion," said Caroline.

Darcy stepped in, turning the conversation away from such dangerous waters.

"Tell me, Bingley, who have you invited to the ball?"

"You must ask Caroline," said Bingley. "She is the one who has managed everything."

"She seems to be a very managing young woman," said Mr. Bennet with an innocent air.

Elizabeth hid her laugh behind her cup of tea.

"Caroline has been a great help," said Jane fairly.

Caroline smiled graciously and was soon reciting the guest list. It consisted of all the local worthies, together with some good neighbours with whom Jane and Bingley had become friends.

"A fair-sized ball," said Darcy.

"Not as splendid as the balls at Pemberley, but I believe it will do," said Caroline. "Charles means to buy a house in London soon, and the guests there will of course be more refined."

"A house in London?" asked Mrs. Bennet.

Jane's face fell at her mother's eagerness.

"Why, that will be the very thing," said Mrs. Bennet.

Fortunately for Jane's nerves, the gong rang. It was a sign that it was time for them to retire to their rooms and dress for the ball.

The weather had remained snowy, but the local roads were still traversable. Jane had had only had three letters from more distant neighbours excusing themselves. The rest were looking forward to the evening's entertainment.

Mr. Collins's brother, who had been unable to join them earlier on account of business, was to arrive for the ball and then stay for a few days. It was an event which Kitty did not relish. She had told Mary and Maria that they must on no account leave him alone with her, and she sought her married sisters' help as well.

"Never fear, you will not have to marry him," said Elizabeth.

"You do not know how determined Mama can be," said Kitty.

"I know exactly how determined she can be," said Elizabeth, "but Papa will be on your side. He will not want you to marry a stupid man, and he will not see you forced into a marriage that is distasteful to you, you know."

"I wish I had never heard of Mr. Collins's brother," sighed Kitty.

Elizabeth could not help but agree. Her mother had talked of him constantly for the last few days.

They parted on the landing. Elizabeth retired to her room, where she chose an amber muslin to wear. It suited her complexion, but she felt out of sorts as she caught sight of her reflection in the mirror, and when Darcy entered her room, looking immaculate in a ruffled white shirt with a black tailcoat and tight fitting breeches, Elizabeth gave a sigh.

"Are you unwell?" he asked in concern.

"No, not unwell, just…"

"Unhappy?" he asked searchingly.

"No, not exactly. I was just thinking that you look every bit as handsome as the day I met you, whereas I"—she looked down at her bloated figure, clothed in a tent-like dress—"I am not the same at all."

"No," he said, taking her hands. "You are far more beautiful."

She laughed, but there was no laughter in his eyes. His words were sincere.

"What did I do to deserve you?" she said. "I must have done something very good."

"I believe you played a sonata without striking one false note," he teased her.

"Ah, so that was it! Yes, I remember it now. You are right, of course, that feat entitled me to such a husband. I believe I deserve you after all."

"That is better," he said hearing her laugh. "Are you ready to go down?"

"Yes, I am."

He gave her his arm and together they went downstairs.

Some of the guests had already arrived and there was a buzz of conversation. Elizabeth and Darcy went through into the ballroom where the musicians were tuning their instruments before striking up the opening chords of the first dance. The guests took their partners and arranged themselves around the ballroom.

Elizabeth took Darcy's hand, causing a few raised eyebrows, for it was not customary for husbands to partner their wives, but she did not care. She saw no reason why she should not enjoy herself. When the dance ended, however, she was too fatigued to dance any more, so Darcy fetched her an ice and sat down beside her.

"You must not ignore the other guests," she said. "You will shock everyone if you spend the evening with your wife."

"I am used to shocking people at balls. I might as well enjoy myself into the bargain," he told her.

But when one of Jane's neighbours, Mrs. Withington, drew near, accompanied by a plain young girl, Darcy's enjoyment was at an end. Mrs. Withington made it clear that her niece did not have a partner. Without precisely asking Mr. Darcy to offer the girl his hand, it was obvious that, as a gentleman, he could do no less.

"I hope Miss Withington will do me the honour of partnering me," he said, standing up.

The girl blushed prettily and Darcy led her onto the floor.

Elizabeth could not help thinking of another similar occasion some years ago, when he had refused to dance with another partnerless young lady, who had just happened to be herself, and she was pleased to see how far his manners had improved.

Mrs. Withington sat down beside Elizabeth.

"It was very kind of your husband to ask Susan to dance. I did so want her to enjoy herself this evening, but it is difficult for the girls; there are not enough young men to go round."

As if to underline the point, Kitty and Maria approached and sat down close by.

"It is a pity," went on Mrs. Withington, "for Susan loves to dance, and I do not know where she is to find another partner."

She looked around the room, assessing each gentleman

in turn. "She has already danced with young Lindford and Captain Collins…"

"Captain Collins?" asked Elizabeth. "I did not know he had arrived."

"Yes. In fact, here he is now with my husband."

Coming towards them were two men. The elder, Mr. Withington, was a plain but affable looking man of about fifty years of age and next to him was a very handsome young man indeed, with a good bearing and a good-humoured countenance. Elizabeth's eyes widened in surprise. He was nothing like Mr. Collins!

Mr. Withington saw his wife and walked over to her, bringing Captain Collins with him. He made the introductions and Elizabeth greeted him warmly.

Kitty, hearing the name of Captain Collins, kept her back firmly turned towards him and talked to Maria with a determined animation, but when Mr. Withington addressed her by name she was forced to turn round, her face a picture of mulish resignation. But on seeing Captain Collins, her eyebrows rose and her expression brightened so much that the transformation was comical.

"You look surprised," said he to Kitty. "Have I done something to startle you?"

"No, not exactly. It is just… well, you are not what I was expecting, that is all."

"I did not know that you were expecting anything, but perhaps my reputation precedes me," he said.

"In a way it does. You see, I know your brother."

"Indeed?"

"Yes. You are not very like him. In fact, you are not like him at all. You do not seem like the sort of man who would have a brother in the church."

"We are four brothers. Out of so many, one of us was almost certain to be a clergyman."

"Four of you?" asked Kitty. "I had no idea. And are you all so very different?"

"Yes, I believe we are. Your friend is the cleverest of us—"

Kitty looked startled at this, and Elizabeth was no less surprised, for it did not seem possible that Mr. Collins should be the cleverest of any family. But she concluded that Captain Collins was being kind.

"And my brother Samuel, who is in the navy, is the handsomest," went on Captain Collins. "He has broken a dozen hearts already and he is only nineteen. Henry is the pompous one. He is already making his mark in politics and is such a windbag that he cannot fail to do well. But enough of them. Would you consent to tell me more about yourself as we dance?"

And so saying, he offered her his hand.

She accepted with alacrity and the two of them, making a handsome couple, went onto the floor.

"Well!" said Mrs. Bennet. She had seen everything from the other side of the room and she had now joined Elizabeth in her desire to talk about it. "Did I not tell you how it would be? I knew it. Another daughter married. What luck!" She looked around the room for Mr. Collins and beckoned him over. "I must congratulate you on your brother," she said. "My girls have just been introduced to him. Such a handsome man!"

Mr. Collins looked surprised but was quick to accept the

compliment and said that his brother had been called an unusual looking gentleman by no less a personage than Lady Catherine de Bourgh.

"And so he is, for such looks are not often to be met with," said Mrs. Bennet. "He has all the advantages of a fine face and a fine person. Height, address, manners: all good. You must be very proud of him."

"Indeed we are. I may say that, after myself, he is the most notable member of the Collins family. He has not the good fortune to be patronised by such a great lady as Lady Catherine, but he has drawn down some very estimable patronage of his own."

"Yes, I am sure he has. Such a worthy young man will not fail to attract attention amongst influential people. He will quickly rise in life, I am sure. You must invite him to visit us at Longbourn. We would be very glad to have him with us."

"You are too kind," said Mr. Collins.

"Not at all. He is welcome at any time."

Mrs. Bennet watched Kitty and the Captain whilst Mr. Collins turned his attention to Mr. Bennet, complimenting him on his fine house, his elegant daughters, and his notable son-in-law.

To put an end to the fulsome compliments, Mr. Bennet began to ask him about his brother and laughed quietly to himself as Mr. Collins continued to talk.

The dance came to an end. Captain Collins escorted Kitty back to her family but then bowed and withdrew.

"But what is this? Where is Captain Collins going?" asked Mrs. Bennet. "Why is he not staying to talk to us?"

"He is engaged to Miss Porter for this dance," said Kitty. "But never fear, he has asked to take me into supper."

Mrs. Bennet was in raptures.

"What did I say? I knew how it would be. Kitty, my dear, you have never looked better. You are becoming quite a beauty. You are in looks tonight. And dance! I have never seen anyone lighter on their feet. We will have another wedding this year, you mark my words. Did I not say that Captain Collins was just the man for you? And what a life you will have! All the fun of being married to an officer, and then Longbourn when your father dies. What a thing for Mary and me, being secure in our home!"

Elizabeth raised her eyebrows, but Kitty was too happy to mind about her mother's matchmaking, and even the thought of living with her mother after her father's death did not dampen her spirits. Indeed, she said she was sure that, by then, she and her husband would have enough money to build a dower house for Mrs. Bennet.

Elizabeth was by this time so far rested that she was able to dance once more. She had not taken more than a dozen steps, however, when she gave a grimace.

"Is anything the matter?" asked Darcy.

"No, just a twinge," she said. "But I think I had better sit down."

He gave her his arm and they rejoined her family. Mrs. Bennet asked if she was quite well and Jane looked at her in concern, but Elizabeth reassured them. Fortunately for Elizabeth, after a few minutes' fussing, Mrs. Bennet saw Captain Collins coming towards them, for supper had just been announced.

"Now, Kitty, stand up straight," she said.

"Mama!" replied Kitty.

"Ah Captain Collins, there you are," said Mrs. Bennet. "All set to claim Kitty. It is a pleasure to see you both together, never were two people more well suited. I am sure your brother must feel it as much as we do. How fortunate for us that he was able to visit you this week."

Captain Collins looked surprised and said that he was not aware that his brother was in the neighbourhood.

"Not in the neighbourhood? Why, Captain Collins, here is your brother before you," she said, stepping back to reveal him.

Captain Collins looked at her enquiringly, but Mrs. Bennet did not notice his perplexed expression, for she was too busy congratulating Mr. Collins on having such a delightful brother.

"But that is not my brother," said Mr. Collins. "He sent his apologies this afternoon, business preventing him from attending this most worthy and illustrious gathering."

"Not your brother?" asked Mrs. Bennet, staring at Mr. Collins. "Of course he is your brother. He was introduced to us by Mr. Withington and Mr. Withington would not lie about such a thing."

Elizabeth stifled a gurgle of laughter. "Mama, Mr. Withington introduced him as Captain Collins; he said nothing about him being Mr. Collins's brother. Collins, you know, is not an uncommon name."

Mrs. Bennet was dumbfounded. But she quickly recovered herself.

"No, indeed, it is very common," she said, sounding very much aggrieved. "I never met with such a common name in my life, indeed it is very vulgar. Twice now my girls have been deceived by a man named Collins."

"Mama!" said Elizabeth.

But Mrs. Bennet was unrepentant until Captain Collins apologized most gallantly—and with laughing eyes—for not being the brother of their friend.

"He is no friend of mine," said Mrs. Bennet bitterly.

Elizabeth was mortified, and Darcy touched her arm in silent sympathy.

Mr. Collins, meanwhile, apologized so many times for not being related to the most admirable captain that Mrs. Bennet at last recovered her good humour. A good-looking Captain was not to be overlooked, even if he was not in line for the entail.

It was time for supper. Captain Collins escorted Kitty, and the rest of the guests began to file through to the supper room.

As Elizabeth took Darcy's arm she gave another grimace and said to Darcy, "Do you know, I do not feel like eating. In fact, I am feeling a little unwell. I think I will retire for the night."

Jane, who had been following Elizabeth into supper, said, "Would you like me to come with you?"

"Yes," said Elizabeth. "I rather think I would if you do not mind leaving your guests."

"They are all going into supper and after that, you know, they will be going home," said Jane. "The weather being so bad, we thought it best to set an early end to the evening. I will stay with you until supper is over and then I will come down again to bid them farewell."

Supported on one side by Darcy and on the other by her sister, Elizabeth made her way slowly upstairs, but by the time they reached her room it was clear that she was feeling more than a little unwell.

The baby was on the way.

Darcy, feeling suddenly helpless, stood awkwardly beside the door.

"The doctor is downstairs," said Jane. "Go and fetch him?"

Glad, for once, to be told what to do, Darcy ran downstairs and went into the supper room. He looked about him and caught sight of the doctor at the end of the table. He went over to him and spoke to him in a low voice. The doctor nodded, excused himself, and rose to his feet. Bingley, sensing something was happening, followed them, leaving the rest of the guests to enjoy themselves.

"I think it would be as well if you were to have a message sent to the midwife," said the doctor as he began to mount the stairs. "Her name is Mrs. Parsons, and she lives on the far side of the village green. The footmen will know where to find her."

Darcy gave instructions for the midwife to be fetched, then made to follow the doctor upstairs.

"No," came a voice at his ear. "You cannot go up. They will not let you in the room. I know. I tried."

Darcy noticed Bingley for the first time. His thoughts had been so full of Elizabeth that he had not seen him, but he was very glad of his friend's presence. There was something reassuring about Bingley's good-natured countenance and his friendly voice.

"Of course. You know. You have already been through this," said Darcy.

He tried to speak lightly, as though his wife had a baby every day of the week, but his voice was full of anxiety and his face was strained.

Bingley put a friendly hand on his arm.

"Come and eat some supper," he said. "Nothing will happen for quite some time, believe me."

"Some supper?" asked Darcy incredulously, looking at Bingley as if he had run mad. "You cannot expect me to eat at a time like this."

"It is difficult, I know, but you must make the effort. It is going to be a long night and you must keep your strength up." As Darcy continued to look scandalised at the mere thought of eating when Elizabeth was suffering, Bingley added, "Elizabeth might need something, and you will be no use to her if you are weak from lack of food."

Darcy's attitude changed at once and he followed Bingley into the supper room, but his eyes kept drifting upwards as though he thought that, by straining them, he might be able to see through the ceiling.

Bingley led him over to a spare chair and with difficulty Darcy drew his eyes away from the ceiling and sat down. The long table was laid with a snowy cloth on which porcelain and silverware glistened. Pyramids of fruit were set in the middle on ornate stands, and every kind of dish was set on silver platters in between.

Darcy looked at the appetising food as though it were ashes, for he could not think how he was going to eat any of it, but he knew he must make the effort, and with reluctance, he took some chicken and cold beef. He lifted a forkful of chicken to his mouth but it tasted like sawdust.

Around him, the other guests talked. He tried to take an interest in their conversations, but everything they said seemed shallow and inconsequential and he could not bring himself to join in. Indeed, he scarcely knew how to answer them when they asked him a question.

The grandfather clock's pendulum seemed to swing in slow motion, as the seconds seemed like minutes and the minutes passed like hours.

After answering one particularly stupid question he found himself wishing the guests would hurry up and leave, but when they had at last all departed and he had retired to the drawing-room, he realised how much more difficult it was without their presence. The noise and the necessity of making the odd response to a question had kept him turning outwards, but now he found his thoughts turning inwards. So it was with relief that he heard the door opening and Bingley entered the room.

"Well, that is the last of them. They have all gone," said Bingley.

"And your sisters?" asked Darcy.

"Louisa and her husband have retired for the night. Caroline offered to help with Elizabeth, but Jane told her there was nothing she could do and so Caroline too has gone to bed. Mrs. Bennet was with Elizabeth, but as she would talk of nothing but Kitty and Captain Collins, Jane has managed to persuade her that she should retire."

"So Elizabeth is with Jane as well as the doctor and the midwife?" asked Darcy.

"Yes." He spoke reassuringly. "She is in good hands."

Darcy nodded, then walked over to the fireplace where he stood lost in thought.

"Come, you cannot stand about like this," said Bingley. "You must do something. Have a hand of cards with me."

"I cannot think of cards at a time like this."

"A game of billiards, then."

"No!" snapped Darcy. Adding more gently, "No, thank you."

"You must do something, you know."

Darcy paced to the other side of the room and took up a book, but he quickly dropped it again.

"It will be all right," said Bingley sympathetically. "I imagined every kind of tragedy when Jane was giving birth, but here I am with a fine son and a healthy wife. It will be the same for you."

"If only I could believe that," said Darcy, coming to a halt. "But I keep remembering..."

He broke off.

"Yes?" asked Bingley.

"I keep remembering the night Georgiana was born."

"Ah."

Darcy sat down opposite his friend and leaned forwards with his elbows on his knees. He was not one to talk of his feelings in general, but there were so strong they would no longer be denied.

"It was a terrible night," he said.

"You were ten years old at the time, I think."

"Yes."

Darcy could not help remembering the events of that night, although he tried to shut them out. The house had been strange. It had not been the safe and familiar home he had always known; it had been full of hurrying feet and anxious whispers.

He remembered the maids running up and down stairs with bowls of hot water and armfuls of clean sheets, and their worried faces. He had tried to talk to them but they had not had time for him and so he had gone down to the drawing-room, drawn there by the light, hoping to find someone to comfort him. His father would be there, he thought, to give him some manly words of advice. But instead he had found his father crying. He had been so shocked by the sight that he had crept back to bed again unnoticed.

The following day, he had been taken into the nursery and he had seen his little sister, Georgiana, but he had not been allowed to see his mother for three days, and when he had finally been allowed to see her, she had been sickly and pale.

"My mother… I thought she would die," he said.

"But she did not die," Bingley reminded him.

"No. But she was never the same again. Before she had Georgiana she was always riding or dancing or going out in the carriage. Afterwards she was sickly, and she died young. What if the same happens to Elizabeth? What if I have ruined forever her delight in roaming round the countryside? What if I have taken from her, her pleasure in dancing? What if I have turned her into an invalid—or worse."

"Come, now, these are morbid thoughts," said Bingley bracingly.

"I cannot expect you to understand," said Darcy with a sigh, rising to his feet and turning away.

"You are wrong, I do understand. I thought exactly the same. But we do not make things better by worrying about them. Time enough to worry if worry is needed."

Darcy roused himself.

"You are right," he said, making an effort. "Let us have a game of billiards. Lead on."

The two men went through into the billiard room, with Bingley speaking cheerfully all the time but not burdening Darcy with the trouble of expecting a reply. He set up the table and handed Darcy a cue and the two men began to play.

Darcy did his best to keep his mind on the game, but his shots were wild and Bingley won easily.

"Perhaps I should go up," said Darcy when the game was over. "I could just see how she goes on."

Bingley advised against it, but his words fell on deaf ears, for Darcy was already halfway up the stairs.

At the top, he met Jane just coming out of Elizabeth's room. Jane was looking tired, but she smiled when she saw Darcy.

"How is she?" he asked.

"She is doing well," said Jane reassuringly. "There is nothing to worry about. I will come down and tell you when there is any news."

"Come down regularly," he beseeched her. "Let me know how she is going on—but not if Elizabeth needs you," he added.

"Very well," she promised him. "I will come down often. Now go, and try not to worry. Everything will be all right."

Reluctantly, he went downstairs and joined Bingley in a hand of cards, though he threw away his chances through inattention and lost miserably when he should have won.

At three o'clock, Jane came downstairs to tell him that things were progressing nicely and to chide Bingley for not having ordered some sandwiches.

"If you are going to sit up all night, you will need something to eat," she said.

"And so will you," said Bingley.

He made her sit down, for she was looking tired, and he ordered some soup and sandwiches for all three of them. It was just what they needed. Jane was clearly revived and Darcy at least had something to occupy him for a quarter of an hour. Having finished her soup, Jane went upstairs again and the two men were left together. They talked in a desultory fashion and from time to time indulged in a game, and the night dragged on until grey light started to filter through the curtains, and they realised that morning was on its way at last.

The silence was broken by the church bells ringing and when Darcy wondered aloud why they were ringing so early, Bingley said, "It is Christmas morning."

"Of course!" said Darcy. "I had quite forgot."

A cry came from above.

"And what a Christmas it is turning out to be," said Bingley with a smile.

Darcy sprang up and was out of the door before Bingley could stop him. He met Jane on the stairs, coming down to tell him the news.

"How is she?" he demanded. "How is Elizabeth?"

"She is well, very well," said Jane.

"And the baby?"

"Well."

"And?"

"And a girl. As bonny a baby as I have ever seen," said Jane, adding, "apart from little Charles, of course!"

Darcy caught her hand in thanks and then turned his steps towards Elizabeth's room.

"Go quietly. She is sleeping," said Jane.

He nodded, then went on. He was excited but also a little apprehensively too, for although Jane had said that everything was well, he would not be content until he had seen that it was so with his own eyes.

He turned the handle softly and went in. It took his eyes a few moments to accustom themselves to the gloom, for there was only one candle lit. The nurse was dozing in a chair by the fire, and in the bed, Elizabeth was sleeping. Her hair was spread around her on the pillow. Her colour was healthy, and there was a smile playing about her lips. He went over to her and kissed her. She stirred a little but did not wake.

His eyes moved across her to the cot beside the bed. In it was a baby, red and crumpled, but for all that, the most beautiful thing he had ever seen in his life.

He heard a slight stirring beside him and turned to see that Elizabeth had awoken. He went over to her and kissed her again. She sat up and he put the pillows behind her to make her more comfortable, then she reached towards the baby. Eager to prevent her overtiring herself, he picked up his daughter and then wondered what he had done, for he had no idea how to hold her and he was suddenly afraid she might break. But she settled into his hands trustingly and he carried her over to Elizabeth. As he put her into Elizabeth's arms, he thought he had never known a moment so perfect.

"There remains just one question to be answered," said Elizabeth with a smile. "Is she your Christmas present to me, or is she my Christmas present to you?"

Darcy remained with Elizabeth all day and, despite the protestations of the nurse, he refused to move. Elizabeth further scandalised the nurse by talking of going downstairs after dinner. Her robust constitution had stood her in good stead and she had recovered quickly from the birth, so that Jane had no qualms about seconding Elizabeth's determination. And so it was that Elizabeth joined the rest of the party that evening.

Lady Catherine declared herself scandalised and Mr. Collins agreed with her, saying that his own dear Charlotte had remained in bed for every day of the accustomed lying in period.

Elizabeth, knowing Charlotte's nature, doubted it, but she was too happy to argue with him.

"Well, Lizzy, this is a joyful Christmas," said Mr. Bennet. "Two daughters married and two cribs by their sides." He turned to Mary, who was playing the pianoforte. "Excellent, my dear, a wonderful sonata, but today we want something different, I think. Play us some carols if you please."

Mary determinedly finished her sonata, but once it was done she obliged the company by playing a selection of carols and the festive strains mingled with the crackling of the fire to create a cheerful scene.

"Another grandchild," said Mrs. Bennet, smiling dotingly at the new baby.

Kitty and Maria were cooing at the two babies.

"And have you decided on a name?" asked Mr. Bennet.

"Something festive, in honour of the occasion," said Caroline. "Carol, perhaps, or"—as though she had just thought of it—"Caroline. That would suit the occasion very well."

Mr. Hurst said, "Humph," from his place, reclining on the sofa, but Mr. Bennet said, "An excellent idea!" He twinkled at Elizabeth. "Or perhaps Catherine," he added.

Lady Catherine looked graciously pleased.

"Oh, yes, a most illustrious name," said Mr. Collins at once. "If I may say so, any child would be fortunate, nay graced, by so noble a name."

"Or *Lady* Catherine," said Mrs. Bennet.

Elizabeth laughed, but her father, never slow to indulge his wife's follies, remarked, "True, Lady Catherine would be a fine name. But I believe there might be some little difficulty about christening the child with a title she does not possess."

Darcy put a stop to their guesses by saying, "We have already decided on the name. She will be Elizabeth, like her mother, but we will call her Beth."

"Well, to be sure, that is as good a name as any," Mrs. Bennet conceded. For, having given it to her own daughter, she could hardly disagree. She gave a happy sigh and looked around the room with glossy sprigs of holly tucked behind the mirrors and red berries glowing in the candlelight, then letting her eyes come to rest on the cribs. "What a Christmas this is turning out to be. Three daughters married and now two grandchildren. If only Captain Collins should happen to call in the next few hours and ask for your hand, Kitty, my dear, my happiness would be complete."

A Darcy Christmas

SHARON LATHAN

CONTENTS

PROLOGUE

HE SET THE PAINTING onto the sofa, assuring it was well supported before stepping away. He gazed at the canvas, a smile spreading as he looked upon his family. His family. The family created by him and his wife, just as he had dreamt for so many lonely years. They stood on the portico of Pemberley flanked by their precious children on the steps. All of them were smiling at the artist. A sentimental man by nature, he silently examined the newest portrait of his family and lost himself in happy memories. Unsurprisingly, since it was Christmas Day, his reminiscences focused on holiday celebrations of the past. So lost was he in quiet contemplations that he did not hear his study door opening. But he did smell the lavender water habitually worn by his wife and extended his arm without averting his attention from the painting. She slipped under his arm, nestling against his side as naturally as a bird takes to its nest, her arms encompassing his waist.

"I plan to hang it there," he nodded toward the wall above the settee. "As much as I love Gainsborough's landscape, I would prefer to have you and our children watching over me as I work. Someday it can join the others in the Portrait Gallery, but not yet."

She nodded in agreement. "I concur. We look wonderful here. It is an amazing portrait, arriving at a perfect time."

"How true. It induced me to reflect on Christmases past. All of them have been wonderful since you came into my life." He looked at his wife then, his blue eyes tender and inundated with love.

"All of them?" she repeated, teasing and meeting his eyes with the same intense emotion.

"Even those Christmases that were sad or difficult were special, my heart. My life is complete since we married and I would change nothing. This Christmas is the most recent in a long line of incredible memories."

"It is not over yet!" she reminded him, both of them laughing as they returned their gazes to the painting.

Silently, in sweet harmony, they admired the canvas testimonial to what they, through God's grace, had achieved in the long years of their marriage. They studied the painted images, each beloved beyond measure. The portraitist had easily identified the individual characteristics, capturing them brilliantly. Especially manifest was the love, unswerving commitment, and supreme happiness verily shining from their faces as proud parents to the next generation of Darcys. Memories of Christmases together flowed through both their minds, time seeming to halt as they reminisced.

She broke the quiet contemplation, tugging gently on his waist. "Come, love. Our family awaits and I have a special present for you."

"I thought we were finished exchanging gifts this year."

"It is something special I have held in reserve."

"Secrets?"

"Of course! It is Christmas after all!"

With laughter and a final glance at the mute and fixed images, they exited the parlor to rejoin the boisterous reality.

CHRISTMAS
LONELINESS

THE SNOWFLAKES DRIFTED SLOWLY downward. They were enormous flakes and floating so delicately on the air that, even in the inky darkness behind the thick glass with only the faint glow of lamplight reflecting, Fitzwilliam Darcy could visualize the minute crystals and unique geometry of each flake. It was mesmerizing and oddly calming to his tumultuous thoughts. He sipped the cocoa that was now lukewarm, watched the snow fall and gather into piles on the panes, and struggled to stir up the Christmas cheer one was supposed to enjoy on Christmas Eve.

It was not working.

He couldn't readily recall the last Christmas that was truly joyous. Surely it was before his mother died, but the memories were faded and supplanted by so many years of forced gaiety. Oh, they exchanged presents and decorated the house and went to church and delighted in a lavish feast. Often they visited Rivallain for the day, the estate of his uncle and aunt, the Earl and Marchioness of Matlock, and once or twice they had dwelt at

Darcy House in London for the holiday activities there. But like all festivities since his mother's passing, and now his father's, the celebratory atmosphere was muted.

Of course he strived to celebrate the day for his sister Georgiana's sake, understanding that a child needed the merrymaking. And lauding the birth of their Savior was indeed a commemoration he took very seriously. Yet personally, he often felt that the entire season could easily pass by without him noticing or caring.

Darcy had grown so accustomed to the attitude that it hardly registered any longer. Even while plotting and planning for Georgiana and purchasing gifts—that a delight he truly did enjoy—his internal zeal for Christmas was dim. He did not dread the holiday nor was he particularly gloomy over it; he just did not care all that much.

So why was this year so different? Why did he feel a melancholy blanketing his soul? And why did the dreams continue to invade his sleep? Why was *she* persistent in burrowing into his mind and hea…? No! He refused to even think it! This Christmas of 1815 was no different than the previous twenty-seven.

He sighed unconsciously and continued with his rapt contemplation of the falling snow and abstracted sipping of the cooling cocoa.

Georgiana Darcy sat on the sofa near the fire. She had been reading aloud but halted several minutes ago when it became clear that her brother was not listening to her. Now she studied him in perplexity. Georgiana was well aware that Christmas was not exactly a period of crazed jubilation for her brother, but he usually showed some enthusiasm. He never failed to create a special atmosphere for her and showered her with expensive gifts. Since she knew no different, it honestly never occurred to her to yearn for more. Georgiana was a girl quite complacent and content in her life. Her only desire was to please her family, that being primarily her adored older brother. Thus, she was disturbed by his current distraction and somberness.

None would refer to Fitzwilliam Darcy as gregarious or buoyant, but the private man was one of tender humor and affection. That he was overwhelmingly devoted to his sister could be denied by no one, especially Georgiana. She held him in tremendous awe and respect, but also took his love and playful teasing for granted. Yet ever since his return from Town and the sojourn in Hertfordshire with Mr. Bingley, he had been… odd.

She shook her head. It made no sense whatsoever. Naturally it distressed her. Not for her sake but because she loved him too much to think of him as being in pain. Yet, with the overconfidence of youth and the towering admiration of a worshipful younger sister, she shrugged it off. In her mind, her brother was fearless and capable of solving any dilemma.

So she smiled and rose to bid him goodnight. He smiled genuinely in return and held her close for several minutes, wished her sweet dreams and gave a teasing reminder not to wake him at the crack of dawn, and after a tender kiss to her cheek, she retired to her room no longer fretting over her complicated sibling but losing herself in dreams of presents.

Darcy watched her gracefully exit the parlor, his heart surging with happiness as it always did when considering his sister. But as soon as she left, seemingly taking the light and music and laughter with her, the pensiveness drenched him once again. It was late and he felt simultaneously weary and jittery. He stared at the faint light beyond the doorway, imagined the shadowy corridors between this chamber and his suite of cold and empty rooms—*Where did that thought come from?*—and actually shuddered.

Then, just as abruptly as the sadness, he was jolted by a flare of anger. He muttered a harsh curse, strode briskly to the low table where the tea and snacks sat, and placed the drained mug onto the silver tray with a plunk. He squared his shoulders, straightening to his full and considerable height, and marched purposefully from the room.

His thoughts were darker than the illuminated hallways. What was it about Elizabeth Bennet that had bewitched him so? He truly felt as if under a spell that consumed him and made no sense whatsoever. She was so completely unsuitable! She was infatuated by George Wickham, for goodness sake. That spoke volumes. And her family? He shuddered anew.

Oh, but she was beautiful. Indeed, so very beautiful.

He paused outside his dressing room door, one hand on the knob as his throat constricted and heart lurched with longing. He cursed again, a habit that was quite unlike him normally but lately seemed to be occurring frequently, and reached to loosen the cravat that was strangely now choking off his air supply. He pivoted and entered his bedchamber. For tonight, he would manage to undress himself. Facing the calmly professional presence of his valet Samuel while he was in what could only be termed "a mood" was intolerable!

Yet as he resisted slamming the door violently behind him with tremendous restraint, he discovered his steps slowing. He halted in the middle of his room. He gazed at the comforting surroundings, savored the warmth of the crackling fire as it seeped into his chilled skin, and awaited the peaceful relaxation that inevitably washed over him when alone in his sanctuary.

It did not come.

Rather he recalled the dreams that had, in one shape or another, been haunting him nearly from the moment he encountered a vivid pair of brown eyes within the crowd at an obscure dance assembly in Meryton.

He wanted to be angry.

He wanted to be disgusted with himself.

And he wanted to forget her.

At least that is what he told himself. But even now, as he remembered his dreams and remembered their conversations in Hertfordshire, he knew a smile was spreading over his face and heat was flushing through his body.

Some of that, he knew, was due to the nature of many of his dreams. It annoyed him to a degree, and he was embarrassed to a degree. But he logically deduced that it had nothing to do with Miss Elizabeth personally. No, indeed not! It was simply that he had reached the point where needing a woman, a wife, was a physical necessity. Surely that was the primary reason why increasingly erotic musings were causing him to bolt awake in a sweat of unfulfilled desire.

If it was always Elizabeth Darcy—*Bennet!*—who brought him to such a state, well that could be logically explained as well. Right?

Of course! It was because she had enchanted him in some way that he could not comprehend. Her passionate personality, her fire as she argued with him, her intelligence as she countered every last one of his held beliefs, her teasing smile and sparkling eyes as she laughed at him—*At him! Mr. Fitzwilliam Darcy of Pemberley!*—drove him virtually insane until he no longer controlled his faculties. Until his dreams, both day and night, were invaded by her.

Yes, that was it.

And if he was beginning to dream of her as the mother to his children?

Well, that was more troubling.

He again scanned the room, only now he was seeing it as in the recent dreams. Elizabeth curled up in his chair, wearing a soft gown of blue with a baby at her breast. He and Elizabeth reclining on the bed with several children jumping on the mattress as they all laughed. The door to the unused dressing room once belonging to his mother ajar with Elizabeth brushing her incredible hair and smiling at him via the mirror while he held a child in his arms. Elizabeth pregnant and standing before him while he caressed the swell of her belly with his hands. Elizabeth…

He shook his head to clear the strange and disturbing visions that had started in earnest these past two weeks.

Since returning to Pemberley.

Since preparing for Christmas.

He passed a hand over his face.

You are lonely, Darcy, he thought. *Admit it. You want a wife and a family.*

Of course this was not a huge revelation. He had longed for a family of his own for most of his adult life. He had envisioned the silent halls of Pemberley echoing with the noise of childish laughter and running feet. He had desired a relationship as his parents possessed. He had searched endlessly for a woman to love.

Did he love Elizabeth Bennet?

He crawled under the counterpane, the cold linen upon his flesh a sharp contrast to the imaginary fever he felt flowing over his skin while dreaming of her. The flames of passion and tranquil warmth of affection were so incredibly real. Yet, he did not know the answer to his question. Did he love Elizabeth Bennet? Or did he merely desperately crave a connection that presently eluded him? Was he simply weary of searching and being alone?

He no longer knew. But as the tendrils of sleep claimed him, he recognized that his anger and disgust were a sham. The edges of his unconscious mind accepted the love he refused to acknowledge in broad daylight. He reached for the dreams, however they would come to him on this night, Christmas Eve, as an intoxicant that he wanted and required.

"*Elizabeth*," he whispered as sleep overtook him, not even aware that he had done so.

And eventually the dream came.

This one was different, as they all were, although the essence was the same.

He walked down the main floor corridor toward the parlor with a spring in his step that was utterly inconceivable in his real world but completely normal in this imaginary world. Happy voices, laughter, and singing reverberated down the hall, growing in volume as he neared the gaping portal. He distinguished each one of them, placing names to the individual tones with warm, deep emotion attached. Many of the names would escape him when he woke—this he knew on some level—but in his dream they were dear and intimate.

There was Richard and Georgiana, his Aunt Madeline and Uncle Malcolm, even Jonathan and Priscilla. These were not a surprise. But as he turned the corner and crossed the threshold, his eyes instantly scanned the room and alit upon the one voice dearest of all.

Elizabeth.

He always knew she would be there, somewhere in the midst of those he loved most in the world, belonging there as surely as he did.

She stood next to Richard laughing at some joke his cousin had made. Her ringing laugh, the one he insisted annoyed him while in Hertfordshire but he knew never had, was now the sweetest music. It filled him to bursting with a joy unlike anything he had ever experienced. Even not directed at him, her happiness was a profound balm to his soul, and the smile that had been forming before entering the room grew wider.

Then she noted his presence and turned in his direction, her glorious eyes engaging his. And there quite simply were no words in the English language to describe what passed between or to relate how he felt. Yes indeed, it was magical, and the enchantment feared in his waking moments was wholly understood in this visionary place as the purest form of bonded love.

He accepted it. He relished it. He claimed it. And he returned it wholeheartedly.

He took a step toward her, intending to enfold her into his arms and press her against his heart, but his legs were abruptly engulfed.

"Papa! Papa!"

The dreaming Darcy was not the slightest bit surprised by the chaotic assault of several tiny arms and piping voices. In fact, his spirit soared higher, the missing pieces of his puzzled real life snapping together instantly, into a masterpiece depicting earthly paradise. A booming laugh launched from his mouth and he knelt to administer hugs and kisses to the surging mass of children clamoring to accept his love.

Then Elizabeth was there. His wife. He stood, gazing at her with his entire soul visible in his eyes. She smiled simply, raising one hand to lightly touch his cheek, and said, "Happy Christmas, William."

On some level his rational mind knew it was fantastical, as the number of offspring defied what was physically possible unless Elizabeth had birthed triplets once a year! But of course, dreams have a way of melding reality and allegory. Besides, it was the emotions attached to the fabricating dream that counted. The power of hearing her utter his name, the shortened name only those dear to him used, was so strong. Add to that the intensity of affection from a multitude of quarters and his sleeping mind was soothed as it never was in his waking life.

The dream proceeded as all dreams do. It flipped incoherently from scene to scene, some bizarre in their content and hazy while others were crystalline. The strange mingling of credible specifics—such as Georgiana a grown woman and the heirloom Christmas decorations adorning the Manor—with points impossible—like his parents conversing with Elizabeth—seemed normal within the boundaries of the dream.

It wasn't the details that resonated but the themes of family and love. And as happened every night, he jerked awake before the final consummation of expressing his love to his wife. The ache of need with heart pounding and perspiration rapidly chilling his skin brought on tremors and groans.

He lurched to his feet, crossing the room to stir the smoldering logs. He stared into the flames, his body warming as he tried to make sense of it. The questions flashed through his brain as they did every night. Why her? Was it possible to love in such a way? Was it fated for him as he hoped? Had he childishly imagined his parents possessing such a love? Would he ever have a family of his own? Was he a romantic fool destined to be disappointed?

Did he love Elizabeth Bennet?

And then it dissolved, as it inevitably did. The cold air restored his clarity, the fuzzy sentiments dissipated, his rational intellect reinstated, and logic took over. It was only because he was lonely. It was due to the nature of the Christmas holiday focusing on love and felicity leading to nonsensical musings.

He could not be in love with the lowborn, argumentative, fiery Elizabeth Bennet!

The dreams were nice, pleasant, and passionate, but harmless. *Just enjoy them while they last,* he thought to himself. Why not? They will pass. You will never see Miss Bennet again. God will bring a suitable mate to you. The years will unfold sensibly and composedly. Indeed, serenity will prevail, as it should.

So with that comforting thought conquering the turmoil, his mind calmed and heart beat a regular rhythm. He returned to his bed, his slumber, and his dreams.

CHRISTMAS HONEYMOON

A YEAR AFTER THE torturous dream-filled weeks of 1815 presented a Christmas Eve as different as night is from day. Pemberley was adorned with a wealth of green vines and branches with candles both large and small flickering in nooks and creatively decorated crannies. The holiday family heirlooms were repaired and now graced their customary locations, mistletoe ornaments lurked at practically every hallway junction, and the aromas of savory food wafted tantalizingly from the kitchen. Guest rooms once layered with dust were inhabited by visitors from afar, increasing the lights and laughter blazing from the game rooms and music chamber. Topping it off was the enormous Yule log burning in the main parlor's hearth.

Happiness, deep love, and Christmas cheer echoed down the lengthy corridors and invaded every chamber of the Manor. But in none were these positive emotions as high as in the Master's chambers on the upper floor of the south wing.

You see, this Christmas was Darcy's first as a married man. A newlywed of less than a month, in fact, and to his indescribable joy, his wife was Elizabeth. The numerous questions of the prior Christmas were answered beyond his wildest imaginings. Any delusions or doubts were erased.

Was he in love with Elizabeth Bennet, now Elizabeth Darcy?

Yes! A resounding *yes*, and to a depth that continually staggered him.

She was amazing in every definition of the word and astounded him at every turn. Celebrating Christmas in an unrestrained manner was her idea, the planning begun days after entering the house as its Mistress and executed flawlessly. Darcy quickly recognized that his newly found joy would not have allowed for the quiet commemorations of the past even had he wished it, which he did not. His heart was simply too full. Thus, the festivities had started several days ago with visitors and music, the perpetually smiling and laughing Darcy surprisingly loving each moment and always with Elizabeth Darcy at his side.

However, it truly was the private holiday observances that topped his list. Sharing his bride with others was not as painful as it might have been since they ensured special time alone. So far today, Christmas Eve, they had kissed under the hanging mistletoe, cuddled in the library, ice skated, and then explored the delights to be found in bathing together—the latter an extremely pleasurable activity they agreed must be repeated as often as possible!

After a wonderful evening involving fine dining, games, and singing with their guests, they retired to the chamber they shared and sat before the fire on the newly acquired, exquisitely tanned hide of a brown bear, propped against a dozen down-stuffed pillows with her body nestled between his legs. The legs still weakened from the shocking but blissful *gift* given to him in her dressing room! Her frank, verbal proposal of precisely how she wished for her husband of one month to love her—*in her dressing room*—all while unveiling her gorgeous body, was quite simply the best gift he had ever received in his entire life. He was yet reeling, but in a completely satisfied manner.

The glow yet flushed their skin as they cuddled, sipped wine, shared an abundance of tender kisses, and talked. Darcy read aloud from Lord Byron's *The Corsair*, the melodramatic poem of love and pirates additionally thrilling when rendered in his resonant, storytelling voice. Lizzy, absently toying with the bookmark that had kept their place since last evening's reading, was mesmerized by his surprisingly expressive face.

"Be careful not to fray the fabric. That bookmark is precious and I wish it to remain intact forever."

She stayed her fidgeting fingers, holding the bookmark in question up for close inspection. The wide strip of fine silk with a quilt backing had been a gift from Lizzy to her then fiancé upon his twenty-ninth birthday. She had embroidered two linked hearts bearing their names with a verse from Genesis above. The promise of their future as one soul was a treasured possession that Darcy kept in whatever book he was reading.

"It is undamaged, but I apologize. Of course, you know that it cannot endure forever?"

"I intend to ensure it does," he countered stubbornly, ignoring Lizzy's chuckle and reaching under a nearby pillow. "Speaking of gifts, I have an early Christmas present for you."

He handed her a small, ribbon-tied box contained a key that belonged to a locked cabinet filled with his personal journals and mementoes. Lizzy laughed when she saw the key, because also hidden behind the secured doors was a collection of sexually instructive books that were a source of continual jesting between them.

Elizabeth, of course and to his never-ending delight, had to tease.

"Books? How sweet of you, William. Always desiring to improve my mind. I promise I shall apply myself diligently and will practice as often as feasible."

"You minx!"

He drew her against his chest, reclined onto the warmed fur, and opened her robe all in one smooth motion. They kissed and caressed, enjoying the tactile sensations and hearts beating in time while the longcase clock in the corner ticked a regular rhythm.

"This is vastly superior to every dream I had of how Christmas with you would be. In fact, this is undoubtedly the best Christmas of my entire life."

"It isn't over yet," she whispered. "But as sweet as that is for you to say, how could it be the best of your life, William?"

He met her eyes. "I am not exaggerating. Never has a Christmas transcended this one, Elizabeth. And I do not refer to the incredible passion we have together, although that surpasses every fantasy my feeble mind conjured. And certainly that facet alone adds a delicious dimension to 'celebrating' Christmas that I never experienced before. But, at the risk of sounding woefully quixotic, my love for you enhances all aspects of my life to a degree that overwhelms me."

"I adore my quixotic husband, so do not stop." She pulled him in for a long kiss.

"Yes, most assuredly better than any of my dreams."

"You dreamt of us celebrating Christmas?"

"Last year I was tortured, if you want to know the truth. I could not stop thinking of you, Elizabeth. It took me awhile but it was consistent dreams of us as a family that finally convinced me that I was in love with you." And in gentle tones and vivid recounting, he told her of the visions that had haunted him.

"I wish I could say that I thought of you last Christmas, my love."

He shook his head. "Do not be sad, dearest. We are together now and that is all that matters. Besides"—and he grinned, lifting his left brow—"you are thinking of me now, are you not?"

Lizzy laughed, nudging him until he rolled onto his back with her body draped partially over. "Indeed I am. Thinking quite seriously, as a matter of fact. I have promised to practice until an expert on the subject…"

"Then I shall pray you never become an 'expert' as I would not wish for the practicing to cease," he interrupted.

"I am sure there is always something new to learn," she assured him. "I am very clever, you know."

"Yes, I know!"

"Do you still wish for serenity and composure? Or does a little fire and argument now exhilarate you, Mr. Darcy?"

"No and yes." He wrapped his fingers within her hair, bringing her closer for an intense kiss. "I have repented of my foolish misconceptions. You may scorch me with your fire any time you wish, Mrs. Darcy."

The antique clock of gleaming mahogany chimed through the midnight hour, alerting the busy occupants that Christmas Day had arrived. The final chime's echo still rang when they were finally able to speak.

"Merry Christmas, my lover."

"Indeed it is!" he rasped. "I knew it was unwise to give you access to the books if you can devise such methods all on your own. I think you may kill me!"

But Lizzy just laughed.

CHRISTMAS
TOYS

THE MID-MORNING SUN SHONE brightly through the wide
windows lining the west-facing wall of the huge main parlor.
Dustings of snow lay upon the terrace stones, but the fair
weather and unobstructed sunlight had melted the bulk of it.
It was cold outside, as one expected on Christmas Day, but
the combination of blazing fire for interior warmth and golden
rays from without created a false summertime atmosphere. The
mood amongst the Pemberley inhabitants was as gay as one
might expect at a spring picnic or festival. But rather than
focusing on fine finger foods or catching butterflies, the adults
were cheerily focused on one thirteen-month-old infant.

A pile of presents surrounded Alexander Darcy, the heir
to Pemberley, who accepted the ridiculousness with his typical
stoicism and intense concentration. He did not quite seem able
to grasp that something special lurked *inside* the package. He was
perfectly content to look at, play with, or chew upon the ribbons,
wrapping, or box itself. The adult assistants allowed this for about
two seconds before impatiently "helping" him open the gift to

reveal the treasure within. Alexander tolerated the interruption to his play with extreme forbearance, continually amazed when a new toy was miraculously revealed. Then he would squeal with glee, bouncing and waving his arms in the air, and joyfully clutch the prize to his chubby chest.

It was a lengthy process, mainly because Alexander had just recently learned how to walk proficiently. His stumbling early steps and need to hold on to a solid foundation were gone in the wake of new maturity. He was quite proud of his skill and also well aware of just how much more of the world he could explore on two legs that functioned fairly well most of the time. Suddenly sitting on his bottom confined to a small space was wholly untenable! Alexander was an oddly complacent child, but even he grew cranky and annoyed at being compelled to stay put. Luckily he was easily distracted, as most infants were, and readily calmed when a new sparkling bauble was thrust under his nose.

The loving adults thought it was the greatest fun ever.

"Here, Alexander," Dr. George Darcy said as he loosened the ties holding the maroon and yellow cloth concealing the spongy item inside. "Jharna's son, Nimesh, had this made for me. It is a hoolock gibbon, my favorite of all the primates in India." George, younger brother to Darcy's deceased father, freed the exquisitely crafted stuffed animal from its wrappings, grandly plopping it onto the toddler's lap.

"Uncle! He is remarkable." Darcy leaned forward from his cross-legged perch behind his son to finger the soft brownish-black fur. "This is incredible taxidermy. Are you sure you want Alexander to drool and chew on such a masterpiece?"

George waved his hand dismissively. "It is well preserved. Allow him to play with it for a while, then perhaps it can be put aside temporarily to extend its life. But I wanted it for a toy. See how the long arms wrap around you, Alexander. He is bigger than you so will be great for cuddling."

Alexander was mesmerized. He pressed the black bead eyes, ruffled the thick white fur rings around the eye sockets, pried open the toothless mouth to peer inside, squeezed the thin arms, and wiggled the long toes. He looked up at his father, smiled widely, and released a string of nonsense intermingled with "papa" and a smattering of intelligible words as he proudly showed off his newest animal.

Darcy smiled, pulling his son onto his lap for a tight hug. "You are assuredly the only child in Derbyshire with a stuffed gibbon, my sweet."

"Papa, see? M'key? Mine, Unc Goj?"

"Yes, he is yours and 'monkey' will do, I suppose. Your Uncle George spoils you."

George snorted. "Somebody has to. Poor baby would have no toys to play with if not for his favorite uncle."

Georgiana laughed. "Yes indeed. Nothing to play with! Poor Alexander. Now, open this one from your *favorite* auntie, my precious."

"Thank goodness it is only you two here this Christmas or we not only would never get through the gift unveiling, but we would also have a brawl on our hands. Jane may take exception to the 'favorite' appellation." Lizzy spoke from her lounging location on the chaise, her voice weak and rough from coughing.

Darcy had returned from an eventful visit to London several days ago and discovered his wife extremely ill with a vicious cold. Darcy was still furious over not being informed of her illness. She was gradually improving under the care of their resident physician and her diligent husband, but remained lethargic and symptomatic. Yet, as sick as she was, Lizzy refused to lie abed for her son's first Christmas of consequence, the prior one occurring when he was not yet a month old. Darcy understood—his attempts to dissuade feebly offered—but he was worried. He directed a glare at his uncle, who ignored the not-so-subtle reminder of his nephew's irritation at not being notified, before closely examining his wife's face for the slightest sign of increasing distress.

"Cease staring at me, William. I am fine."

"Drink all your tea and then I will cease staring at you."

Lizzy lifted the cup reluctantly to her lips, grimacing with each swallow. "This is exceptionally foul." She shuddered, it now her turn to glare at the doctor.

"If medicine was delicious, people would stay sick," George asseverated. "It is a psychological inducement to get well if the medicine is bitter and fetid."

"Alexander's medicine was a sweet, berry-flavored syrup," she grumbled sulkily, already knowing his response since they had had this argument several times, the physician always winning and the tonics suspiciously tasting worse.

"Babies must be tricked into taking their medicine. Adults apply reason."

"Or force," Darcy added, pointedly nodding toward the half-filled cup.

"Lizzy may be ill and you larger, but I am not so sure who would prevail in that contest of wills," Georgiana offered. "Here, Alexander, open this one from your Aunt Giana." She knelt onto the floor, handing her nephew the wrapped bundle and winking at Lizzy.

Darcy made no attempt to dispute Georgiana's allegation, knowing his wife's temper, but he held no doubts he would indeed prevail even if he had to physically restrain and pry open her jaws! Luckily that course did not appear imminent, as Lizzy finished her tea in one pained gulp.

An enthusiastic upward launch from Alexander with hard skull cracking against an equally hard, firmly set jaw effectively diverted attention from ill wife to giddy son. Wiping tears of pain from his eyes, Darcy examined the collection of sock puppets spread between the happily gibbering toddler and delighted aunt.

"Papa! Papa, see?" Alexander grabbed the top two, one in each fist, swinging them directly into Darcy's face.

"Yes, son, I see them. No need to hit me. Let me look."

Georgiana leaned forward. "This is a grandfather and this a grandmother. She is the pretty blonde shepherd girl and here is her sheep. This is a footman in livery, perhaps Phillips or Watson. And the soldier like Uncle Richard." She inserted her hand into the latter, her pinkie bringing the puppet's arm up for a salute.

"Most impressive, Georgie. A judge, a frog, an elegant lady, and a horse. Well done." George slipped his bony hands into the frog and horse, "hopping" and "galloping" around Alexander's head while the infant laughed and wiggled.

"These are very thick, woolen socks. Where did you get them?" Darcy asked, one arm firm about his son's squirming body while examining the shepherd girl with his free hand.

"Mr. Clark gave me a dozen. The groundsmen wear them in the winter. They are the thickest stockings I have ever seen. Perfect for warmth and sturdy puppets, is that not so my sweet, sweet Alexander? Give your Aunt Giana kisses."

Georgiana was nuzzling Alexander and did not notice the strange expression on her brother's face until Lizzy began to hoarsely laugh. She glanced from Lizzy to Darcy, and then rolled her eyes. "I was not looking at the gardener's legs, William, only their attire."

"I was not imagining *that*. I am merely surprised you noticed the workers' leg coverings as suitable for creating puppets."

She shrugged. "I noticed the socks years ago and asked Mrs. Reynolds to get them for me to wear in winter. They are the warmest woolens in all of England, I am sure of it."

Darcy's mouth dropped open in shock. "You wear these ugly, roughly woven things?"

"Not in public!" She flushed but lifted her chin. "Not all Darcys are impervious to the cold of Derbyshire." And she nodded significantly toward his muscular legs, thinly sheathed in lightweight wool breeches, silk stockings, and low soft-leather house shoes.

"Lord knows I am not," George interjected with an excessive shiver, his thirty years in India's kinder clime meaning the gesture was only slightly overblown. "I wish you had shared your secret with me sooner, Georgiana. I would wear those socks, public or private."

"They might clash with your garments, Uncle. Plain grey and bleached beige? Unacceptable!"

George flashed his toothy grin at Lizzy, winking at her jest. "Not a problem, my dear. I can dye them fuchsia or maroon or blue to match. I even have the red left over from coloring my Christmas outfit." He lifted one long, thin leg, the bright red, loose, Indian-style trousers a stunning complement to the flowing kurta of three shades of green that covered his broad chest. They were all so familiar with Darcy's eccentric uncle's chosen way of dressing that none had even blinked when he strutted into the dining room that morning proudly modeling his "Christmas ensemble." George had been visibly deflated at the lack of response, prompting Darcy to take pity upon him and mutter grumpily that, "In this one instance, it is fortuitous Elizabeth's illness prevents me the embarrassment of attending church with you and witnessing the elderly ladies fainting in fright." George had beamed, his mood instantly improved.

"Apparently our son agrees with Georgiana's opinion."

All eyes swung to Alexander, still sitting in Darcy's lap, but now seriously intent upon the task of pulling sock puppets onto his chubby legs. The elegant, ball gown dressed lady puppet encased his left leg, but the grandfather puppet was not cooperating as well. Alexander frowned, deep creases between his thick brows, azure eyes squinting with concentration as his dexterous fingers manipulated the knitted edges from between his toes where they kept getting caught.

Everyone laughed at the humorous picture. Darcy reached to assist but was given an irritated glare and elbow nudge.

"I do it! No he'p, papa!"

Darcy buried his face into his son's wild, curly locks, shaking with laughter. Present opening shifted to gifts for the adults as Alexander refused to veer from placing sock puppets onto the stuffed, gangly extremities of his gibbon. He approached the procedure with the single-minded focus inherited from his father, finally managing to garb the ape before turning to the next glittering box.

Alexander next acquired a miniature kaleidoscope, the brass tube gripped and twisted with glass lens pressed against his eye for a full ten minutes. The wooden wagon was tremendous fun for three fast-paced circuits about the parlor after which his disenchantment was obvious when he exited the moving vehicle with a nosedive onto the floor. No permanent damage was done, hugs and sympathetic kisses by a remorseful father restoring his good humor.

Each pair of the twenty species of painted animals had to be positioned in a precise line awaiting entry on Noah's balsa-wood Ark ere Alexander was satisfied enough to pay heed to anyone in the room. Only then was the grand finale carried in by two footmen: a three-foot tall, six-foot square, to-scale replica of a medieval castle jointly created by Darcy and George. It was complete with functioning drawbridge and portcullis, crenellations, towers at each corner, arrow slits, and a painted moat. Tiny cannons and catapults were manned by enough tiny knights of shiny tin that, if added to the tin Regimental soldiers stored in the playroom, Alexander's army could withstand a pretend Saxon siege for years.

Lizzy watched it all from her comfortable roost on the chaise. The effort to control the persistent tickle in her throat, ignore the pain in her chest, and keep her eyes open sapped her already depleted strength, but Lizzy fought the impulses. She sipped the medicinal tea brewed by Dr. Darcy, smiling brightly whenever Darcy pierced her with his hawk-eyed gaze. If some of her sparkle was due to a fever, it was enough to placate her overprotective husband.

Darcy smiled in return, frequently reaching to tenderly caress her quilt-covered body or stooping to kiss her hand or forehead. He wasn't fooled by her brave act but knew it was fruitless to argue, yet he kept one joyful eye on his son and one sharp eye on his wife as the Christmas merriment unfolded.

As the maids gathered up the debris and Georgiana and George organized the gifts, Alexander stood up and toddled toward his mother. The movement was disjointed due to the clutter on the floor and the long limbs of the primate entangling about his legs, Darcy assisting the process.

"M'key, Mama." He held the stuffed toy out for his mother's inspection.

"He is a beautiful monkey, my sweet. Help him up, William, please."

Darcy lifted Alexander onto the chaise, the baby instantly snuggling onto her chest with thumb in his mouth and the gibbon clutched tightly. "I think Dog may have competition," Darcy said. "Is he too heavy, love?"

"No. He feels so good." She kissed his curly head. "Cuddling is not a top priority these days so I must take it when I can get it."

Darcy chuckled. "That is true."

"He is a man of action like his father."

"Perhaps, but I never pass up a chance to embrace his beautiful mother."

Lizzy started to laugh but the sound caught in her throat, inciting a violent coughing episode. Within seconds Alexander was grabbed by George and a breathless Lizzy was gathered into Darcy's arms. She tried to protest as he strode briskly from the room but simply did not have the energy or free air to do so.

"You will rest for the remainder of the afternoon and I shall have dinner brought to you. Do not argue with me, Elizabeth!" But an argument was not forthcoming as she pliantly melted into his stalwart embrace and succumbed to her need for sleep before he reached their upper floor chambers.

CHRISTMAS ADDITION

IT WAS NEARLY MIDNIGHT on another Christmas Eve. The halls, as always, were faintly illuminated with spaced lamps burning low. Darcy and Lizzy crept down the stairs, heading toward the parlor.

"Explain to me again why we are being so stealthy when the boys are soundly asleep in our room? And why we are adding more presents to the sky-high pile in the first place?"

"Very funny, Mr. Darcy. Just because you were too lazy to leave our bed, do not pretend you have forgotten this was your idea in the first place."

"Can I help it if sleeping cuddled with you and our boys is preferable to traversing freezing corridors in my bare feet?"

"You are tough. Now, put those packages right there in front where the boys will see them first off. No, no! Stack them nicely, William!"

She leaned over to meticulously arrange the presents he had dumped onto the carpet, Darcy kneeling beside. He grinned and nudged her shoulder. "You know, I do not recall ever making love on Christmas Eve before the Yule fire."

"If we had, I am sure you would remember it."

"No doubt of that. Seems quite remiss of us, do you not agree? And it is almost Christmas, so I believe it is obligatory. I think it is a commandment in the Bible."

She laughed and shook her head. "Unbelievable. I shall do my best, but considering the condition I am in, I may well fall asleep midway through."

He nuzzled kisses to her ear, one hand caressing the swell of her belly. "I am confident I can find ways to keep you interested."

"Arrogant," she teased, turning to kiss his lips.

"Hmm… Absolutely. But you forgot virile, wildly handsome, supremely masculine, and crazily in love with you."

"I shall consider the notion *after* you help me with these and only if you do an excellent job." She smiled and patted his cheek. "It really was a fine idea, Fitzwilliam. Alexander thinks he is so smart and has all his gifts figured out. Discovering new ones delivered by the mysterious Father Christmas will shake his composure."

"I would not count on it. I have been reading him all the stories so he knows that Father Christmas does not bring gifts but brings good cheer, although I have tried to gloss over the fact that spirits are usually the impetus for all that cheer. I made up a few bits here and there since he cannot read all that well yet, but I am not sure he is convinced about Father Christmas toting presents all over England in the dark of night."

"Well, either way, the boys will be happily surprised. And they did not have enough presents anyway."

"Ha! Tell me that after my aunt and uncle arrive for dinner.

You would think with Richard now adding to the Fitzwilliam flock they would not shower our children with trinkets."

"There," she declared, sitting back on her heels. "It looks beautiful."

Darcy paused to survey the scene, including his gorgeous wife in the tableau, and had to agree. The flickering glow from the perpetually burning Yule log cast a ruddy sheen over the array of colorful tissue and rag-paper wrapped packages stacked on the plush velvet drape spread nearby. It was the perfect corner with the window above kept partially uncloaked so any starlight or moonbeams could enter in. The fire added to the illumination and the holiday atmosphere was further accented by the bundles of mistletoe and holly branches strategically hanging over everything. The newest acquisition was a three-foot tall Father Christmas carved and painted by George Darcy that sat on a small shelf above. It was as if the historical Yuletide visitor was watching over the collection, his mischievous grin casting some doubt on his intentions!

They tarried in the parlor to enjoy the holiday scene, comfortable atop a layer of cushions, and snuggled under a fire-warmed blanket before the burning log. Darcy caressed Lizzy's abdomen. Approximately two or three weeks away from the anticipated birth, her belly was smaller than in previous pregnancies. Lizzy was carrying this baby completely different than she had with their two boys, joking with some irritation that she resembled a pear. Darcy thought it was wonderful, convinced that the pronounced deviations meant it *had* to be a girl! Lizzy thought that was ridiculous. Even this close to her date of confinement, the overall growth and weight gain was far less than previously.

George assured them that it was still within normal parameters and that the baby appeared quite healthy if constant activity was any indication!

Finally, as the mantel clock chimed one o'clock, they rose to return to their bedchamber. They knew they would be woken in a mere four or five hours, Alexander catapulting onto his father with all the exuberance of a youngster anxious to open his presents.

Darcy halted her at the top of the Grand Staircase, pulling her into a firm embrace where they stood just under the enormous kissing bough that was yearly redecorated with fresh greenery and polished until gleaming.

"One kiss under the Darcy bough," he whispered, lowering his mouth to brush over hers. "It shall bring us luck."

"You are a superstitious man, Mr. Darcy."

"Or simply grasping onto another opportunity to kiss my stunning wife."

Who knows how long the kiss may have continued if not for the strange popping sensation Lizzy felt from the recesses of her loins that was followed by a gush of warm fluid streaming down her thighs into a puddle on the marble floor. She gasped, jerking out of Darcy's arms, and exclaimed a shrill, "Oh my!"

Darcy was perplexed for about two seconds before processing the information and meeting his wife's embarrassed and startled eyes. He was jubilant! His eyes sparkled, the grin spreading over his face reaching from ear to ear. "A Christmas baby! Ha! Once again, my dearest, I am immeasurably thrilled that you never do anything as it is expected of you!"

And with a booming laugh he swept her into his arms.

"The boys will be disappointed that I ruined their Christmas!"

"Nonsense. They will consider their sister the best gift of all."

And he was correct on both counts. The boys were overjoyed to greet their newest sibling later that afternoon, loving her wholeheartedly and forever, even if Noella Holly Jane Darcy would prove in time to be puckish, high-spirited, and fiery as often as she was loveable, generous, and jocose.

CHRISTMAS
MORNING

THE BED CURTAINS WERE drawn tightly with only a mere slit allowing Lizzy to see the darkness of the chamber. There was nothing within her eyesight to hint toward the time of morning, but an internal clock gave the impression of a pre-dawn hour. For a few seconds she wondered what had roused her. Surely it was too early for the children to be awake, even as anxious as they were to open the presents in the parlor. No, it wasn't the patter of feet and shouts of tiny voices raised in enthusiasm. Rather, it was the muted sounds of her husband adding a log to the fire and then the metallic click of the door's bolt being thrown that woke her.

She smiled, stretching her limbs under the sheets still warmed by his body. Christmas guests and customs varied, and new traditions were added each year, but the one established on their first Christmas together had been kept. Whether later in the day due to their children sharing the bed with them or before being disturbed for the Christmas festivities, they allotted time for intimacy.

Lizzy may have wanted to sleep longer and was certain by the stealth employed as Darcy tread about the room that he did not propose to wake her quite yet, but she discovered that she was more than ready to greet their eighth Christmas as a married couple, even if the sun was hiding below the horizon.

Darcy gingerly pulled the heavy burgundy velvet drape aside and carefully slid his tall, muscular body under the thick coverings so as not to lift them off his wife's bare skin. He slithered across the cool expanse until reaching the burrow created by where he had lain nestled against her back. Fully intending to resume his customary sleeping position with Elizabeth clutched within his arms and legs, snuggling on the edges of sleep for an additional hour or two, he was surprised when she rapidly flipped over and pulled his face down for a hard kiss.

"Merry Christmas, my dearest," she breathed minutes later.

"I apologize for waking you. I did not mean to."

"I am happy you did, intended or not. I find that I want you far more than sleep."

He chuckled. "I love the increased ardor of pregnancy." His lips traveled over the sensitive skin along her neck while one hand caressed the soft abdominal swell barely palpable under his palm.

"I am not convinced it is primarily due to pregnancy. It may simply be that you are so desirable that I cannot resist you."

"If you insist that is the reason I will not argue. But I have noticed a pattern after three previous children. When you are not leaning over a chamber pot, that is."

Lizzy grimaced. Like with Noella, her morning sickness for the first trimester had been horrific. Doing anything besides vomiting was nearly impossible. Darcy smugly announced that the similarity meant they were blessed with another girl, a declaration Lizzy was willing to accept primarily because she was too unwell to argue. Now, with perfect health restored, she was making up for lost time—in every aspect.

After fulfilling tradition, they dozed for a few more hours, Lizzy rousing when the clock chimed six o'clock. She nudged Darcy's inert side, earning a weak grunt. "We should dress in our night clothes before the children arrive pounding on the door."

"Mrs. Hanford will not let them invade us until seven at the earliest," he muttered. He cupped the bulge that was more prominent when she lay on her side, wishing the baby were large enough for him to feel when moving. "Did you hear that Richard felt their baby move last week for the first time?"

"Yes. Apparently he was as ridiculous as you always are, and as ridiculous as he was with Emery."

"I honestly never thought I would be sharing these paternal moments with my cousin. And the fact that you and his wife seem to conceive at roughly the same time is a nice bonus."

"Indeed it is, for all of us. I am so happy they are here this year. I think our Noella has decided Hugh Pomeroy is her personal knight."

"He is a fine lad to put up with our volatile daughter. The soul of a saint, I believe, and he sure knows how to calm her temper. I should take lessons."

"Don't be silly. She melts around you, love."

"She has me firmly wrapped about her fingers, and she knows it," he said affectionately. "I cannot believe she is three today. And already such a little lady. Beautiful, smart, and spunky like her mother." He kissed the nape of her neck, his hands instinctively caressing.

A mere fifteen minutes later loud knocks sounded upon the door separating their bedchamber and private sitting room. Solid oak did not greatly mute the three voices demanding immediate entrance. Darcy laughed, sweetly kissing his wife before rising. He tossed her the nightgown lying on the chest and then donned the trousers and robe left just for this occasion. He unlatched the lock, Noella and Michael nearly tumbling face first onto the carpet when the door was opened.

"Papa! We knocked and knocked for ages!"

"Mama, today I three!"

The two youngest Darcys dashed to the bed, climbed the steps like little monkeys, and leapt into their mother's outstretched arms. All the while they jabbered about presents and birthdays and food and dreams. Alexander stood with slightly more composure but was grinning and bouncing excitedly. Darcy bent and swept his eldest son into his arms, the smaller arms encircling his neck as soft kisses were planted to cheeks and lips. Together they walked to the bed, joining Lizzy and Michael and Noella, who were chattering non-stop.

"Mrs. Hanford made us dress and drink our juice," the six-year-old said with disgust. "She said we had to wait until seven-thirty." Alexander's tone conveyed astonishment at such a baffling commandment, but then he brightened. "Uncle George saved us early. He came to the nursery and said it was time to wake Eros and Psyche. He brought us here. Were you and mama reading Mr. Adlington's translation of Apuleius?"

"No. Nor should you be reading that! Your uncle likes to tease and exaggerate, son. And cause trouble." He tweaked Alexander's nose, the serious boy's dismay at the very idea of doing something wrong etched upon his face. "Relax, sweetling. Mrs. Hanford was performing her duties as I ordered, but it is fine that Uncle George rescued you from the nursery. Mama and I were waiting for you three. We need special Christmas hugs and kisses from our children before we join the others."

"The new baby cannot kiss yet, can she mama?"

"Not yet, but you can give kisses and happy Christmas wishes." This they did, tenderly touching the soft swell of Lizzy's abdomen. The reality of a baby in her belly was mysterious and comprehended to varying degrees by their immature minds, but they all knew a sibling was to join them and they were eager.

"Christmas kisses need mistletoe, yes, Papa?"

"It isn't a requisite, miss, but it does add to the fun."

"Mr. Rothchilde must think so. He was kissing Miss Betsy for a long time outside the ballroom."

Noella nodded in agreement with her brother. "Samuel too, Papa. He and Marguerite were kissing yesterday."

Lizzy laughed aloud. "Now that is a shock. Not Rothchilde and Betsy..."

"No?"

Lizzy squeezed her husband's knee, chuckling. "They have been courting for months now, darling, but it does not surprise me that you are unaware! I am more surprised that Marguerite managed to waylay your valet. Poor Samuel must have been red as a beet."

Darcy grunted. "Be that as it may, what I am curious about is how you two seem to be catching so many clandestine kissers under mistletoe. Wandering the halls freely after escaping your nannies?"

"Yep!" They declared simultaneously with nary a hint of remorse. "We saw Aunt Mary kissing Uncle Joshua. Caleb kissing Miss Cassie. Aunt Giana kissing…"

"Very well," Darcy dryly interrupted the flood, "I believe we get the idea."

"And Uncle George showed us the hidden passageway behind the King Arthur tapestry!"

"Oh did he now?" Darcy growled, Lizzy bursting into laughter.

"Be calm, dearest. It only leads to the music room so no harm can be done. I have never understood what the purpose of that secret route could be."

"Mysteries of Pemberley aside, you two are hereby forbidden to evade your caretakers and wander the halls, understood?"

"Yes, Papa," they quickly agreed, heads nodding in unison.

Lizzy chuckled under her breath and Darcy briefly closed his eyes, both knowing the admonishment would be as ignored as the promise. Prim Alexander sat on his father's lap through the whole commentary with his lips pressed tightly together and brows knitted. Lizzy ruffled his curls, leaned for a kiss, and whispered for his ears only, "Occasional misbehaving is healthy, Alexander. You should give it a try now and again." But he truly looked aghast at the idea, Lizzy only laughing harder and pulling her firstborn onto her lap for a snug embrace.

"Can we go now? Please!" Michael and Noella pleaded,

bouncing on their knees, for once not irritating each other in their agreement over Christmas entertainments.

"I am hungry."

"And I have Christmas presents and birthday presents and cake!"

"It's not fair that *she* gets more presents," Michael grumbled, the truce obviously over as he glared at his sister.

"It's my birthday!" Noella smugly declared, smirking as she added, "Christmas is *my* special day, not yours."

"Christmas is everybody's special day. It's Jesus' day, not yours, silly!"

"Today is God's day first," Lizzy interrupted what promised to be full-scale war. "But we will manage to celebrate both special events. Just as Alexander's birthday falls on mine and your papa's anniversary and we always celebrate both."

"But..."

"No 'buts' young man," Darcy caressed the thick brown locks so like his. "Look at it this way, son: You have a birthday all your own. A day not shared with any other holiday or person."

"So can we open presents now?" Noella asked, ignoring Michael's cheery expression and protruding tongue.

"Your birthday will be celebrated later today, after church and Christmas."

"But I am three!" she wailed, tears instantly forming.

"Technically you will not be three until late this afternoon, Noella, because that is when you were born."

"But, Papa! That is silly. Today is my birthday and today happened at midnight!"

"You cannot argue with that logic," Lizzy murmured with a smile.

Darcy laughed. "All right, Miss Three Years Old, let your mother and me get dressed..."

"Dressed?" Michael whined. "That will take forever!"

"My goodness, such high drama. Wonder where you two inherit your theatrical tendencies from?" She glanced sidelong at her husband, who grinned and blushed. "You can go ahead to the dining room. I am sure others are there and will assist, although apparently you have supreme dominion of the entire Manor. We shall be along shortly. And don't even think it, you two," she sternly interrupted with their mouths half open for an objection, "presents are never opened until after church. You may as well accept it."

They frowned for approximately two seconds until Alexander nudged and reminded of Mrs. Langton's famous Christmas breakfast pastries. Significantly cheered by that news, fresh hugs and kisses were administered before they clamored off the high bed and exited the room with as much noise and energy as when they entered.

CHRISTMAS STORYTELLING

"'THE GRATE HAD BEEN removed from the wide overwhelming fireplace, to make way for a fire of wood, in the midst of which was an enormous log glowing and blazing, and sending forth a vast volume of light and heat: this I understood was the Yule clog, which the squire was particular in having brought in and illumined on a Christmas eve, according to an ancient custom. Herrick mentions it in one of his songs:

"'Come, bring with a noise,
My merrie, merrie boyes,
The Christmas log to the firing;
While my good dame, she
Bids ye all be free,
And drink to your hearts desiring.'"

"Why does he call it a 'clog,' Papa?"

Darcy paused in his reading and smiled at his eldest daughter. "It is an older term for a large, heavy piece of wood, Noella.

Not so commonly used today, but one of the reasons I adore Mr. Irving and encourage you to read him is his command of our language."

Michael snorted, muttering disdainfully, "Everyone knows what a clog is."

Noella flared, piercing her brother with a withering glare. "I bet you did not know it! You are more stupid than me!"

"Am not!"

"Are too!"

"Children," Darcy interrupted the familiar exchange with his patented tone: calm and quiet but with a firm edge that clearly conveyed the penalty for disobeying. "You will refrain and hold your tongues. It is Christmas Eve and we will have a lovely family time. Understood?"

"Yes, Papa," they intoned meekly, ducking their heads. Darcy, however, knew his children well and did not miss the smirk on Michael's lips or the elbow nudge Noella gave her brother.

Neither did Alexander. "Bets on how long peace reigns?"

He spoke in French, his father responding in the same language, "Five minutes? Ten?"

"Ten what?" Michael asked.

"If you attended to your French lessons then you would know more than merely counting to ten," Darcy answered in English, reaching to pinch his second son's nose.

"I can count to more than that," he countered churlishly. And then he brightened, turning his crooked grin upon Alexander. "You win in languages, brother, but I can still wrestle you to the ground in seconds."

Alexander shrugged, unconcerned. Nor did he deny it since it was the truth. Alexander was nearly two years older than his brother and a foot taller, having inherited his father's stature, but Michael was brawny and incredibly strong. Lizzy lovingly referred to him as her bear. Noella said he resembled a block, always following the slur with a comment comparing his intellect to a stone. Practically from the moment Noella could talk the two had grated on each other's nerves. Yet underneath the incessant pestering and insults, the two Darcy children closest in age were deeply devoted to each other. Of course, they would deny the affection vociferously! Nevertheless, denials aside, the fact that they clearly enjoyed the bantering and baiting and were forever together revealed the truth.

Such as now.

Michael and Noella sat cross-legged next to each other, their shoulders and knees touching. The family congregated in their parents' bedchamber, the enormous bed large enough to accommodate all seven of them with ample space to sprawl out. Yet Michael and Noella chose a position next to their father's long legs, bodies brushing together as they proceeded to irritate each other.

The family held a tradition started upon Michael's first Christmas Eve. Alexander joined them in their bedchamber while Lizzy nursed Michael, Darcy cuddling his two-year-old son against his chest and opening a book to read a story. Naturally, given the date, he chose the Bible and a collection of Robert Herrick's Christmas poems. Both boys fell asleep to the comforting sound of Lizzy humming carols and Darcy reading poetry, neither parent having the heart to return them to the nursery. The special interlude of holiday celebrating was unplanned but thoroughly enjoyed, the perfect memory of Christmas Eve play and storytelling thus becoming a tradition.

The addition of more children only enhanced the delight, so the once-a-year event continued. Following a lavish dinner and entertainment with carols in the parlor with whatever guests were dwelling at Pemberley, they dressed in sleeping attire and reclined upon their parents' enormous bed in the fire-heated chamber while Darcy read a collection of Christmas themed stories. Songs were sung, prayers were recited, and upon occasion, everyone slept in the room rather than returning to their own chambers.

The story choices varied year to year, but always concluded with a Bible reading of Christ's birth. This year Darcy chose the writings of Washington Irving from *The Sketchbook of Geoffrey Crayon*. After disappointing Michael and Noella by refusing to read the tale of Ichabod Crane and the Headless Horseman of Sleepy Hollow, he began with "Christmas Eve" and had not gotten far when the first of what would probably be several sparring interruptions had occurred to discuss the origins of clog.

Lizzy laughed from her comfortable location leaning against Darcy, propped on a large goose-down pillow and holding the youngest Darcy asleep on her chest. She met her husband's eyes and smiled, and then she winked at her eldest son. It certainly was annoying at times, but the antics of Michael and Noella were amusing. Alexander smiled, bending his head to nuzzle a kiss to the head of the fourth Darcy offspring who sat curled on his lap.

"Papa, finish the story, please." The four-year-old's tiny voice, sweet and velvet, brought instant tranquility to the room. Everyone smiled, even Noella and Michael, tender eyes alighting upon the fragile child encased in her protective brother's embrace.

"As you wish, angel." Darcy resumed his reading, the tendrils of peace touching all of them as if a spell had been cast.

Such was the natural power of Audrey Faine Bethann Darcy.

She was born under tremendous stress, with Lizzy experiencing the most traumatizing birth of her five children. Dr. Darcy's superior skills were sorely tested to deliver a living baby. The combination of malpositioning that impeded her easy descent and a severe gush of blood that signified a premature detachment of the placenta led to the birth of a limp, weakly gasping infant requiring swift intervention. Darcy and Lizzy did not doubt for a second that if George had not been present their second daughter would have died either before her arrival or in those critical moments after. Perhaps Lizzy as well, as she bled profusely, was delirious from the pain, and could not help with the final stages of the delivery in any way. The physician's professional deportment and staggering mastery in any crisis saved both of them, but it would be some months before they knew their daughter had not suffered brain damage along with the left-sided partial paralysis that was a permanent fixture.

Her name was chosen carefully to reflect their hope for her future and thankfulness in her survival. It also presaged her unique character. Audrey was a favorite name of Lizzy's since reading Shakespeare's *As You Like It*. Darcy loved the tale of the seventh-century Anglo-Saxon Cambridgeshire Saint Æthelthryth, or St. Audrey in the common tongue, since reading of her life in a Latin translation of the *Anglo-Saxon Chronicle* while at University. But primarily they agreed that the name's meaning of "noble strength" was apropos. Faine was an Old English name meaning gladness, joy, and good nature. Bethann, obviously, was a tribute to Elizabeth and Darcy's mother Anne.

In time it became clear that she not only was mentally sound but incredibly bright. Her intelligence promised to rival Alexander's. Audrey was already able to speak French and Latin quite well, could read above her level, and possessed a phenomenal memory. The muscle damage that disfigured her face by causing a droop to her left eyelid and mouth, and weakened her arm and leg so that grasping was difficult and walking a chore, was unable to mar her dainty beauty and saintly disposition. She truly was an angel—a miracle child with features delicate and fair. Her body was waiflike, hair like fine silver, eyes pellucid blue, and skin of snow. Her temperament matched her appearance. She was gentle, lovable, and soothing. Serenity surrounded her, the aura so strong that it touched all who encountered her.

She and Noella were polar opposites in every way. Noella was darkly beautiful with olive-tinged skin, lustrous ebony curls, eyes the color of fire-glazed raw umber, and bold features. She greatly resembled her mother, her temperament taking Lizzy's stubbornness and wit to extremes. Michael and Noella combined were a definite challenge to parenting skills! Darcy was convinced that God in His wisdom and grace had granted them the steady

Alexander and halcyonic Audrey to buffer the severity of the middle Darcys.

The baby, just four months of age, was probably their most "normal" child. The personality of Nathaniel Marcus Charles Darcy was still emerging, but he did not seem to live on one or the other edge of the spectrum as his siblings always had.

Darcy managed to read through all four of Irving's Christmas related essays, but with several interruptions for questions, two more arguments between Michael and Noella, and a half dozen bursts of laughter.

"I want to learn to play the guitar," Michael declared when the instrument was mentioned, jumping up to prance about the bed while pretending to strum. He sang the stanza of Herrick's "Night Piece to Julia" as just read by his father, dramatically and comically serenading Noella and Audrey as if a lover. Audrey gave her brother a soft kiss of thanks but Noella punched him in the knee, stating firmly that she would sooner die a spinster than allow anyone like him to woo her. Laughter rang out, minor wrestling ensued, and order was difficult to restore.

Audrey interrupted only once, her euphonious voice commenting that having peacocks running free as they were in the story would be nice. "Pemberley is stately and magnificent. Peacocks are pretty, don't you think, Papa?"

"I think that is a marvelous idea!" Lizzy agreed. "How does one obtain peacocks, William?"

"I know several gentlemen who have them on their estates. Purchasing a few would be an easy task. I am sure Mr. Holmes or

Mr. Burr would know how to care for them. If it is peafowl you wish for, princess, we can find them."

Irving's mention of minstrels playing during the Christmas dinner was appealing to Alexander. "A harper or violinist playing softly in the background is a nice touch. How about hiring one for next year, Father? He could play hymns and carols."

Darcy and Lizzy nodded, sharing an approving glance, but Michael enthusiastically burst in. "Oh! I can play my guitar! I will have all year to learn, yes, Papa? Or, better yet, we can hire the fiddler who plays at the Village pub! He plays a hardingfele and is amazing…"

"When have you had occasion to hear the fiddler at the pub? And know what type of viol he plays?"

Michael paled, eyes wide as he stared into his father's stern face.

"This will be good," Noella murmured, her eyes glittering.

"Be silent, miss. Michael?"

"Only once, Papa, I swear it. Mr. Drake is Howard and Milton's cousin and they kept on about him, dared me, they did, to come listen! I only peeked through the window, I promise! Then Mr. Drake came out and talked about his instrument. It was carved and decorated with roses, and it was rounder than your violin, and—"

"While I am impressed by your sudden wealth of knowledge regarding stringed instruments, I believe you have failed to mention that you would have needed to leave the house after dark to hear Mr. Drake. Since this is incredibly difficult to accomplish given how well we secure the Manor and the abundance of servants guarding, I can only surmise you have a clever way to sneak out? Care to illuminate us, Michael Darcy?"

"William," Lizzy lightly laid her hand on his arm, "perhaps we should discuss this on the morrow?"

Darcy frowned but nodded. He fixed his delinquent son with a harsh glare. "We *will* be discussing this, young man, and do not forget it."

"Yes, sir," Michael mumbled, knowing very well that the "discussion" would undoubtedly involve a lashing. Darcy administered corporal punishment rarely, but when he did it was memorable!

The reading resumed with Michael quite downcast. His self-pity increased under Noella's snickers that he could not retaliate against without incurring fresh displeasure from his father. Of course Noella knew this, the subtle taunting continuing until Darcy reached the paragraph where the Christmas delicacy of peacock pie was detailed. This information made the tender-hearted Audrey—who was still dreaming of colorfully plumed peacocks strutting across Pemberley's vast lawns—burst into tears. Everything stopped at this point with everyone offering comfort to the stricken girl. Only Darcy's sworn oath never to harm one of their peacocks or ever serve a peafowl pie, along with dozens of kisses, finally calmed her and the reading recommenced. The mood-vacillating, Michael forgot his impending punishment in the midst of assuaging his beloved baby sister and gaiety ruled for the remainder of the story.

An interlude of play and treats broke up the Christmas story-telling. Warm spiced cider and gingerbread cookies were served. Nathaniel woke at the sound of rambunctious laughter and Lizzy permitted him to suck on each sibling's finger dipped in cider. Michael and Noella jumped and tumbled on the firmly stuffed mattress. Nathaniel and Audrey were passed about for hugs and cuddles. Alexander retrieved his flute and entertained, even loosening up enough to pipe a couple of rollicking, non-Christmas tunes.

Eventually Darcy called them to order, reaching for the dog-eared Bible to read the original Christmas story. He opened to Matthew, removing the worn bookmark and handing it to Audrey for safekeeping.

"Mama's bookmark has frayed on this edge, Papa." Audrey lifted it for his inspection, her eyes sad and his disturbed.

"I suppose I need to store it in one of my memento boxes for safekeeping, but I hate to part with it." He looked at his wife with a soft smile. "It is precious to me. The first gift I ever received from your mother, after her heart and love, that is."

"Oh! Tell us the story again, Papa! Tell us about your birthday surprise with Uncle Charles and Aunt Jane and how Mama made you a cake with a candle! And how mama embroidered your names in the hearts! And how…"

"You've already told the entire story, Noella!" Lizzy said with a laugh. "We have told it and others dozens of times. Now it is time to read about Christ's birth."

Darcy agreed, turning his gaze from the loose stitches on his bookmark to the page of Scripture. However, before finding the beginning verses he was stayed by Alexander.

"Mother, Father, this year the Darcy children wish to bring you the Christmas story. We have prepared a theatrical entertainment for your enjoyment."

"And we want you to see it first before we perform for Uncle George, Grandmama and Grandpapa, and the family tomorrow," Noella threw out, already dashing toward the sitting room where they had secreted their props and costumes unbeknownst to their parents.

It was a surprisingly bravura enactment with dramatically delivered lines, rehearsed acting, authentically designed costumes, and cleverly used props. Alexander narrated and acted as Joseph. Audrey was the perfectly cast virginal Mary, a tiny pillow at her abdomen the unborn baby Jesus, and she sat astride the rocking horse that served as a donkey. The "donkey" was pulled about the room, arriving at the inn where Noella informed them there was no room except for in the barn. The birth went amazingly easily, glossed over considerably with the Christ child played by a large Nathaniel who was not particularly thrilled to lie on his back in the doll cradle. Stuffed animals—many of the jungle rather than barn variety—functioned as witnesses. Noella and Michael stole the concluding act as the exalting angel and worshipping shepherd, high drama an inherited forte.

Applause was loud and enthusiastic. Parental kisses and hugs were lavish. And the longcase clock in the corner struck the twelve o'clock hour before the final skirmish over Michael and Noella sharing covers—sleeping side-by-side of course—was quelled by a stern rebuke from Darcy with peace and slumber finally reigning.

CHRISTMAS
MERRYMAKING

LIZZY STARED OUT AT the spitting of snow falling from a sky dotted with pale-gray clouds. She frowned and bit her lip while absently fastening the lacings of her thick wool coat. Years living in Derbyshire had given her a sense of typical weather conditions so she was fairly certain the weak clouds would disperse once they squeezed the last drops of moisture into the frigid air, leaving behind a cold but clear day. Traveling to Matlock over the frozen roads should be easy and the sturdy coach packed with seven bodies would remain warm. Yet they had decided it best to leave their youngest child, Thomas, not quite two and recuperating from a minor respiratory affliction, in the care of Mrs. Hanford for the day rather than expose him to the winter chill. It was a wise decision, Lizzy knew, but it was always difficult to leave her children behind.

"We will only be gone for the day," a deep voice interrupted, the speaker divining her thoughts. She nodded, turning toward her husband where he sat on the nearby bench assisting Audrey with her gloves and fur-lined bonnet. He wasn't even looking at her or the weather outside, focusing instead on his youngest daughter's accessories for proper placement to protect against the bitter cold, continuing without a pause, "And I assure you the storm, if it can be called that, will pass within an hour. We will be home before dark and Thomas will not even miss us."

"Are you sure the snow will not worsen?" Darcy glanced up then, lifting one brow and delivering a you-must-be-joking look. "Well, someday you may be wrong in predicting the weather, Mr. Darcy! What if today is that day and we are stranded at Rivallain?"

"I am *not* wrong. We will *not* be stranded at Rivallain. We *will* be home to celebrate our family Christmas Eve with *all* the children. And Thomas will remain largely oblivious to the fact that we were away."

"Will we bring his presents back home, Papa?" Audrey's question halted Lizzy's sharp retort, Darcy chuckling as he again focused on his daughter.

"Of course we will, princess. You can help him open them tomorrow. He is too young yet to accomplish the task alone, nor is he old enough to be fully aware of the festivities surrounding him."

"He loves to look at all the decorations. He laughs and tries to touch everything. Yesterday he escaped Nanny Lisa and climbed onto the table while we were mixing the dough and fell face first into the bowl! He was covered with flour and molasses. Oh, you should have seen him, Papa. It was very funny."

"I heard about it. Another reason to keep him here rather than running amok at Rivallain. Here he will be safe, warm, and happily playing with his toys between naps and meals."

She nodded her agreement, but then stayed his hand with a gentle clasp of her delicate, gloved fingers. "But you are wrong, Papa. He will miss us."

Darcy flashed a warning glance to Lizzy while answering. "Perhaps a little, but it is the wisest decision." Lizzy snapped her lips shut, knowing he was correct but remaining disturbed at the idea. "His grandpapa and Uncle George will dote upon him while we are away. And then we shall make it up to him with an abundance of kisses and hugs when we return. How is that?"

"Ow! It is too tight! You pinched me on purpose!"

"I did not. And you wouldn't have been pinched if you would just hold still!"

Darcy engaged his wife's eyes for a brief reaffirming exchange, Lizzy smiling and nodding before rolling her eyes and indicating he deal with the squabbling duo. With a smile of relief that his wife was appeased followed by an exasperated sigh at the bickering Noella and Michael, he rose from the bench. "Enough, you two. Michael, help Nathaniel with his coat. Here, Noella, let me button that."

"He did do it on purpose, Papa. Is my neck red?"

"Not in the least. Flawlessly beautiful, as always."

"Good," she said, lifting her chin so Darcy could finish clasping her bonnet, "I must look my absolute best."

"And why is that?"

"Hugh will be there."

"Ah, yes. Young Mr. Pomeroy. Still sporting a crush on your cousin, are you?"

"Papa," she sighed, piercing him with her patented longsuffering look, "Hugh is *not* my cousin, not really. And I do not have a crush," her tone clearly conveying her derision for that definition.

"Of course not," he smiled, brushing her cheek with a soft kiss. "How foolish of me."

"I intend to marry him."

Her announcement was firm and completely matter-of-fact, Darcy stammering slightly in a combination of amusement and surprise. "Do you now?" He finally managed, noting Lizzy's attempt to refrain from bursting into laughter. "And is Mr. Pomeroy aware of this arrangement? After all, he may not be so pleased at betrothal to an eleven-year-old."

"I will be twelve tomorrow," she informed him flatly, as if that made all the difference in the world, "and will tell him eventually."

"Perhaps I should break the good news to him," Alexander interjected dryly. "He may need the next eight years to prepare for the concept. Bolster his fortitude, practice the proposal speech, save up for the ring, and so on."

But instead of erupting into a tirade, as they all expected—Michael dying to chime in on his opinion of poor Hugh's bleak future—Noella merely shrugged and calmly pulled on her gloves.

"Well, since I do not foresee any of my children becoming engaged in the next day or so, I say we put the topic aside and get into the carriage so we can arrive at Rivallain for breakfast as planned. Mrs. Darcy?"

Darcy's prediction proved correct. The feeble snowfall ceased before they reached Beeley, and clear, crisp skies remained throughout the day. Their celebration with the Fitzwilliam clan and local friends at Lord and Lady Matlock's grand estate was lively, entertaining, and wholly wonderful. The wrapped gifts, hampers of Mrs. Langton's favored holiday fare, and baskets of Christmas cookies and pies baked by the Darcy women were exchanged for fresh piles of gifts, restocked hampers of feast remnants, and different cookies and pies.

To the fascination of the adults, Noella utterly ignored Hugh all day!

"Strange way to capture your chosen man, don't you think?" Darcy asked the group in general.

"She is a female and who can understand the subtle intrigues of a woman?" Richard responded, winking at his wife and Elizabeth, who laughed.

"Noella's declaration apparently isn't trammeling Mr. Pomeroy's roving eye," Lady Matlock pointed out with a chuckle, indicating the object of Noella's infatuation. The handsome nineteen-year-old Hugh was one of several unattached gentlemen brazenly flirting with a cluster of young ladies sitting near a far window. Alexander had shared his sister's intentions with his friend, Hugh laughing so hard that tears sprang to his eyes. Whether it was his flippancy at the idea or some female machination on her part was unclear, but Noella pointedly pretended he was invisible, even to the degree that she endured Michael's taunts in stoic silence. It made for a humorous afternoon amid the typical holiday festivities.

Just as the sun touched the horizon, the seven Darcys said their adieus and crammed into the spacious coach that was rapidly becoming too cramped even with the smaller children sitting on laps. They embarked on the hour-long ride back to Pemberley with hearts and stomachs filled to bursting. It was Alexander's idea to play a memories-and-forfeit game reciting "The Twelve Days of Christmas" and using evenly distributed candy canes as the "payment" for blundering in remembering the proper sequence. The first round made it as far as "seven swans a-swimming" when Michael, who possessed a memory as reliable as a rusted bucket holding water (according to Nathaniel), stumbled over what came after "four colly birds."

"Three French hens! How could you forget that?" Noella dramatically wailed, collecting her hard sugar cane and taking a bite just as the carriage rocked ominously, causing them to collectively gasp and grab onto the nearest body.

The occupants had no time to process the aberrant break from the normal rhythm of bobs and sways when the loud crack of splitting wood was immediately followed by the strident sound of twisting, scraping metal. Mr. Anders, the coachman, shouted a warning to Mr. Darcy and barked an order to the horses just as the carriage abruptly lurched to the right. An audible crunch shuddered through the walls and ceiling of the carriage, mixing with the loud snap of a leather strap on the roof and the crash of a dozen packages as they tumbled onto the solid ground. The carriage came to a sudden stop, careening dangerously off-balance as it continued to shake from the stress.

"Be still!" Darcy bellowed, his voice rising above the shrieks. Relative silence fell as a blanket, harsh breathing and muted whines low enough to hear the coachman and footman warily leap to the ground. Darcy scanned the white faces of his family before cautiously shifting his weight and unlatching the window shade. "Mr. Anders? Watson?"

"Here, sir. Hold fast and don't move. The rear felloe shattered and the wheel is bent beyond repair. We need to brace before I trust ye to move. Those rocks there, Watson. The bloody thing is sittin' on the axle. Can't fathom how it happened…" And his voice lowered into mutters of disgust at what the proud coachman would perceive as a failing on his part.

Eventually, he was sufficiently satisfied with the carriage's stability for the family to disembark. It was a procedure, with Darcy personally lifting his wife and children to the ground and sending them well away from the precariously perched carriage. Darcy took one look at the damage and knew they were stranded.

Lizzy and the children gathered the scattered packages, amazed that most appeared to be intact. Darcy surveyed the surrounds, immediately recognizing where they were. "Mr. Anders, unhitch the horses and ride to Pemberley. Bring back the other coach. Watson, I request you stay here with the carriage and horses on the off chance thieves are about on Christmas Eve. Elizabeth, we cannot stay out here in the dark and cold. It will take near two hours for Mr. Anders to return from Pemberley." He pulled her gently against his side, brushing a light kiss over her temple and whispering softly, "I know you are distressed, love, and I am sorry for the delay. But we will be home with Thomas before he falls asleep for the night."

She smiled through the tears that threatened to spill, bravely shoving the emotion aside. "'Accidents happen. That is why they are called accidents,' as I always say to the children. He is safe and warm, but we are not. Do you have a plan?"

"We seek shelter until Mr. Anders returns. A bit of a walk will do us good."

"There isn't much here, William." She nodded toward a cluster of faintly lit buildings off to the east a good quarter-mile. "Is that a village?"

"Of a sort," he answered. "This is Haversmith's land and that is Hogslow."

"Hog's Low? You're joking? That hardly sounds reassuring."

Alexander laughed. "It isn't as it sounds, Mother. Mr. Spane works this parcel, does he not, Father?" Darcy nodded, the prideful expression at his fifteen-year-old heir knowing the residents this far south of their lands evident even in the gloom. "That is his cottage there. The village isn't much and there isn't a pub, but it is clean and I am sure we can find warmth and shelter."

"That building is well lit. See, Papa?" Audrey pointed to a large barn-shaped building set apart.

"Indeed. Perhaps they are having a Christmas celebration. Good eye, princess." He bent to pick her up, holding securely to his chest. "I have Audrey. Nathaniel, Alexander can carry you."

"No, Papa! I can walk!"

Lizzy chuckled. "Of course you can. But mama insists you hold Noella's hand. No letting go. Boys, grab those baskets. If we are going to barge in on a party the least we can do is bring a gift."

And thus the small company of marooned travelers walked into the shadowy farmland, thankful for the moonlight when it appeared in the cloudless sky. It was difficult to discern in the growing twilight, but as they neared the structure indicated by Audrey, it was obviously not a barn but a large assembly hall. It was also obviously the site of a gathering of merrymakers! The festive scene unfolded before their dazzled eyes, far removed from the more sedate and spiritual celebrations offered to the Pemberley tenants on a yearly basis.

Enormous three-foot logs split down the middle and criss-crossed in a stack burned within a stone ringed pit, the bonfire blazing in a clearing before the wide-open doors. The snap of fiery pitch, reek of rising smoke, and heat of hungry flames was evident from yards away, yet did not deter the bustling bodies moving in a flood of enthusiasm between the dirt expanse and inviting building. The flickering illumination of candles and fireplaces glowing from within promised additional warmth from the steadily chilling air.

Children dashed amongst the adults, laughing and chasing one another while blowing whistles, ringing bells, and banging drums. Folks of all ages circled the flames, dancing and singing in time with the rollicking music filling the air. The sound of lutes, guitars, fiddles, and assorted pipes brought an instant grin to Michael's face, but they all unconsciously responded to the lively rhythm as they drew closer.

The scene of merrymaking outside the assembly hall was a preview to the play visible inside. From holly-draped wall to mistletoe-adorned corner, the Darcys absorbed wonders.

Six musicians were upon a wooden dais, some sitting and some standing, feet stomping and heads bobbing to the beat they created. The line of dancing couples only vaguely remained

straight as frequent errors in the steps or exaggerated twirls led
to unrestrained laughter. Other couples did not even bother with
the line, dancing together in whatever free space was available.
One old gentleman in well-worn breeches and shirtsleeves
danced a jig all by himself, the circle of cheering observers clapping out the tempo.

Clusters gathered along the walls playing an assortment of
games. A group of eight played blind-man's bluff to the right with
an animated charades tournament a few feet away. At a line of
tables and chairs to the left sat people playing loo, whist, and
gleek. Other coveys segregated into ages were talking, laughing,
and flirting, especially those near the mistletoe.

It was a sea of humanity joyously commemorating the season.

One body separated from the overwhelming whole, noticing
the new arrivals just as Michael spied an entertainment more
intriguing than anything he had ever seen.

"Mr. Darcy! What a surprise! What brings you to my lands?"

"Mr. Haversmith," Darcy greeted the rotund, flushed, and
sweating man before him with a slight incline of his head. "I
apologize for barging in uninvited. Our carriage broke an axle
and we sought shelter until a replacement vehicle can arrive
from Pemberley."

Haversmith was already waving away Darcy's explanation
with a hearty welcome and shouted orders to bring mugs of ale
and spiced cider to their honored guests. Elizabeth was greeted
with profuse flattery and hand kissing—Darcy and Alexander
hiding identical frowns of irritation—as they were herded toward
a raised platform with a trio of white-linen covered tables. The

Haversmith family, mostly male and liberally partaking of the wassail, tipsily received the newcomers, shuffling chairs and place settings amid raucous laughter and Christmas best wishes.

The baskets containing pies and Rivallain feast remains were taken amid generous thanks, but it was instantly apparent that food was not lacking. Long tables groaned under the weight of roasted turkey and pheasant, haunches of beef and mutton, mince pies, plum-puddings, wooden bowls of wassail, casks of malt-brewed ale, loaves of grain breads, rounds of cheeses, freshly roasted chestnuts and apples, cakes decorated with fruits and berries, and dozens of platters heaped with steaming vegetables.

Space for seven Darcys was readily made and platters of steaming food plopped down by smiling servants before the introductions were complete. The merriment continued unabated and such was the tumult that no one noticed the missing Michael.

Michael Darcy, thirteen, mischievous, and curious, had slipped away to investigate the activity taking place on the far side of the room in a darkened corner.

Resting on a crude wooden table was a shallow, wide-mouthed bowl filled to the brim with brandy, almonds, and large raisins. The brandy was ignited, the eerie blue flames flickering and dancing over the surface of the amber liquid as the raisins glistened and swelled and the almonds sizzled. Brave lads approached the fiery bowl while the girls observed with tense excitement. Their faces illuminated dramatically as they rapidly reached into the bowl and snatched a burning raisin. Quickness was the key. One must grab the fruit and pop it into the mouth to instantly extinguish the flame. Fingers had to be licked clean as well or the brandy would continue to burn. But for a split second the strange blue fire engulfed the fingertips, highlighting eyes that were wide and sparkling devilishly, the boys' faces demonic in the play of shadow and flame.

The awed onlookers cheered and clapped. After the first daring trio snatched their plump, hot raisins without major mishap, several others stepped forward. Their eyes glittered and waves of bluish light swept over their cheekbones as they searched for a gap in the flames. Someone in the growing crowd of spectators began a song that was rapidly taken up by all:

Here he comes with flaming bowl,
Don't he mean to take his toll,
Snip! Snap! Dragon!
Take care you don't take too much,
Be not greedy in your clutch,
Snip! Snap! Dragon!
With his blue and lapping tongue
Many of you will be stung,
Snip! Snap! Dragon!
For he snaps at all that comes
Snatching at his feast of plums,
Snip! Snap! Dragon!

Michael did not hesitate for a second, stepping boldly up to the fiery bowl and unerringly plucking an almond from the middle. He watched the capering flames lick over his fingers for a span of heartbeats before extinguishing behind his lips, chewing the crispy nut with delight. Two girls inched toward the bowl and Michael wasn't the least bit surprised to note that one was Noella. She glanced to her brother, her grin and dark eyes fey in the lambent light, and proceeded to shoot both hands into the flames, grabbing not one but two raisins from the bowl! She made sure he saw her catch, only then popping them into her mouth. The barest tightening at the corners of her eyes was the only indication that the hot fruit scorched her palate.

Michael threw back his head and laughed. Contending with his sister was second nature, and he would gladly suffer stinging burns to prove he was braver and tougher than she, but secretly he knew that the main reason he so enjoyed taunting Noella was because of her fearlessness.

The game was on! Snapdragon competition raged for a good while. Fresh batches of fruit and nuts were added as more people, young and old, entered into the contest. Alexander was content to retrieve an almond once, just enough to prevent ceaseless jibs of "coward" from his younger siblings, before moving on to more sedate entertainments. Lizzy flatly refused to allow Nathaniel to play, earning his deep displeasure for the remainder of the evening.

At an appointed hour, all activity and music stopped and everyone in the hall was called to order by Mr. Haversmith. His deep bass reached each ear, his speech of welcome and praise to God for Christ's birth delivered in practiced oratorical tones until the end, whereupon he turned to Darcy with a devilish twinkle in his eye. "And now if those Cambridge alumni among us will pardon the boasting, we here on Haversmith lands yearly uphold a tradition this Oxford man holds dear to his heart."

He paused, inclining his head humbly in Darcy's direction. Darcy laughed out loud and lifted his tankard of ale as a salute. "Carry on, Mr. Haversmith. We Cambridge men can appreciate traditions, even those with dubious origins."

"Thank you, Mr. Darcy. However, all who walk the hallowed halls of Queen's College in Oxford know the legend to be true." And abruptly his voice dipped into a dramatic timbre with a perfected storyteller fluency that would rival Dr. George Darcy at his best. "It is a well-known fact that in 1341, an Oxford student walked through the forest of Shotover on his way to Christmas mass, innocently reading Aristotle as he strolled, until"—his voice rose on the last word, a smattering of gasps heard in the spellbound crowd—"suddenly he was viciously attacked by a wild boar! The slathering beast bore down upon the hapless youth, all snarling maw and sharp tusks designed to maim and kill. The unarmed man was doomed. Then, inspiration struck! With outstanding presence of mind he slammed the huge, metal bound tome shut and rammed philosophy into the open mouth of the advancing animal. He held on tight, pushing with all his might, bravely ignoring the wrenching strain to his arms, until the book was securely lodged. Then he leapt away as the raving monster thrashed about, tearing apart bushes, gouging the turf, and knocking over trees as he choked to his death. It was a fair kill. The courageous cadet shared his bounty in a Yuletide feast with the boar's head dressed and displayed in honor. It is this event commemorated yearly to this day at my alma mater."

And he bowed, hand lying against his heart. Applause burst forth, Darcy shouting "Bravo!" as loudly as the rest.

"In honor of that resourceful Oxford student and the subsequent tradition, or, if you wish, in remembrance of our Anglo-Saxon ancestry with their Norse rituals in sacrificing a boar to Freyr for blessings in the coming year, or perhaps Saint Stephen whose feast day centers on the mightiest of men slaying the savage boar, this year I give you"—he swept his hand toward the front entrance and lifted his voice to a booming roar—"the head of the boar felled by my son!"

A blast of trumpets heralded the procession of four servants carrying an enormous, ornately designed silver platter upon which rested a massive rosemary and bay garnished boar's head with a gleaming red apple stuck in its mouth. Mr. Haversmith's eldest son stood, his expression proud as he gazed upon the soused head, initiating the boar's head carol in a clearly heard chant:

> The boar's head in hand bear I
> Bedecked with bay and rosemary
> I pray you, my masters, be merry
> *Quot estis in convivio.*
>
> I bring the boar's head,
> giving praises to the Lord
>
> The boar's head, as I understand,
> Is the rarest dish in all this land,
> Which thus bedecked with a gay garland
> Let us *servire cantico*

Our steward hath provided this
In honor of the King of bliss
Which, on this day to be served is
In Reginensi atrio

On the heels of the boar-toting servants came a roisterous troupe of mummers costumed elaborately, as everything from animals to medieval characters and from royalty to peasants. They pranced about, banging hand-held drums and clashing cymbals, and pantomiming comically until the platters were safely placed and the food served. Then, once silence reigned, they acted their allegorical play for the enraptured audience. Always in rhyming verse, sometimes serious and ofttimes humorous, they spun a unique offering of the standard theme of triumph over death and the battle between good and evil.

The Darcys spent about two-and-a-half hours celebrating with Mr. Haversmith's tenant farmers and staff before Watson arrived to inform his master that Mr. Anders had returned with the other carriage, after thoroughly inspecting all undergear for potential problems. Lizzy continued to fret over Thomas being asleep before they arrived home, and Darcy fretted over her unhappiness, but they both pushed the worst of their emotions aside. The entertainments were too varied and delightful not to enjoy and the food too delicious not to partake of.

They arrived home to discover Thomas happily playing with Alexander's castle in the playroom. The collection of soldiers now numbered in the hundreds and included Prussian troops, Napoleon's *Armée du Nord*, a handful of Spartan warriors, Royal

Scots infantryman, medieval armored knights complete with lance and horse, the odd Celt and Viking and Mongol, and a partial regiment of Crusaders to augment the dozen different English regimentals. Alexander had no problem sharing the castle with his siblings and even managed to bite his tongue when the pretend wars did not follow the truth of history! Grandfather Bennet and George sat in the midst of fallen soldiers as Thomas proceeded to kill every last one of them with his lone Spartan.

In fact, King Leonidas had to complete the job ere Thomas would allow his parents to carry him into their bedchamber and lavish him with kisses and hugs, whereupon he promptly fell asleep in his mother's arms. Whatever entertainments Darcy may have planned for that particular Christmas Eve were left undone. Even the obligatory reading of the Biblical first Christmas was rendered hastily before they collapsed in exhaustion, *after* rehashing the day's events.

CHRISTMAS GRIEF

"You are beautiful, dearest," Darcy spoke from the doorway, gazing at his wife where she stood before her mirror.

"I should wear black, but I just cannot bring myself to do so on Christmas day." Lizzy's voice trembled, her hands unsteady as they clasped the ebony earrings in place.

Darcy entered her dressing room, pausing beside her. "Your father would understand. He would not wish his daughters to be grief-stricken to the point that Christmas was not celebrated properly."

"I know." She sighed, smoothing the fabric of her dark blue gown over her slim waist. "But it feels wrong nevertheless. Black is appropriate for my current mood, but I rather hoped the blue would cheer me slightly." She smiled weakly at his reflection. "It is not working thus far."

Darcy said nothing, choosing instead to gently caress her back and bestow a tender kiss to her brow. He watched her closely, waiting for the flood of tears and heavy sobs he had been expecting for weeks now.

Lizzy's eyes moistened but her whisper was restrained, "Two weeks, Fitzwilliam. If only he had lived another two weeks, he would be here now as we planned."

"I know, love. I know."

"But, as you have rightly said, we were all here before the end. That meant so much to him. He was happy, was he not?"

"Very happy. He knew his girls were here, and all his grandchildren. He even bested Uncle at chess just days before."

Lizzy chuckled lightly. "I believe George forfeited."

"Perhaps. But they argued and taunted as ever. Mr. Bennet gave it his all, called Uncle a cheat, and gloated the requisite number of hours." He paused, both of their thoughts affectionately resting upon the departed Mr. Bennet. When he again spoke, it was softly but with a hint of reproach. "He spent several wonderful years with us, Elizabeth, and was pleased to do so. Pemberley was home. His grandchildren from you and Jane were a daily part of his life, and Kitty and Mary visited frequently. The previous two Christmases were here with the bulk of his family. He was content and, I believe, ready to go, waiting only until all of his daughters were with him to say his good-byes. We must grieve, naturally, but life does move on."

"He told us to lift our wassail to the heavens and sing a special carol just for his ears." She smiled, brushing the escaped tear from her cheek. "Ridiculous, really, since he was not particularly religious."

He withdrew his handkerchief, daubing at her face. "Whether he hears or not is irrelevant. He was telling you to celebrate. Celebrate this day and celebrate his life. I sometimes think the

Irish have the wiser attitude in holding a raucous wake to remember the departed loved one."

"My father would love that idea!" She took a deep breath, shook her head, swiped irritably at her watery eyes, and straightened her spine.

Darcy continued to observe her face, wishing she would finally succumb to her sorrow and have a long cry, but also recognizing that this moment was probably not the best time for her composure to be lost. They had a house full of family, Christmas and Noella's birthday to celebrate, and church to attend.

As he expected, Lizzy regained control and gave her appearance a last brief inspection in the mirror before turning fully toward her husband. "Very well. I cannot promise to laugh in utter joy, but my sisters and I will take advantage of our time together and toast the memory of our father. Shall we, Mr. Darcy?"

He offered his arm, Lizzy linking through the bend of his elbow, and leaned down for a thorough kiss. "Merry Christmas, Mrs. Darcy. Did I yet tell you that you are beautiful?"

Lizzy smiled, steering him toward the door.

The manor had been decorated with a lesser degree of glittering opulence than in year's past due to the shadow of mourning, but it was far from somber. Darcy and Lizzy had agreed to restrain the quantity of greenery, festive candles, and multi-hued ribbons, but not erase all indications of the holiday. The heirloom pieces were in place and of course the presents that had grown in number over the years were colorfully wrapped and glittering.

It had been a number of years now that these gatherings were relegated to the massive formal dining room in the north wing. The immediate Darcy family could comfortably fit into the smaller dining room, but Pemberley so often played host to visiting relatives and friends that the once dusty, disused larger chamber was frequently utilized throughout the year. This year the guest list only included Lizzy's mother, aunt and uncle, and four sisters with their families. However, even that added up considering how prolific the Bennet girls were! This fact also made it utterly impossible to maintain an atmosphere of mourning, children not typically able to remain downcast for long.

Nevertheless, all except for the youngest children knew their beloved grandfather was dead. Voices were hushed, laughter dimmed, and indoctrinated manners frequently ignored were flawlessly expressed on this day. The latter miracle may have been commented upon, but it remained difficult to jest amid the sadness.

Jane's tears, freshly rekindled when greeting Lizzy with an embrace in the upper hallway, pooled in the corner of her blue eyes. Mary sat at the tiny pianoforte playing a light but solemn tune. Kitty performed the motherly duties of assisting one child with cutting a slice of ham while shoveling steady spoonfuls of mashed squash into her baby's mouth, but with an occasional wipe of a handkerchief to an escaping tear. Even Lydia, still wayward and egotistical after three marriages and a dozen personal imbroglios, was sitting sedately and absently chewing a slice of jam-smeared toast.

"Maybe it was not a wise idea to place Papa's portrait in the room," Lizzy mumbled.

Darcy nodded, glancing at the ornately framed painting of Mr. Bennet commissioned shortly after he settled at Pemberley nearly four years ago.

Longbourn Manor and the surrounding lands gradually became unmanageable and too isolated for the elderly gentleman, whose vision was failing. Nevertheless, pride and stubbornness kept him tied to his familiar environment despite Mrs. Bennet's incessant complaining about boredom and loneliness with all her daughters married and busy. Her long absences to dwell with her brother and sister-in-law in Cheapside brought him a measure of peace but led to further isolation and the estate's decline.

A broken leg resulting from a minor stumble upon the stairs prompted George Darcy to drive to Hertfordshire to rescue his friend. He goaded the cranky older man into a heated shouting match while the physician reset the bone misaligned by the local hack; verbal insults and expletives were flung back and forth with anger masking the residual pain not dulled by heavy draughts of brandy. George's nagging and harassment persevered for days until finally convincing Mr. Bennet to relocate to Pemberley, which, of course, was the main purpose of the trip. Lizzy and Jane were profuse in their thanks, which George also quite enjoyed!

The years that followed were joyful ones for all the inhabitants of Pemberley. Mr. Bennet delighted in exploring the vast library that appeared to have a magically inexhaustible supply of new books. His friendship with Dr. Darcy was a sincere one that brought pleasure when the busy physician was available. And the immensity of Pemberley meant that privacy and quiet were easy to find even with the ever-increasing number of Darcy children, constant visitors, and a shrill wife, when Mrs. Bennet chose to reside at Pemberley rather than in London.

Thus the skillfully wrought portrait depicted an aged, snowy-haired man with twinkling, intelligent eyes and a faintly mischievous smile.

"Mother, I have your tea poured and sweetened as you like. Noella is filling a plate with your favorites." Alexander bent, planting a soft kiss to his mother's cheek.

"Thank you, darling." Lizzy clasped her son's offered hand, smiling into the face that was a youthful image of her husband's.

"Happy Christmas, Father. Aunt Jane, I believe Michael and Ethan are yet fighting over who should be allowed to bring your breakfast, but Charlie has your tea waiting."

"He won that battle, did he?" Charles laughed, glancing to Jane's designated table placement where their second son stood behind the chair, steaming cup of tea waiting.

"Only because Michael and Ethan were too busy arguing over boiled or scrambled eggs."

"I never eat boiled eggs."

"And of course Michael knows this, Aunt. Irritating cousin Ethan is the impetus, but I am sure he will relent before you perish from hunger."

"Let us pray so," Darcy murmured. "I would hate to be forced to publicly admonish my ornery son on Christmas Day."

"Do not worry, Darcy," Charles said. "Ethan is far too gullible. Michael is good for him."

"Perhaps, but I rather doubt Michael has Ethan's best interests at heart."

"Merry Christmas, Mama! Papa! Your plate is ready, Mama. Shall I dish yours, Papa?"

"Thank you, Noella, but I can manage. A hug would be appreciated," he said with a smile, opening his arms as Noella readily embraced him. "Happy birthday, holly berry." He kissed her head, whispering for her ears only, "I have a very special gift for you."

"Oh! What is it, Papa! Tell me, please!"

"Christmas first. One party at a time, as we always do, and then this afternoon I will reveal. No pouting, miss," he tugged on her protruding lower lip, "and the sad eyes shall not sway me." He winked at his wife, Lizzy smiling and shaking her head, well aware that Darcy was pathetically vulnerable to weepy manipulation from his daughters.

Noella knew this as well, but she laughed, tossing her head and causing her black curls to bounce prettily. "Oh, very well! I shall be patient. Does not Grandpapa's portrait cheer the room, Mama? I still feel as if he is here, and Audrey said she knows he is watching over us. Do you think that is true?"

"Only God knows for certain," Darcy answered, "but he lives on in our hearts to be sure."

He glanced to the table setting nearest Mr. Bennet's easel-propped painting where Audrey sat, her lips moving in a steady stream of quiet conversation to her adored grandfather's image, relaying the antics of his daughters, sons-in-law, and grandchildren. Nathaniel sat beside his sister with Mary's oldest girls across, all of them adding to the observations as had become a custom due to Mr. Bennet's diminished far-sight. The gift of descriptiveness with colorful language and exaggerated recounting was possessed by all of them to varying degrees, their talents perfected via theatrical performances on a regular basis and later used to entertain their grandfather. It appeared to be an ingrained habit that would be slowly relinquished.

Lizzy left to assist Thomas with his plate while Darcy crossed to the breakfast sidebar where his Uncle George stood talking with General Artois, Kitty's husband; Mr. Joshua Daniels, Mary's husband; and Mr. Gardiner. Greetings and holiday well wishes were extended as Darcy poured his coffee.

"Is the birthday girl still clueless as to her present?" Artois nodded toward Noella, who now sat between Michael and Nathaniel, inhibiting the latter from pouring a sixth spoon of sugar into his porridge, a pronouncement he was clearly not pleased about.

Darcy nodded his head. "As far as I know. I have been most adamant that she cannot have a full-grown horse until she is fifteen, so she is not expecting it. And thank you again for supplying the headgear. Cleo is quite small, that being why I chose her for Noella, and none of our bridles or halters fit her. The decision was a sudden one—"

"And displeasing to Mrs. Darcy," George added with a chuckle.

"—and I did not have time to order a new one from London," Darcy concluded, ignoring his uncle's remark. Lizzy had relented all opinions ages ago when it came to the boys riding horses with their equestrian obsessed father, but she fought the notion with Noella. However, the reality that Noella was far more enamored with and competent on a horse than Michael could not be denied, so Lizzy was gradually learning to accept defeat. Nevertheless, they had argued over gifting Cleo, and it was only the mare's smaller stature that convinced Lizzy to agree, albeit reservedly.

"My pleasure," Artois said. "It will be fun to see her face. Cleo is an excellent mount for a first horse. Thankfully the weather is pleasant enough for her to ride today."

"Pardon me, Mr. Darcy," the ever-polite solicitor to the Pemberley Estate began, Mr. Daniels forever maintaining his formality despite years as a brother-in-law, "but when is the birthday party to commence? Mrs. Daniels wanted to take the children to Mr. Bennet's graveside sometime this afternoon but we do not wish to place a damper upon the festivities."

"Not until after present opening is completed and luncheon has been served. I think Elizabeth has arranged three o'clock with the kitchen staff for Noella's portion of the day. At teatime, more or less, with birthday cake and sandwiches. Elizabeth already discussed visiting the cemetery before the party. Grief is a part of this Christmas, as it is often a part of life. The two frequently coexist—a reality the children need to learn."

"Perhaps the stark combination will finally be the catalyst to Elizabeth's proper grieving," George said softly.

Darcy nodded. "I pray so. She needs to release her grief. I worry for her."

"She will, William. Soon. Elizabeth takes her duties as Mistress and hostess too seriously. Her responsibilities have given her a structure to hold on to, but that task is almost done, with Christmas here and the family returning to their dwelling places in the next week or so." George squeezed his nephew's shoulder. "Just be there, as you always are, when the dam breaks. I do not envy you!"

Darcy said nothing. Observing tears from any of the women he loved was never easy, but when it came to his wife he preferred her grief manifest with him there to comfort.

George's chuckle brought him out of his reverie. "I suppose there is no point taking bets on what Michael and Charlie are harassing Alexander about?"

The men's eyes returned to the table. Alexander sat in perfect repose, calmly dining, and, if not for the slight color to his cheeks, presumably oblivious to the smirks and gibes directed his way. Lizzy, sitting several chairs away, was clearly trying not to laugh and pretending not to hear what the younger boys were saying as she conversed with her mother and Kitty.

"It might help if he did not carry Miss Lathrop's card in his jacket pocket and take it out every few minutes," Mr. Gardiner said.

"I honestly do not think he cares," Darcy said with a faint laugh. He looked at his brothers-in-law, explaining, "You should have seen his face when the Royal letter carrier delivered it yesterday. It was like he was witnessing the most brilliant, heart-piercing sunrise of all time. He actually smelled the envelope—it was perfumed—and his eyes lost focus for a solid ten minutes! Even I could not resist joining the taunts. I am still not sure when that relationship shifted from friendship to love but they seem certain. Time is needed to be sure for the future, however."

"He reminds me of James with Anne," George interjected, his old eyes misty in remembrance of his brother. "They knew almost instantly and never questioned. Merely bided their time until your mother was old enough. Of course, we tortured him as mercilessly as they are Alexander." He grinned, years dropping from his countenance as the devilry of youth took over. "All part of the fun!"

"How are Mr. and Mrs. Lathrop accepting the arrangement? The two are quite young."

"Indeed, Mr. Daniels, you are correct. At this juncture we are maintaining our peace. None of us have any misgivings to the match. In fact, it is delightful to think of our children married. However, they are far too young."

"In years Alexander is young, yet he has ever been mature for his age. A serious and tenacious lad as I have never seen. I was not at all surprised when Lizzy wrote us that he insisted on enrolling at Cambridge at sixteen and after only two years at Harrow. I surmise this is a young man with a goal in mind, and that may not just be to co-manage Pemberley with his father."

Darcy frowned at Mr. Gardiner's comments. "Alexander's studies at University keep him too occupied to dwell upon affairs of the heart."

"So you hope." George winked, his grin downright salacious. "I tend to agree with Mr. Gardiner as to his diligent application. The sooner he pleases his parents and himself with all that book learning, the sooner he can please other appetites."

"Precisely why Lathrop is keeping Fiona at home. Alexander may be starry-eyed, but his sense of propriety is more rigid than mine. She, on the other hand, is fiery like her mother." Darcy shook his head. "God knows I adore her, but we all feel it best to limit contact to censored letters for now, as distressful as that was for Lathrop to allow for his un-betrothed daughter. Elizabeth reports from Mrs. Lathrop that the pleading was fervent and highly dramatic. Poor Stephen was doomed to acquiesce."

"Seems we have our fair share of headstrong women in this family, with the probable exception of your three daughters, Mr. Daniels." The solicitor blushed, but appreciatively inclined his head at the General Artois, who then turned to Darcy, continuing with a smile. "I overheard Noella exuberantly sharing with her cousins a recent encounter with Mr. Pomeroy. I daresay it was highly embellished, but the females were appropriately swooning."

Darcy shook his head and grimaced. "My stubborn daughter has her mind so set, and Hugh pays her scant heed. I truly do not know how she will cope when he finally marries. At least that does not seem probable any time soon, according to Richard. Hopefully she will mature out of her infatuation and set her sights on another, since he apparently quite enjoys his bachelorhood."

"Well," George declared with a deep breath and broad grin, "all this youthful zeal and drama keeps us young, yes?"

"Indeed it is amusing. Quite difficult to wallow in sorrow when the children persist in theatric entertainments. Now I think it is time I play my part as disciplinary figure before the teasing turns to physical blows. By now I am certain the playful harassment is bordering on provocation. Alexander is losing his composure and as proud as I am of my eldest's strength, he is no match for Michael in a brawl."

"This you know from experience, I take it?"

Darcy grunted, pouring more coffee as he answered Kitty's husband. "Years of experience. Michael applies equal commitment to athletics, especially pugilism, as Alexander does to books. I fear that only on a horse would he prevail over Michael."

"They could joust."

Darcy lifted a brow as the men laughed at Artois' sally. "Not a bad idea. I shall suggest it."

The Christmas hours ticked by with standard events transpiring alongside the unusual. First, church at the Village chapel with the requisite Scripture readings followed by a nativity themed play starring the children of the community and orphanage. The opening of gifts was barely finished before luncheon at one o'clock.

A somber walk to the Pemberley cemetery followed.

The ancient family burial ground was situated to the southeast, beyond the maze and rock pond, in a gated greensward surrounded by trees. The gardeners kept the flowers blooming as long as possible, although there were few to be found in December. Still, the sacred area was immaculate and oddly peaceful, even in the midst of winter's gloom. Mrs. Bennet broke into loud sobs before they opened the gate, leaning heavily on Lizzy and Jane as they wound past the desultory plots, to where Mr. Bennet was buried. The fresh mound of overturned dirt was lightly dusted with snow, the marble gravestone glaringly recent compared to all the others. Sniffles and coughs were plentiful, a few weeping anew, but none as strident as the widow. Soothing Mrs. Bennet required every ounce of Lizzy's absorption, and the flood of lamentation Darcy both dreaded and hoped for did not occur at this predictable moment.

Noella's birthday celebration overshadowed the previous hour of woe. Mr. Bennet's portrait traveled into the orangery where the party was held, his grandfatherly gaze cherished as an angelic onlooker, before being permanently hung in the portrait hallway with due pomp. The late afternoon passed in outdoor activities. The younger children napped or played together in the playroom under the supervision of their nannies while the adults walked Pemberley's gravel pathways zigzagging the manicured gardens and hedged maze. Noella on Cleo led the adolescents on a vigorous ride across the moor, returning to the warmth of the manor well after sunset.

Through it all, Lizzy fulfilled her role as the perfect hostess. Darcy kept one eye upon her, but she never once lost her composure. Finally, as darkness fully enveloped the land, and with stomachs filled to bursting with Mrs. Langton's fine cuisine, their guests retired to the largest parlor for subdued conversation, music, and games, and he relinquished his vigilant concern.

Of course it was then, to the surprise of all, that Lizzy's grief would overwhelm her.

"Aunt Elizabeth? Forgive me for forgetting to return this to you as soon as we arrived. It was in with my other hair combs, wrapped safe in your handkerchief. Thank you for lending to me. I was the only girl at the Michaelmas banquet with Michaelmas daisies adorning. It was perfect." Deborah stammered to a stop, glancing toward her mother in confused concern. "Aunt Lizzy? I am sorry…"

"Lizzy?" Mary leaned forward, touching her immobile sister lightly on the knee. "Deborah was careful with it, I assure you. She meant no disrespect in her delay to return it…"

"No," Lizzy choked, shaking her head and rapidly blinking her eyes to clear the sting of hot tears. "Deborah, dear, it... it's fine, truly." Her voice cracked and she swallowed a dry gulp. All moisture had vacated her mouth and throat, traveling, apparently, to her palms and lachrymal ducts.

Stupefied, the seconds stretching, she stared at the white linen draped over her trembling hands and the item cushioned therein. The four-inch long hairpin was silver, embedded with tarnished spots that were impossible to polish, aiding the appearance of antiquity. The cluster of lavender Michaelmas daisies covering the top were exquisitely detailed, but the color was faded in places with tiny chips in the porcelain petals and one of the yellow garnets set in the center of each flower was newer and scratch-free. It was a lovely hair accessory, obviously well used and finely wrought, although a close inspection by anyone moderately familiar with jewelry would reveal a piece of no great worth.

Yet Lizzy stared as if hypnotized, emotions assaulting her in a deluge. She did not see a shabby hair clip. She saw shiny, brilliant lavender daisies with centers of sparkling garnet nestled in a tiny velvet-lined box resting on a broad palm. She saw her father's face caught between a loving smile and teasing grin as he said, "Lavender because it is your favorite color, Lizzy, and Michaelmas daisies because they mean 'farewell,' although in your case not because I am saying good-bye, but because I know you shall always fare well in your life. You are my brightest daughter and have the greatest potential."

"I remember that clip!" Lydia's slurred voice boomed from over Lizzy's shoulder, shattering the echo of Mr. Bennet's voice.

"Papa brought each of us a flowered hairclip that year when he returned from Town. Mine was buttercups, if I recall, and Jane, yours was carnations. Or was it chrysanthemums?" She shrugged and took a hasty gulp of wine. "That was ages ago. I can't believe you still have it. Look how tarnished it is!" She leaned over the sofa back and pointed to the splotched silver filigree leaves, and then hiccupped loudly, spilling a drop of red wine onto the end daisy. "Oops! So sorry…"

But Lizzy had risen to her feet, the flowered clip clutched to her chest. Her shimmering gaze swept over the expressions on the faces of the women sitting in a circle around her: Lydia annoyed that the abrupt action had caused her to step unsteadily backward and splash wine onto her bounteous exposed bosom, her other sisters sympathetic, and her mother baffled. Beyond their intimate circle of chairs the remaining family members carried on unaware, including Darcy, who was scowling intently at the chessboard located between him and George.

Yet Lizzy barely registered any of it, not even Charles Bingley's questioning look. Focusing on any one person was impossible. A vise was tightening about her chest, making breathing difficult. She struggled viciously against the images of Mr. Bennet that slammed over everything in the room and the gruff timbre of his voice that drowned the laughing children. Her efforts were in vain and the Christmas merriment faded into a background shadow and murmur, yielding reality to the plethora of visions and conversations spanning years past with her father.

The final shred of hope that dignity might be retained was dashed when Mrs. Bennet declared with a disgusted sniff, "Why you would bother with that old piece when you have a closet full of jewels to rival a queen is beyond my comprehension. Mr. Bennet brought me one with roses along with you girls'. It was nice enough, I suppose, and he commented when I wore it, but my goodness, it was tarnished and bent! I couldn't wait to part with it once he was gone."

Lizzy stifled a cry, wet, blazing eyes piercing her mother before she mumbled an apology to the group and rushed toward the exit.

"Darcy."

"Hmm?"

"I think something is wrong with Elizabeth." Darcy's head snapped up at that, his eyes swinging to where she had been sitting last he looked. "No," Bingley answered before his friend could ask, "she left the room visibly upset."

Darcy reached the empty hallway, hesitating briefly, then taking a chance that she had headed toward their private chambers. His guess was correct, but his wife had halted midway up the sloping staircase. She was leaning into the wall, her body bent at the waist, arms hugging her torso as she shook with silent sobs.

He paused for a moment, his heart painfully twisted. He empathized wholly with her suffering, having lost both his parents and a grandfather who was dear to him. Yet he knew that it was not words she needed. Only his love and support. He took a deep breath, ascending to where she hunched, gathering her gently into his arms just as she released her pent agony in a keening wail and her knees buckled.

The final hours of their nineteenth Christmas as a married couple were spent alone in their bedchamber. Darcy held her before the fire, rocking gently until her gasps diminished, cries turned to whimpers, and speech lowered to levels a human could hear. Then the stories came. Lizzy related dozens of conversations with her father, humorous incidents from her youth, books they read and discussed, arguments and debates, their unspoken communications at the antics surrounding them, his earthy witticisms, and the numerous gifts he gave his favorite daughter.

"He hated Town," she whispered, "yet every time he was forced to travel there he purchased presents for us." She opened her hand, running one fingertip over the petals. "I was thirteen when he gave me this. I can't say why it became so special to me, but I love it." She glanced up at Darcy's face, snuggling deeper into his firm chest and smiling softly. "Do you remember when I feared I had lost this at Caister-on-Sea? After we made love on the sand?"

"Of course," he answered, cupping her cheek and rubbing the pad of his thumb over her lower lip. "That was a magical morning high on my list of special memories." He bent to kiss her lightly. "And not only for the obvious reason. I knew how precious this clip was to you and I am glad I found it."

"And also why you had the garnet replaced when it fell out. Did I thank you adequately for that, William?"

He chuckled. "Indeed. You profusely expressed your thanks. But only after sternly chastising me for stealing it away to surprise you, leaving you frantic that you had lost it. I believe that lesson is indelibly etched in my mind."

"Well, I do like most of your surprises." She smiled, pulling him in for a slow kiss and then looking back at the old clip. "It is odd how small, insignificant items become vital. The mundane happenings or casual remarks that now linger as momentous." She inhaled, pressing knuckles against her trembling lips. "They are priceless now, and I wish..."

"What do you wish?"

"There were so many other... gifts. Trinkets that I did not value... gaps in my memory... words that should have been said... his personal effects that... Oh William! I do not trust Mama to..." She waved her hand frantically, breathless sobs falling faster between the gasps and sniffles as she tried to talk.

"Cry, dearest. You need to let it out. You are safe here with me to share your pain. Fret not over Mr. Bennet's personal effects. I haven't allowed anything to be touched until you are ready. The staff has orders."

"What if I forget? I feel... already as if I.... have to force the memories. As if they are slipping from me and... all I see is his face.... His cold face lying there... How old he was!"

He tightened his arms as shivers raced through her body and the cleansing weeping continued. "Only because that was your last images, love. Trust me. That will fade in time as you grieve, to then be supplanted by images of your youth. All of your memories and devotion to your father will carry you through and be with you forever."

And then he began to speak of his parents, his richly reso-nant voice and vivid remembrances reassuring and pacific. She listened, her weeping lessening gradually as his stories mingled with her own past remembrances. Sadness washed away with the tears he tenderly dried, and grief-coiled muscles released their tension. Finally, sleep claimed her.

He carried her to their bed, nestling close all through the night. And within his stalwart embrace, gentle caresses, radiant heat, and enduring love, her emotions began the necessary journey of settling into a balance of sorrow and joy.

CHRISTMAS PRESENT

"OUCH! DAMN!"

The whispered curse forced her to burrow her face into the pillow, stifling the giggles that finally erupted after the past five minutes of listening to her husband attempt to sneak quietly about the dark room. He had already missed the chair back when tossing his robe onto it, the plop of heavy velvet hitting the floor surprisingly loud in the silent room. And the noises rendered by an ungainly one-legged hop and frantic rescue of the oil lamp that tipped when he lost his balance while taking off his shoes and stockings still echoed across the ceiling's beams. She felt some sympathy for what she knew was a toe painfully jammed into the solid wood of the bed's frame, but the humor of the situation overruled her pity. When would he learn?

"A single candle would have saved your poor foot, you know."

After a long pause and bumbling search for where the edges met, the bed curtains parted and the vague outline of his head appeared in the gap. "Forgive me, dearest. I tried not to wake you."

She laughed, rising up on one elbow to better see his face. "Amongst your many talents, stealth is not one of them. I would have thought that evident by now. Next time you choose to prowl about the halls in the middle of the night, please take a candle. I may still waken from the light but it will prevent damaged digits leaving blood on the carpets."

"As you wish, Mrs. Darcy. Although in this case it is not the middle of the night but nearly dawn, and may I remind you that the halls of Pemberley are well lit? Only in here is it pitch dark."

"What induced you to leave our warm bed at this hour anyway?"

"I wanted to ensure the tree had been properly erected in the ballroom as ordered."

"And was it?"

"All twelve impressive feet of it. I daresay it is rather lovely and festive, despite my misgivings at the notion of a tree inside the manor." The curtains opened further as he leaned in to kiss his wife.

"So now that you have satisfied your curiosity, how about you and your injured toes join me in bed?" But before he could answer, she balled her fists around the loose linen of his shirt and yanked him flush onto her body, a position he did not protest after the initial startled grunt.

After a long kiss he whispered huskily, "You are so demanding and impetuous, love. A trait I much admire although in this instance a modicum of restraint would have allotted me the chance to remove my clothing and join you *under* the blankets."

"I'll release you long enough for that task, but try not to injure yourself further."

With a speed and precision at odds with his earlier clumsiness, he lit the bedside candles, disrobed, and was under the blankets nestled against her bare skin in record time. The faint glow of the rising sun mixed with the light from the candles, igniting the fiery red strands of her hair as he buried his fingers into the mass spilling over the pillow. He inhaled her scent and kissed the soft bend of her neck repeatedly.

"Happy Christmas, Alexander," she murmured into his ear.

"I love you, Fiona," he responded, burrowing deeper beneath the covers and preparing to establish their own Christmas tradition.

Far on the other side of the upper floor of the enormous manor house, the master's chambers were silent. Fitzwilliam Darcy, the Master of Pemberley, was soundly asleep and dreaming.

Christmas was one of his favorite seasons of the entire year and this one promised to be particularly spectacular and joyous for a number of special reasons. This indisputable awareness was why a sliver of his unconscious mind recognized how odd it was that his dreams were troubled. As the unsettling dream escalated to a true nightmare, that sliver of consciousness began to exert more force, sending signals to his twitching muscles and pounding heart, urging him to wake up.

However, it would not be his own will that ended his sleep and shattered the disturbing images.

"Hmmm… You're moving finally. Are you waking up, William? It is dawn and I tire of waiting for your touch and kisses."

Even his distressed, sleep-fogged brain dimly perceived the moist, full lips raining kisses over his bare shoulder and up his neck while a small, firmly caressing hand traveled over his chest. The jumble of negative dream sensations and visions collided with the pleasant impression of a woman possessively touching his skin with the utmost tenderness.

"Elizabeth? Is that you?" His rough voice cracked, one hand grabbing the tiny fingers winding a determined path down his chest. With the other he scrubbed at his gummed eyes, turning toward the face that was now floating above him and laughing.

"After three and twenty years you expected someone else? For that, I should leave in a huff and make you suffer." But she only laughed harder and brushed a kiss over his slack mouth. "I shall forgive you, my dearest husband, as I know what a deep sleeper you are. Unless, of course, you confess to dreams of another woman in *our bed* waking you with kisses? In that case your punishment will be severe."

She was still smiling, an impish quirk to her brows as she stared into his gradually clearing eyes. She was not the slightest bit concerned about his dreams involving another woman, knowing with full certainty that even in his sleeping state, only she appeared.

He exhaled in a gush, blinked, and pressed two fingertips tightly against the bridge of his nose as he shook his head. He then brought the slim hand he yet held to his lips, kissing her wrist and palm, and finally opening his eyes to focus on her face. His naturally sapphire-blue eyes were dark in the shadows, but they were lucid, piercing her with his familiar intensity.

Now that he was fully awake he snorted at her teasing and draped his free arm around her shoulders until his fingers were entwined in the hair at the nape of her neck, the rest spilling over his arm. "Never," he answered decisively. "Rather I was enduring a nightmare where you were not a part of my life. I was old and wrinkled, grayer than my uncle, shuffling my body arthritically through the empty corridors of Pemberley, depressed and lonely. It was horrible."

"I am sorry for your nightmare, love," she said with true sincerity. "You should not suffer unpleasant dreams of that sort. I am your wife now and always." She played with his thick, brown hair, trailing her fingertips over his features as her rich voice caressed and soothed. "We are all here as we have been and will be for a long while to come."

She paused for a long interlude of tender kisses, withdrawing to continue reassuring, only with a playful lilt to her voice. "And you, my darling, are as robust and healthy as the day I married you. I only see three or four grey hairs—"

"Each placed there by Michael, I am sure."

"—and tiny laugh crimps at the corners of your eyes are the only wrinkles on your perfect body. Fifty-one is far from old and considering how active your uncle still is, I doubt your virility will be an issue for many years to come, if ever."

"Well, when you clarify it in those terms, the nightmare fades into oblivion." He pulled until she lay completely atop him with limbs entangled.

"Since it is Christmas morning, we have a tradition to uphold," she reminded him.

"Breakfast with the family?"

"Before that."

"Waking the children before they pound upon our door?"

She giggled. "You know they will head directly to the ball-room and the tree sparing no thought of their parents. Try again."

He continued the teasing questions. "Bathing together so your back will be adequately cleaned?"

"Now that is a fine idea! What say we squeeze that in between dressing in our Christmas finest and attending to our customary private celebration?"

She wiggled her brows, Darcy erupting in laughter and flip-ping her onto her back. "You are insatiable. I love you, Elizabeth."

"And I love you, Fitzwilliam. Now how about *showing* me your abiding devotion and passion."

"As you wish."

It was over three hours and one extended bath later when a whistling Darcy exited his dressing room. Hair trimmed, face shaved and splashed with cologne, and garbed in an impeccable, fashionable suit of dark blue wool, he exuded dignity and refine-ment. The jaunty spring in his steps as he headed toward the staircase flowed naturally and did not mar the aura of authority he wore. At the bottom of the stairs he paused, a wide grin spreading over his face before he quickly dashed to hide around the corner.

"Stop! Would you two listen to me? When I catch you there will be hell to pay! Are you listening to me?"

Darcy held his chuckle inside. His sister's unheeded com-mands mixed with high-pitched peals of laughter and the stomp of small, running feet. The sounds grew louder by the second until two bodies barreled around the corner. Darcy shouted and leapt into their pathway. They shrieked in unison, but smoothly veered to either side of his legs, their wild rush not slowed in the slightest as they raced by. "Happy Christmas, Uncle William!" floated on the air behind them as they plunged down the corridor, still laughing.

Georgiana rounded the corner seconds later, pulling up short before crashing into her brother's much larger body. "You didn't stop them?"

"I tried, but…"

"Never mind! Oh thank God. Richard! Harry! Grab those two ruffians please."

Yells and laughter rang out as the two men jumped into the fray, making a grand procedure out of capturing the two five-year olds. With a kicking and squirming boy tucked securely under an arm, Richard and Harry walked toward Georgiana and Darcy.

"What is the penalty, Aunt Giana? Twenty lashes? The rack?"

"Mr. Burr was talking about a huge ant hill he discovered," Richard offered with a wink not seen by the twins, who were now limp and quiet. "I hear that is an ideal form of torture."

"Mama! We promise to be good!"

"We just want to see the tree!"

Georgiana rolled her eyes. "Everything is 'the tree this' and 'the tree that.' Whose idea was it to have a tree?" It was a rhetorical question, as the three men knew, and they all laughed. "Just take them to the dining room if you don't mind."

"But Mama!" They cried with identical whines and pouting faces.

"We will take you to the ballroom first, how about that? But you must promise not to try climbing the tree, agreed?"

"Yes, Uncle Richard." Pledged in tandem, and after merry Christmas wishes and proper good morning greetings, Colonel Fitzwilliam and his son jogged away briskly with the cheered boys dangling from their hips.

"Those two will be the death of me, I swear. Why me? The girls are so dainty and mild. Then I am cursed with twin hellions. Now I find out that their father was a crazed child before he became the sedate man I married. Why did he not tell me this beforehand?"

"Would it have changed your heart, my Lady Essenton?" Darcy asked with a laugh.

Georgiana flushed prettily. "Unlikely. But I would have been forewarned!"

"Where is your husband anyway?"

She grunted. "Leaving me to flounder while he hides in the music room practicing the piece we wrote for today." She brightened, squeezing her brother's arm as they strolled the wide corridor leading to the north wing. "It is very good, William, if I say so myself."

"I have no doubt it will awe and delight, dearest sister. And the tree is a fabulous idea, despite the overzealous enthusiasm displayed. Your frequent excursions abroad for concerts and study have paid off in numerous ways, this German custom only the latest inspiration."

"This 'German custom' has been practiced by our royal family for years. Queen Victoria has written of her fondness for a decorated tree. You wait, my skeptical brother. Soon everyone in England will have a tree for Christmas. Once the Pemberley tree is decorated with the glass ornaments we obtained while in Lauscha and the German *lametta*, silver tinsel, in addition to the ornaments the family has made, the ribbons, and candles, you will be as awed as we were while living in Hamburg and Vienna. The Christmas markets, they call them *weihnachtsmärktes*, are incredible. I have trunks of ornaments at home, but brought a large box of my favorites."

"You misunderstand me, Georgiana. I am quite delighted at the concept of a tree. I personally chose the Scots pine hewn and now erected in the ballroom. Days spent on horseback scouring the woods, mind you, before we found a gorgeous specimen that may not contend with your German varieties, but is stunning and will decorate nicely."

"Are we talking about the Christmas tree? It seems to be the prime subject these days, even to the point of wandering dark hallways and injuring body parts."

Georgiana and Darcy turned at the sound of Fiona's voice, noting her amused smirk and Alexander's wince. Lizzy was walking alongside her faintly limping son and by the twitching of her lips it was clear she was privy to the story behind Fiona's remark.

"Our son may look exactly like you, my love, and we know his temperament is remarkably similar. But apparently he did not inherit your uncanny ability to sneak quietly."

"Oh? I have never noticed. He is adequately stealthy when we hunt."

"Very well! Since I know my humiliation will be publicly broadcast, I may as well recount my clumsiness to the entire family all at once and get it over with."

Fiona nodded and continued to smile brightly. "Indeed it is a perfect Christmas story. My father will love it!" Alexander blanched, immediately remembering what happened minutes after his embarrassing stumble. Fiona merely laughed and lifted to kiss his cheek. "Do not fret. I promise not to mention how I alleviated your pain."

Her dimpled smile and wink made Alexander groan and redden. The others burst out laughing.

The formal dining room was nearly filled to capacity. Between the recent wedding of Alexander and Fiona, Noella's eighteenth birthday, and the advent of the Christmas tree to this year's holiday, nearly every relative and friend of the Darcys had been invited to celebrate this Christmas at Pemberley. Most were housed in the manor, with every bedchamber in use for the first time in memory. Other friends from the neighborhood would be arriving after church for the tree decorating and luncheon birthday extravaganza. Due to the multitude of people anticipated and the size of the tree selected by the Pemberley groundsmen and Master, the massive ballroom had been converted into a comprehensive parlor, music room, and gift repository.

Breakfast was an organized affair, unlike the usual free flowing manner, with food kept at the sidebar. Place settings were assigned and courses served in a regimented schedule. Of course, this controlled timetable in no way meant that calm and serenity reigned.

The Master and Mistress of Pemberley entered the room arm-in-arm, taking in the gay atmosphere with happy smiles. But before either could speak, the birthday girl's voice interrupted their thoughts and cut through the lively air.

"As far as I am concerned, Hugh Pomeroy can fall off a cliff. Good riddance, I say. He better not say a word to me or I will give him a piece of my mind!"

They turned to see their eldest daughter flouncing angrily toward them, her face a thundercloud. She was talking to Jane and Mary, both women trying hard not to laugh.

The object of Noella's harsh dismissal stood several paces inside the door talking to Michael. He glanced up at the irate declaration, but instead of looking worried he grinned and started chuckling. Michael grabbed his arm and forcefully propelled him across the room to a curtained alcove.

"All right, what did you do to my sister now?" He looked at his friend with murder in his eyes. "I saw you two sneaking away last night but trusted your honor, Hugh Pomeroy. I can and will beat you to a bloody pulp if you hurt my sister."

Hugh pointedly stared at the colorful bruise encircling Michael's swollen right eye. "That I am well aware of, my friend. Your beating me, I mean. Your success in the boxing ring leaves me no doubt of that. But quit glowering at me, will you? I think it is rather what I *didn't* do that has her up in arms." And then he began to laugh. He snuck a peek through the drapes to see a visibly furious Noella ranting on to Audrey and several of her female cousins. "Oh, this is too rich!"

"What in blazes are you talking about?"

Hugh opened his mouth to respond but was interrupted by the abrupt parting of the curtains. "Are you two hiding in here?"

"Go away, little boy. This is a man's conversation."

Nathaniel merely rolled his eyes at his brother, ignoring the severe glare, and stepped into the alcove. "You might want to stay out of sight for a while, cousin. Unless you enjoy tongue-lashings. Noella may well sear the skin off your bones this time. What did you do anyway?"

Hugh shrugged. "Miss Darcy *may* have been informed by a reliable source that she was to be proposed to last night."

"She did?"

"And you didn't?"

"Yes," he nodded to Nathaniel, "and no I did not," he directed to Michael, who whistled and shook his head.

"Who told her that?"

Hugh flushed slightly but flashed a cocky grin. "I *might* have mentioned my intent to Hannah and Audrey, and Deborah and Margaret, who *probably* shared the secret information with Noella. Just speculating."

"And then you *didn't* propose? Are you insane? If you want to die an early death, let me do it. It will probably be less painful."

"Thanks," he said dryly, "I'll keep that in mind. Relax, I have a plan."

"Napoleon had a plan too. Look how well that turned out."

"I am confused," Nathaniel frowned. "Have you spoken to Father yet? I mean, we all know Noella's been after you for ages, and frankly I think you're a loon to marry her, but are you or not?"

Hugh stared at Nathaniel, weighing carefully before speaking. "Listen, Nat. This is serious, so you must remain silent. Your sister's happiness depends on it." Suddenly sober and exhibiting maturity beyond his ten years, Nathaniel nodded. Michael looked as solemn as his younger brother. "Here it is. I spoke with Uncle William and my father months ago, before Noella's debut in Town, as a matter of fact. Your father was firm on waiting until after Noella experienced one Season." He grimaced, the momentary flash of pain as the confident cast fell from his face more telling than his words. "Blast, that was awful. Her dancing at Almack's, flirting with those blighters, watching them fawn over her. I wanted to wring their scrawny, lily-white necks!" He clenched his fists, then coughed and gathered his wits, finally shrugging again and relaxing, although his voice remained strained. "He wanted me to wait until she was eighteen. I didn't want to hear it, but he was correct. Plus, it gave me time to prepare and establish myself. Father has helped with that, so by the time we marry I will have a proper home for her."

"So..." Michael scratched his temple, "Does that mean you are going to propose today then? Last night was a diversion?"

"Nope!" And the arrogant grin was back. "At the Cole's Twelfth Night Masque!"

Both Nathaniel and Michael stared, more confused than ever. Hugh threw back his head and laughed. Then he clapped them on the shoulder. "Just wait and see. I have it all planned, with the help of Aunt Elizabeth and my mother. What is grander than a spectacular proposal at the preeminent ball of the holiday with all of Derbyshire's elite witnessing? It shall be epic. Miss Darcy will be the shining star, envied and honored, stealing the limelight from everyone, the crowning glory of the evening. And I will be the luckiest man in England when she says yes."

"If she doesn't kill you between now and then. I think it may be the longest twelve days of your life, my friend."

Hugh's dreamy expression and broad smile were assured and slightly lewd. "Trust me. I know how to handle Noella Darcy. I am probably the only man on earth who can. By the time we return from church, she will have forgiven me and will be expressing her adoration fervently."

Nathaniel muttered something about that being disgusting while Michael renewed his threat to pummel Hugh black-and-blue if he touched his sister. Hugh merely laughed as he bravely exited the sheltered alcove.

Noella's glare may well have burned Hugh's skin with its intensity—her choler not aided by the gleaming smile he flashed in her direction—but the nonverbal exchange was quickly interrupted by the appearance of Audrey. The dainty girl was dwarfed between the towering Dr. Darcy and his burly apprentice, Dr. Vaughan, yet all eyes instantly fixed upon her face. Tranquility radiated from her core, a glamour of peace and innocence that none could resist when she was near, or even in the same room. Her ethereal beauty was breathtaking and wholly untarnished by the slight sag to her left eye and mouth. She was mesmerizing, in a multitude of ways, and none escaped the spell she cast.

"Michael, we have a poultice of arnica, comfrey, and parsley for you to place onto your eye. It will reduce the swelling and diminish the bruising."

"Audrey prepared it herself," Dr. Darcy interjected, the aged but spry physician gazing at his niece with overwhelming pride.

"Excellent work by the best assistant I have ever had. No offense, Dr. Vaughan."

"None taken, sir. And I agree with your assessment. Miss Darcy's apothecary skills and knowledge of herbals exceed any I have seen, even those at college."

Audrey pinked under the praise and penetrating look from the young doctor. But her voice was firm and clinical as she instructed her brother. "You must apply this as a compress as often as possible. If you keep it fresh and in place, your eye will be almost normal by evening."

"Why would I want to do that? I won the fight fair and square, and wear my only wound with honor. Received a purse of twenty sovereigns for the win and plenty from private betting." He winked at his uncle, "I told you not to bet against me, Uncle George."

George winced, glancing nervously at Audrey, who smiled sweetly at her uncle. "Fear not, Uncle George. I won't tell Mama or Papa. But Michael, your wound distresses Mama and we cannot allow that."

Her tone remained dulcet and nonjudgmental, but Michael cringed, glancing guiltily toward his mother. "Oh, very well," he grumbled, "give it here. Probably smells foul and stings to boot." He yanked the bowl out of her tiny hands and slapped the wet cloth against his left eye. "Making a mountain out of a molehill if you ask me. It's just a stupid bruise. I hardly feel it. Now I look the fool and everyone will be laughing."

"No one will laugh, and if they do, you have my permission to punch them. I have plenty more where this came from, after all." She patted his cheek, her angelic face sunny. Then she turned to Hugh, her countenance and voice compassionate, "Cousin, I will arrange a place for you next to Noella in church so you can atone for your mischievousness. Try not to frustrate her beyond measure. She truly does love you deeply."

Hugh hung his head, shame drenching him as he stole a glance Noella's direction. She looked up as if sensing his regard. Her flinty eyes engaged his repentant ones for a moment, flickered to Audrey, and then back to Hugh. Even from across the room he could see their chocolate depths melting, the sparkle brightening their darkness to warm umber. He sighed, lost and lovesick as he had been for two years now.

"Nathaniel, Grandmama has apparently forgotten that Thomas is no longer three. Help me rescue him before he dies of embarrassment?" And then she glided away, her elfin form supported by a polished wood crutch that in no way diminished her grace. Dr. Vaughan sighed, for one unguarded moment his mien showing the rawness of his affection before settling into a mask of neutrality.

The modest chapel in the village burst at the seams with the number of Pemberley guests attending this year. The dusting of snow from five days ago was largely melted and the weather fair enough to permit most of the visitors to walk, a fact the estate's groomsmen and coachmen were fervently thankful for. Of course the number of conveyances driving into the spacious avenue after the service were considerable, but as always the efficient Pemberley staff rose to the challenge.

Sofas, chairs, chaises, and settees were scavenged from every room to accommodate the army flooding into the mammoth ballroom. A cluster of thickly cushioned couches arranged for optimal tree viewing was reserved for the oldest guests, Lady Catherine choosing the middle armchair and imperiously draping her voluminous skirts as a queen. That she was then flanked by the loquacious Mrs. Bennet and outspoken Mrs. Gardiner—both now widows—on one side and the ornery George Darcy on the other added amusement to an already entertaining afternoon.

For once the children were not in a frenzy to open their presents. Rather, the exuberance was centered on the tree. Footmen hauled dozens of boxes and trays into the room, setting the precious ornaments onto waiting tables. The women took charge, doling out the decorations to the children in an age appropriate manner and assisting in the hanging. The men supported the ladders needed to reach the higher branches and assumed the responsibility of wisely placing the tiny candles that would be lit that evening. It was a production to be sure, but one filled with merriment. Background music was provided by those talented with instruments and singing. Snacks and drinks were replenished steadily, and gradually the tagged gifts were distributed and opened. Surprisingly there were no mishaps beyond a few broken cookie ornaments.

The only interruption to the flow was the delivery of an enormous painting. The family gathered close and everything halted when Darcy opened the crating and the masterpiece was unveiled.

The nearly five-foot square canvas, painted in brilliant colors, showed the front façade of Pemberley with Fitzwilliam and Elizabeth standing regally on the topmost step of the columned portico. They were turned slightly sideways with Elizabeth in front of her husband in a semi-embrace. Alexander, equally noble and the image of his sire except for his coiled brown curls, was positioned one step below with Fiona by his side, her flaming red hair tumbling over one shoulder. Michael, dark and brawny, stood with one arm flung over raven-haired Noella's shoulders, their devilish grins identical. The younger Darcy siblings were spaced evenly in between.

The painter had resided all summer at Pemberley, dwelling with the Darcys in order to properly capture their personalities on canvas. The result was amazingly accurate and awe-inspiring.

Lizzy slipped away from the boisterous crowd some minutes after Darcy excused himself to ensure the painting's safe delivery to his office. She quietly opened the door to discover him gazing at the framed canvas propped on a sofa. He did not turn from his serene contemplation of their family, but she knew he was aware of her entry—they always sensed the presence of the other—and sidled up to him, arms naturally embracing.

"I plan to hang it there," he nodded toward the wall above the settee. "As much as I love Gainsborough's landscape, I would prefer to have you and our children watching over me as I work. Someday it can join the others in the Portrait Gallery, but not yet."

"I concur. We look wonderful here. It is an amazing portrait, arriving at a perfect time."

"How true. It induced me to reflect on Christmases past. All of them have been wonderful since you came into my life." He looked at her then, blue eyes tender and inundated with love.

"All of them?" she repeated, memories flashing through her mind and her tone only partially teasing, but her eyes were full of the same deep love when they locked with his.

"Even those Christmases that were sad or difficult were special, my heart. My life is complete since we married and I would change nothing. This Christmas is the most recent in a very long line of incredible memories."

"It is not over yet!" She reminded him, both of them laughing as they returned their gazes to the painting.

Silently, in sweet harmony, they admired the canvas testimonial to what they, through God's grace, had achieved in the long years of their marriage. They studied the painted images, each beloved beyond measure. The portraitist had easily identified the individual characteristics, capturing them brilliantly. Especially manifest was the love, unswerving commitment, and supreme happiness verily shining from their faces as proud parents to the next generation of Darcys.

She broke the quiet contemplation, tugging gently on his waist. "Come, love. Our family awaits and I have a special present for you."

"I thought we were finished exchanging gifts this year."

"It is something special I have held in reserve."

"Secrets?"

"Of course! It is Christmas after all!"

With laughter and a final glance at the mute and fixed images, they exited the parlor to rejoin the animated reality.

The party had continued unabated, none even noting their absence. Lizzy squeezed his laced fingers, steering him toward the tree and the table where a handful of ornaments yet waited to be hung. She reached into a segregated box, unwrapping the tissue paper from a thin, narrow object, and handed it to her spouse.

"I saved this one for you to place," she said softly, her eyes shining.

Darcy stared at the bookmark in his hand, swallowing past the lump in his throat as more memories washed over him: Elizabeth Bennet, his then betrothed, surprising him with a party on the occasion of his twenty-ninth birthday and gifting him with this bookmark, embroidered and sewn by her hand, tucked into a first edition copy of Milton's *Paradise Lost*. Both were among his most cherished possessions. The bookmark maintained the placement in hundreds of books for some ten years, then was relegated to his bedside Bible for several more years, until he had finally been forced to store it in one of his many memento boxes before the frayed cloth disintegrated completely. Now here it was, restored with the embroidered silk sewn onto a new backing and edged with lace that looped, for hanging onto the tree's branch. The meticulous stitches from so long ago were freshly reinforced, Lizzy's delicate hand spelling out their names inside linked hearts with a scripture from Genesis scripted above: *The two shall become one flesh.*

He brushed his knuckles over her cheek. "And so we have, my heart." He placed the bookmark onto a prominent front branch at eye level, turning back to his wife.

"Merry Christmas, Fitzwilliam."

"Merry Christmas, Elizabeth." And the kiss he gave her went on long after everyone in the room began clapping and cheering.

THE END

ABOUT THE AUTHORS

Amanda Grange was born in Yorkshire, England, a few miles away from the town of Bingley. She spent her teenage years reading Jane Austen and Georgette Heyer while also finding time to study music at Nottingham University. She has had sixteen novels published, including five Jane Austen retellings and *Mr Darcy, Vampyre*. Austenblog called *Mr Darcy's Diary*, "a treat"; The Historical Novels Review made *Captain Wentworth's Diary* an Editor's Choice, remarking, "Amanda Grange has taken on the challenge of reworking a much loved romance and succeeds brilliantly"; Austenprose said of *Colonel Brandon's Diary*, "Amanda Grange has actually succeeded in improving upon Austen's character Colonel Brandon"; and her paranormal sequel to *Pride and Prejudice*, *Mr Darcy, Vampyre*, was nominated for the Jane Austen Awards. Amanda Grange lives in Cheshire, England.

Sharon Lathan is the author of the bestselling *Mr. and Mrs. Fitzwilliam Darcy: Two Shall Become One* and *Loving Mr. Darcy:*

Journeys Beyond Pemberley. In addition to her writing, she works as a registered nurse in a neonatal ICU. She resides with her family in Hanford, California. For more information about Sharon, the Regency Era, and her bestselling Darcy Saga series, visit her website/blog at: www.sharonlathan.net or www.darcysaga.net. She also invites everyone to join her and the other Sourcebooks romance novelists at: www.casablancaauthors.blogspot.com

Carolyn Eberhart is a debut author and is a member of RWA. She lives in Charlottesville, Virginia.

WICKHAM'S DIARY

AMANDA GRANGE

Jane Austen's quintessential bad boy has his say…

Enter the clandestine world of the cold-hearted Wickham…

…in the pages of his private diary. Always aware of the inferiority of his social status compared to his friend Fitzwilliam Darcy, Wickham chases wealth and women in an attempt to attain the power he lusts for. But as Wickham gambles and cavorts his way through his funds, Darcy still comes out on top.

But now Wickham has found his chance to seduce the young Georgiana Darcy, which will finally secure the fortune—and the revenge—he's always dreamed of…

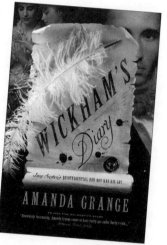

Praise for Amanda Grange:

"Amanda Grange has taken on the challenge of reworking a much loved romance and succeeds brilliantly." —*Historical Novels Review*

"Amanda Grange is a writer who tells an engaging, thoroughly enjoyable story!" —*Romance Reader at Heart*

Available April 2011
978-1-4022-5186-3
$12.99 US

In the Arms of Mr. Darcy

SHARON LATHAN

If only everyone could be as happy as they are...

Darcy and Elizabeth are as much in love as ever—even more so as their relationship matures. Their passion inspires everyone around them, and as winter turns to spring, romance blossoms around them.

Confirmed bachelor Richard Fitzwilliam sets his sights on a seemingly unattainable, beautiful widow; Georgiana Darcy learns to flirt outrageously; the very flighty Kitty Bennet develops her first crush, and Caroline Bingley meets her match.

But the path of true love never does run smooth, and Elizabeth and Darcy are kept busy navigating their friends and loved ones through the inevitable separations, misunderstandings, misgivings, and lovers' quarrels to reach their own happily ever afters...

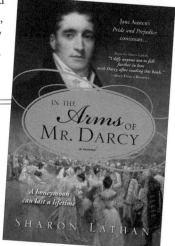

"If you love *Pride and Prejudice* sequels then this series should be on the top of your list!" —*Royal Reviews*

"Sharon really knows how to make Regency come alive." —*Love Romance Passion*

978-1-4022-3699-0
$14.99 US/$17.99 CAN/£9.99 UK

THE WAY OF THE WIZARD

Other Books Edited
By John Joseph Adams

Wastelands
Seeds of Change
The Living Dead
Federations
By Blood We Live
The Improbable Adventures of Sherlock Holmes
The Living Dead 2

Forthcoming Anthologies

Brave New Worlds
The Mad Scientist's Guide to World Domination
The Book of Cthulhu